The gift was offered — and accepted

Perhaps there was only to be this one time for them, or perhaps it was a beginning. There was no way to tell. But Sally understood that she and Neal had been presented with the gift of an innocent, unfettered moment. She would have no more turned it away than she would have denied one of her children a kiss. Strange that she felt this way with this man. Yet she had never felt quite so right about being with anyone before.

Sally knew that all it would take would be to turn her face and look at him. Then Neal would kiss her.

She closed her eyes for an instant and inhaled deeply, drinking in all the sensations she was experiencing. Softly, ever so softly, she touched his mouth first with her fingers, then with her lips.

ABOUT THE AUTHOR

Born in Indiana, Anne Henry moved a lot
during her childhood as the daughter of an
Army officer. She has written a number of
magazine articles and currently raises and
races registered quarter horses in Oklahoma.

Books by Anne Henry

HARLEQUIN AMERICAN ROMANCE
 76—CHEROKEE SUMMER
 90—THE GLORY RUN
114—THE STORM WITHIN

These books may be available at your local bookseller.

Don't miss any of our special offers. Write to us at the
following address for information on our newest releases.

Harlequin Reader Service
P.O. Box 52040, Phoenix, AZ 85072-2040
Canadian address: P.O. Box 2800, Postal Station A,
5170 Yonge St., Willowdale, Ont. M2N 6J3

The Storm Within

ANNE HENRY

Harlequin Books

TORONTO • NEW YORK • LONDON
AMSTERDAM • PARIS • SYDNEY • HAMBURG
STOCKHOLM • ATHENS • TOKYO • MILAN

Published August 1985

First printing June 1985

ISBN 0-373-16114-X

Printed in Canada

Chapter One

Neal fumbled with the key on the front porch of his dark house, vowing to get one of those key rings with a flashlight. After several futile attempts to fit the wrong key in the lock on his front door and several muttered expletives, he finally located the correct key and let himself in the house.

He tripped on a bundle of clothing he had meant to take to the cleaner on his way to work that morning but managed to reach the light switch unharmed. After almost five months, he was still not used to letting himself into an empty house at night.

Neal switched on a few more lights and headed for the kitchen, pausing long enough in the living room to turn on the television in search of a human voice. It sounded hollow in the rugless room. The late news was already coming on. It had been another late night for him at the severe-storms lab.

He got a beer from the refrigerator, put a TV dinner in the oven, and sank down in front of the television on a bean-bag chair he had retrieved from the attic. The chair, the television and a lonely coffee table were the only furnishings in the barren room.

But terminated marriages did make for empty houses, Neal thought regretfully as he looked around the inhospitable room. He was going to have to go shopping for some furniture and for a lamp or two. He hated the glare of overhead lights. And he needed a new rug. At least it wouldn't seem so empty with a rug covering up the bare wooden floors. Or maybe he should sell the house and move closer to his work. He'd thought a lot about that lately. There was really no reason for him to stay in the city. It would be more convenient for him to rent an apartment in Norman, but right now he just didn't have time to tackle apartment hunting or the details of selling his house.

Barbara used to join him evenings here in this room—often with a fire burning in the fireplace—for a cup of coffee or a glass of wine. When he wasn't off chasing a tornado or working late at the lab, this was their time together. At least it had been until the last year or so of their marriage, when her committee work and his job took up so many evenings, and the evenings they were both at home, Barbara took to retiring early. He wondered what she did at night these days. He wondered, as he took a swallow of beer, if she ever thought of him.

The beer was cold and refreshing. A can of beer when he got home was a ritual with him—one of the few pleasures left in his life.

Neal drained half the drink while a television reporter interviewed some striking telephone workers on location in front of their picket line.

Damned chair, he thought with a sigh, then leaned back as best he could in the formless vinyl bag, stretched out his lanky frame, and settled in for a few minutes of relaxation. He supposed he should turn the hose on his parched shrubbery or look over that grant proposal before tomorrow's meeting, but he was bushed.

Springtime was always the busiest time for Neal.

Oklahoma's volatile weather usually acted up in the spring and spawned a rash of tornadoes, and his job was to study tornadoes. His team at the lab not only studied weather patterns from the past that had brought tornadic winds blowing violently across the midsection of the nation, they also plotted, measured and even chased whatever deadly funnels were currently twisting their awesome path of destruction—and sometimes death—across the prairies of Oklahoma and Texas.

Thus far, this had been a particularly active spring, and they currently were shorthanded at the lab, which meant extra work for everyone. If their grant from the National Science Foundation was approved, Neal could hire another researcher and things could ease up a bit.

Of course, he really hadn't minded the busyness so much of late. Busy hands are happy hands, he often reminded himself—or at least they are not quite so unhappy. And busy minds don't keep going over ugly scenes at a marriage's end. At least he could succeed at his work, and that meant a great deal to him after failing so miserably on a personal level.

The telecast moved back to the station after on-the-scene coverage—complete with a hysterical mother—of a wreck on the interstate in which two children were killed. Then the male and female news co-anchors joked back and forth for a minute about the male anchor's golf game before covering a starkly graphic story on teenage promiscuity.

Come on, Neal thought impatiently, *that's not news.* But that was Channel Eight's style—sensationalism, jokes, gimmicks, ambulance chasing. He hated their brand of journalism. He reached for the remote control and started to switch to Channel Four. He toyed with the remote for a minute but didn't make the change. He never did—at least not until after the weather. He drained his beer can and tossed it toward the wastebasket in the corner. He missed.

"And now Channel Eight's lady with the highs and lows—weatherperson Sally Storm," the male newscaster was saying enthusiastically.

"Sally *Storm*!" Neal said out loud. *What those jerks on that channel don't do to meteorolgy in this state,* he thought with a disgusted shake of his head. Wonder what cutie-pie gimmick Miss *Storm* would come up with tonight. Last night she gave the forecast from a hot-air balloon, supposedly symbolic of the city's unseasonably high March temperatures. The night before, her forecast was sung in duet with the six-year-old winner of the Little Miss Oklahoma Beauty Pageant.

He cringed as weatherperson Storm encouraged viewers to stay tuned to Channel Eight throughout the late-night programming for the most up-to-date tornado warning system in the state—and viewers should be sure to write in for their free Safety First Tornado Tip Cards.

The station's "forecasting" equipment probably consisted of a teletype and a rain gauge, he decided. And there was absolutely no severe weather anyplace in the state tonight. Nobody needed to stay tuned to that station for anything except to watch their crummy shows, but Miss Storm made it sound like viewers' very lives depended on their staying tuned to that station and that station alone.

He pointed the remote control at the set again. He should change channels. Such unprofessionalism really galled him. But Sally Storm turned toward the camera and told an amusing little anecdote about an old lady who could always tell when a storm was coming by the way her cow gave milk.

She wasn't exactly beautiful, but there was something about the woman, he had to admit. There was a charming pertness about the way she moved and the way she tilted her head to one side when she smiled—kind of a lopsided smile with a faint dimple on the right side. He admired the way her shiny brown hair waved about her face, and he liked the sound of her voice. Yes, if he could tune out her words and just watch her and listen to her melodious low voice, it would be a whole lot better than having to endure that garbage they called "Channel Eight's Safety First Weather."

She turned sideways so she could gesture at her weather map and still keep an eye on the camera. When she lifted her arm, her navy jacket fell away and Neal could see the contours of her bust under her white blouse. *Nice,* Neal admitted. And he had to admit that she always dealt with the nation's weather picture accurately. Her assessment of the impact of the front coming in from Canada was on the money. She even added a little speculation about the dew point that Neal knew wasn't on the wire-service report. He wondered about her credentials. She did seem to have a meteorology background, but how could a professional have anything to do with that claptrap of a weather show?

"And now for the forecast," she said brightly. The camera came in very close. She photographed quite well; they did lots of close-ups on her. Neal speculated about her eyes. Sometimes they looked green, but tonight they were kind of blue. But it was her smile that brought her face to life. When she smiled, she was quite lovely—gorgeous, in fact. Surely she didn't look that good in the flesh. And just thinking the word "flesh" momentarily sent Neal's ponderings to another level—one that had nothing to do with meteorology.

"We have a special guest with us tonight to help me with the forecast," Sally Storm was saying, her smile dazzling. "Although dog days are usually reserved for the summertime, we are sorry to say one very special dog has been having more than his share of dog days lately. We're hoping to break the losing streak, though, aren't we, Top Daug? Ladies and gentlemen, may I present the one and only Top Daug, mascot of your University of Oklahoma basketball team, which faces the University of Missouri tomorrow night at Lloyd Noble Arena in a game that will be televised right here on Channel Eight."

Neal groaned as a dog-suited figure carrying an umbrella came leaping out onto the news set. The mascot was wearing a red-and-white O.U. basketball uniform complete with basketball shoes.

Top Daug stopped by the newscaster's desk to shake hands with the sportscaster, who was waiting to give the sports news, then hurried over to embrace Sally Storm passionately.

Sally laughed and returned the embrace. Top Daug immediately started fanning himself with his free "paw" and panting furiously as though to indicate that the lady really warmed him up.

"And now, Top Daug," Sally said in a mock-serious tone, "I understand you are going to tell the folks what to expect in the way of weather tomorrow."

At this, the furry creature opened his umbrella, which had Sixty Percent written on it with large black symbols.

"That's right, Top Daug!" Sally said, laughing. "There's a sixty-percent chance of much-needed rain tomorrow morning with the possibility diminishing thoughout the day. We're expecting cooler temperatures, with highs in the high sixties. Tonight's low should be in the low thirties. And now, Top Daug, what's your forecast for tomorrow night's ball game?

The Sooners have lost their last four outings. Any prediction as to what the team will do to the Missouri Tigers tomorrow night?''

Top Daug bobbed his head up and down, then hurried over to the corner of the news desk and lifted his leg in a familiar doggie gesture. The sportscaster and news anchors collapsed across their desks in fits of laughter while the mascot leaped from the set holding his umbrella Mary Poppins-fashion high over his head.

In disgust, Neal aimed the remote at the set like a gun and, with a flourish, switched to Channel Four in time to catch the end of the weather forecast. A sedate, middle-aged man wearing a conservative suit was explaining a satellite photograph of the region. Neal nodded appreciatively. It was the same photograph he himself had been studying a short time before at the lab.

This is more like it, Neal thought, curious to check out the caliber of Channel Four's forecast. Television meteorology could be done professionally. He would have to stop tuning in Channel Eight so much. All it did was irritate him.

But when the weather portion of the broadcast ended, Neal realized with a start that he had completely missed the forecast. His mind had been wandering back to Channel Eight and its more attractive meteorologist.

Neal muttered an expletive in his hollow room and heaved himself out of the ridiculous chair. He put the laundry bundle in his car so he wouldn't forget it again and decided the shrubs had either already died during the long dry winter or would make it until the spring rains came. After all, Top Daug had said we have a sixty percent chance of rain tomorrow.

He got another beer. This one he drank sitting at his

kitchen table waiting for his dinner to finish cooking. He liked his kitchen. It was the only cozy room left in the house. Barbara had left it pretty much intact, with its worn wooden table and chairs that had served as dining-room furniture in their first apartment and the row of kitchen utensils hanging over the stove. A grouping of storm pictures he had taken over the years adorned one wall, and two hanging ferns still framed the window over the sink. As he looked out the window, he could see the treetops swaying erratically in the gusting wind. *Gusts of twenty-five to thirty miles per hour,* Sally Storm had said with her lovely, one-dimpled smile.

SALLY HURRIED off the set, hoping to close up shop quickly and avoid dealing with Barry Clinton, the station's public-relations director, who had been hovering behind the cameras. He had indicated earlier he needed to talk to her, and although Sally was very fond of the sandy-haired young man, she knew from past experience that whatever crazy scheme he had dreamed up for her programs could wait until tomorrow.

She pulled off the latest weather-service maps and hung them on their respective pegs, checked the most recent satellite photos one last time, and thought she was going to get out before Barry made his way across the set to the forecasting center. But over her shoulder she heard his familiar voice.

"Hey, Sally, I need to talk to you."

"Hi, Barry. Look, I'm in a rush. I need to pick up the girls. My mother's not feeling well, and I don't want to leave them over tonight. Can't whatever you need wait until morning?"

"I just need a few minutes," he said pleadingly. *"Please."*

"Oh, all right, but try to make it quick." She sat down at the chair in front of her computer terminal.

"The show looked super!" Barry said enthusiastically as he perched on the ledge in front of the panel of monitors.

"Yeah, wasn't it just great?" Sally said sarcastically. "Meteorology's finest hour. A real dog of a show."

Barry looked disappointed. "I thought the Top Daug spot was fantastic. Everyone else thought I had a great idea when I came up with him."

"You know how I feel about that sort of thing," Sally said wearily as she stacked up the day's assortment of satellite photographs. "We've been over it all before, but if that's what the folks who run this station insist on, I'll try to go along. I need the job."

"Oh, come on. Don't be such a spoilsport. You're a local celebrity! The folks out there in television land love the Channel Eight weather—at least they do when you give it. We get the highest ratings for the evening and late news, and part of that is because we've got the greatest weathergirl in the West."

Sally reached in her bottom drawer for her purse. She didn't even try to raise Barry's consciousness by correcting the "weathergirl" tag. She was a meteorologist, or a television weather reporter—anything except a girl. She was twenty-nine years old and the head of a household. She had ceased to be a girl years ago, but she knew Barry meant well. And she was tired. She'd work on correcting his sexist speech another day. On second thought, however, maybe she was the weathergirl. This job—this station—had turned her into just that. A weather*girl*. She had become a frivolous airhead who dressed up a weather segment of the evening news and didn't put people to sleep. Her job was to be cute and to entertain. Any information she might impart was secondary. Tomorrow night, she understood she would be giving her report from the back of an elephant at Lincoln Park Zoo—supposedly to promote a fund-raising effort at the zoo, but in reality it was another of Barry's gimmicks to increase the show's audience.

Surely some citizens would prefer a serious weather show, but apparently those weren't the viewers Channel Eight was after. Still, the pay was good, and the hours for the past four years had allowed her to spend her days with her daughters. And this job allowed her to move back to Oklahoma City and be near her parents after a difficult couple of years trying to raise two small daughters completely on her own.

Sally hitched her bag over her shoulder and stood facing the boyish-looking Barry. "What was so pressing that you had to talk to me tonight? I really do need to leave," she said firmly.

Barry looked uncomfortable. With Sally standing, he abandoned his perch in front of the monitors. He shifted his weight from one foot to the other, cleared his throat twice and said, "I've got a meeting with management first thing in the morning. You're one of the topics on the agenda. Mr. Vinson is interested in changing your image somewhat." His words came all in a rush, as though he was trying to get a dreaded task over with.

"Oh? In what way does he want my image to change?" Sally asked, not liking the sound of what she was hearing. Mr. Vinson was the new station manger, and in the two months since his arrival, there had been many changes at Channel Eight, including as increase in the "show biz" gimmicks on the weather news. She supposed she'd have to hear this out, she thought, sinking back into her chair.

"Well, they'd like you to dress differently on the air," Barry said, avoiding her eyes as he paced up and down the narrow aisle between the computer and the weather-forecasting apparatus.

Sally looked down at her navy suit. She could see nothing the matter with it. It was the normal sort of attire worn by members of news teams at this and other city stations and any other station of which Sally was aware. Occasionally she wore a dress, but ordinarily she wore a suit, realizing it looked more professional, and goodness knows with all the nonsense required of her on the air, she needed something to give herself an air of credibility.

"Okay, Barry, what gives?" she asked, knowing she wasn't going to like whatever it was.

"They want you sexier, honey. Now don't get mad at *me*." He put his hands up to ward off imaginary blows. He stopped pacing and leaned against the doorframe. "The big guys thought this up. Mr. Vinson's really wild for it. He thinks you haven't been properly exploited. He says you're a hot property, and he wants you on the air more and out there opening shopping centers and making personal appearances—even making commercials—looking glamorous and sexier and ah..."

Sally closed her eyes momentarily to calm herself. She smiled a forced smile at Barry. "Okay, Barry, let's hear the rest of it. Glamorous, sexy and—"

"They think you ought to wear clothing that shows off your figure—sweaters and stuff like that—something that really fits over your..." Barry shrugged and looked away, obviously avoiding even a glance at the part of Sally's body in question. "You know, honey," he tried again, "your *figure*!"

Sally smiled very sweetly and responded in a syrupy tone. "You tell management that I would be glad to wear sweaters or whatever else they want provided all the news team wears similar clothing—anchors, reporters, sportscasters, everyone. Then we can all be *exploited* together!''

"Aw, come on, Sally. The guys have got to wear suits. You know that. It wouldn't look right if they showed up in something else. That's the wrong image. And none of the other women have your..." He paused a moment then held his hands in front of his own chest in a gesture that looked like he was holding two invisible globes. "You know," he said awkwardly. "The boss wants some sex appeal."

"Believe it or not, Barry," Sally said with forced calmness, "I am a trained meteorologist. Look there on my wall. I have my diploma and my membership in the National Association of Meteorologists. My ability to analyze the weather has nothing to do with the size of my bust. Now, please, tell our esteemed station-management team exactly what I told you. I will change my mode of dress only if it is across the board and the entire news team does likewise."

"They're not going to like that, Sally," Barry pleaded. "There are lots of other girls out there who would put on a tight sweater and parade around in front of the weather map. Don't make them reexamine the policy of having trained meteorologists do the weather."

Sally sighed. "Barry, I've gone along with mascots, chickens, full- and pint-sized beauty queens, hot-air balloons, helicopters and waterskiing because I wanted to keep my job. I've gone hang gliding. I've gotten ducked in fountains and given the weather holding a chimpanzee. But on this I draw the line. Do you understand? I draw the line. I'll go to court over this one if I have to. This is sexual harassment!"

"Ah, Sally, you know you can't do that. Just think of

what it would cost to hire a lawyer, and what would you live on while the case is decided? What if Vicky had to be hospitalized again and you didn't have company hospitalization? Come on. Wearing a snug sweater is no big deal. Just strut your stuff. Ratings are bound to go up, and you'll probably get a raise."

Sally got up, grabbed her purse, turned out the light over her computer and plowed past the flustered P.R. man out onto the nearly darkened news set, the only light coming through the glass windows that separated the set from the newsroom.

"Good night, Barry. Go home. Or do you live here?"

Barry offered a forlorn good night in return. Sally stopped and retraced her steps back to where he still leaned at the door to the forecast center.

"Sorry if I was too hard on you," she said with a touch on his arm. "I know you have to spout the party line. Why don't you come see the girls this weekend? They're still talking about the time you took them to the zoo."

Barry's face brightened. "Sure. Tell them I'll take them to see the dinosaur bones at the university museum."

"They'd love it," she said with a soft kiss on his cheek.

He's just a kid himself, she thought, hurrying off toward the parking lot. He tried to act suave and "in the know," but he was still wet behind the ears and trying too hard to keep his job in a very competitive and fast-moving field. He'd never last. He wasn't tough enough—not with the likes of Vinson around.

And what about herself, Sally pondered. Was she going to last much longer? She had gritted her teeth and gone along with the outrageous format laid out for her show in the past. Where else would she have found a meteorology-related job that left her days free to spend with her two small daughters, one of whom was asthmatic and had required a great deal of attention.

The television station where she worked in Shreveport had allowed her to do her job in a more professional manner, but there was only one other meteorologist employed by the station. Sally was often required to work long hours—especially during hurricane season—and often she didn't see her daughters for an entire twenty-four-hour period. When she got the offer from the Oklahoma City station for their weekday evening slot, she had jumped at it. Her parents lived in Oklahoma City, where her father had retired after a career in the air force, and they were only too willing to become doting grandparents.

Sally had formed a pattern of dropping the girls off at their grandparents' late afternoon on her way to the station. Often the girls spent weeknights at their grandparents' house, with their mother coming to fetch them the next morning. The arrangement had been a godsend, and Sally didn't worry nearly so much about Vicky's asthma, knowing that two responsible grandparents were in attendance if she herself wasn't.

Things were different now, however. There were no longer two grandparents. Her father had died last year. At first, Sally worried about her mother managing the girls by herself, but they were older and easier to take care of. And Vicky's asthma was less of a concern than it used to be. She would be in first grade next year, and Amy would be in kindergarten.

With Vicky in school all day, having an evening job would soon not be nearly so attractive as it used to be, and Sally knew Channel Eight would never allow her to go daytime. She was brought to "dress up" the evening news, which aired at the time of day when the audience had a higher percentage of males. Sally realized the station had opted for a flashier delivery in lieu of updating its forecasting equipment. Channel Eight was the only station in Oklahoma not equipped with radar, making her job a sham in many ways. With the outdated equipment available to her at the station, she could often do little more than respond to wire-service reports. In spite of her on-the-air hints to the contrary, she really had no accurate way to monitor the path and intensity of severe weather in the Channel Eight broadcasting area.

Viewers would be far better off watching the other stations, which not only had qualified meteorologists but had up-to-date forecasting equipment, but Channel Eight could claim it had a "qualified meteorologist on duty whenever severe weather threatened." Marketing surveys indicated such credentials were important in an area like central Oklahoma, where people were very aware of hazardous weather conditions. And the station's marketing experts told them to put fatherly men on in the daytime and an attractive woman at night. Channel Eight slavishly followed its marketing reports. Such considerations as professionalism and journalistic ethics would be forgotten if they went against marketing reports. Sally wondered if the marketing firm hired by the station wasn't behind the request that she dress more provocatively.

Sally found it hard to believe that people didn't get tired of Channel Eight's tactics, but the station was doing very well. There were even signs that the other stations were beginning to imitate them, including the ultraconservative Channel Three, which had recently launched a Guess-the-High-and-Low-Temperature-of-the-Month Contest. Winners of each monthly contest would have storm cellars built in their yards. Sally was sure there were people at her station wishing they'd thought of the contest first.

Hank, the station security guard, was sitting by the back door engrossed in a girlie magazine, his chair tipped precariously against the wall. Usually, he rolled the magazine up when he saw Sally coming down the hall. He looked up as she walked by, then sheepishly looked at the magazine.

"Hi, weather lady. Caught me, didn't you?" he said apologetically as he folded the magazine so the scantily clad woman on the cover was hidden from view. Apparently feeling he had to say something to smooth over his embarrassment, Hank blurted out, "I'll bet you'd look as good in the buff as these gals do."

"Oh, Hank, come off it," Sally said, her anger rising. What a night this had been. First she was told she needed to dress to show off her figure, and now some man was speculating as to how she'd look without her clothes! "I'm pushing thirty, have an appendectomy scar and stretch marks from two pregnancies, and I feel about as seductive as an old shoe. So save your fantasies for the perfect strangers in the magazines, and leave me out of them, okay."

Hank reddened. "Sorry, Miss Storm, if I offended you. You sure look pretty in your clothes anyhow," he said awkwardly, trying to make amends. "And I sure liked your show tonight. Caught it before I came on duty. That Top Daug was a riot!"

"Thanks. Glad you liked it," Sally said curtly as she pushed open the heavy door.

It was blustery out—"gusty winds twenty-five to thirty miles per hour from the northeast," the report from the National Weather Service had predicted. The anemometer had read fifteen to twenty, but the stronger winds would come toward morning—nothing se-

vere, however, in spite of her indication on the air that
viewers had best stay tuned throughout the evening to
Channel Eight Safety First Weather. But Mr. Vinson
wanted her to push the "stay tuned" bit anytime the
wind blew harder than usual. He wanted to play on the
fear many people had in this state about severe weather—especially during tornado season.

Vinson was getting to her. The whole station was getting to her, Sally thought wearily. *Everything* was getting to her.

She used to be able to cope with things better—
like that business with the security guard. She would
not have let the remark go unchallenged, but she
would have found some way to do it good-naturedly.
She'd have to be especially pleasant to Hank tomorrow,
she thought, realizing the man had not intentionally
been offensive. And poor Barry—he was just trying to
hang on to his job and please the new station manager.
Yet he bore the brunt of her displeasure when she
should have saved it for Mr. Vinson in person. But
would she face down Mr. Vinson? Would she risk losing her job with two daughters to support?

Everything seemed to be caving in on her at once.
First her father's death, then concern over her mother's health, and now trouble with her job. Even her
on-and-off romance with Stan Edwards seemed to be
off—for good this time, which was just as well, she supposed. While he was nice enough to her daughters,
Sally realized he would just as soon spend as little time
with Vicky and Amy as possible. But he did seem to
care about *her*. That was nice, and she'd miss him.
When she was with him, she felt less lonely, and loneliness was getting to be a chronic condition with her.

Sally unlocked her faded station wagon and wearily
slid into the driver's seat. She grasped the wheel as

though seeking strength. With knuckles tight, she sat there for several minutes reaching deep inside herself. Sometimes the responsibility and the loneliness were too much.

For some inexplicable reason, she recalled a song her father used to sing to her many years ago in his dear gravelly voice. "You've got to accentuate the positive, eliminate the negative," the lyrics began. What was the rest of it? "Latch on to the affirmative, and don't mess with Mr. In-between."

She hummed the tune, then sang the words out loud. "Latch on to the affirmative." She liked that. It wasn't bad advice.

She would not let things get her down, she silently vowed. There was too much good about life to let the bad ruin it. She was still young and healthy, she had two beautiful daughters, and she had a good education. She could either lie down and play victim, or she could figure out some way out of the maze.

Which would it be, she asked herself. But she already knew the answer.

Sally started the elderly car. It coughed a few times, but she didn't even cross her fingers. Somehow, she knew it was going to start for her the first time tonight.

She switched on the radio and found a station playing something upbeat. If the girls were still awake, she'd take them and her mother to get an ice-cream cone. After all, it was Friday night. The girls usually stayed up to watch her show on Friday night. Yes, they would have a celebration! *T.G.I.F.* They would celebrate Friday night and each other. Maybe they should have banana splits. No calorie counting tonight!

THEY WERE STILL AWAKE. As always, Sally was filled with love at the sight of her daughters. At five and a half,

Vicky was a year older but noticeably smaller than her sister, thanks to her lifelong battle with asthma. Amy was taller and plumper and by far the more active of the two blond-haired girls.

The banana splits were wonderful. Always calorie conscious because of the extra pounds a television camera added to her figure, Sally didn't often indulge in such concoctions. Amy managed to get chocolate and whipped cream on her dress and on the end of her blond pigtails. Vicky was neater—but just barely. Even Margie Hampton dug into her ice cream with enthusiasm. She seemed to be feeling better this week. Sally knew her mother had been bothered by dizzy spells lately, and it was good to see her feeling better and enjoying herself.

Margie worked on Amy's sticky fingers while they waited for Vicky to finish. At last, the solemn-faced youngster gave up, announcing her tummy was "stretched full."

"Mine, too," Sally said. "Now let's get home to bed. We've got to clean house in the morning. Maybe if we get done in time, we can see if Barry will take us to see some dinosaur bones."

"Real ones?" Vicky wanted to know.

"What are sour bones?" asked Amy.

HIS DINNER HAD BEEN AWFUL. He really should start cooking again, Neal thought as he cleaned off the table. He was hungry for something Italian—*really* Italian. When he and Barbara had people in, he had always cooked lasagna or perhaps chicken parmigiana. He should at least make some spaghetti sauce—even if it was just for himself—but he knew he probably wouldn't. For him, cooking was a way of sharing and not something he did just for himself.

He felt like doing something for himself tonight, however. He started a fire in his long-dormant fireplace, fixed a small plate with some pear and cheese — Brie that still seemed okay after he cut off the mold — and poured himself a glass of brandy.

He slipped a tape of *Lucia di Lammermoor* in his portable stereo and tried to lose himself in the entrancing music. When the mixed male and female voices sang the opera's incomparable sextet, he joined them.

But the sound in the empty room was all wrong. This empty house was all wrong. He supposed he missed Barbara more than he realized, and he just didn't like empty houses. They echoed. They were inhospitable. But most of all they were lonely.

Even the cat was gone. Barbara had taken the cat. Neal would have like Mr. Chips to stay with him, but he hadn't been willing to fight over the custody of a cat, or over anything else, he thought as he looked around his empty house. She had taken everything that was worth taking, but then most of it had been hers in the first place — except his easy chair. She should have left that. Then he wouldn't be sitting in here in this stupid lump and pretending it was a chair. Of course, he still had the house itself — such as it was. It was a fine old house, but Barbara never had liked it or the city in which it was located very much. When she inherited a small fortune from her grandmother, she left him and moved back to New Orleans.

He wished her well, he thought as he lifted his brandy glass to her memory. Maybe they should have parted years ago, but he had been determined not to be a two-time loser. Geez. Married twice, and nothing to show for it except an empty house and a lonely life. He supposed the loss of cats, favorite chairs and the like was a small price to pay for the termination of a relationship that was more habit than joy. He should be relieved that something had finally been done about his and Barbara's stalemated lives.

He wondered if he had tried harder, they might have made a go of their marriage. He realized Barbara placed a lot of the blame on his involvement with his work. He spent more time chasing tornadoes than he spent chasing her, she was fond of telling anyone who would listen—particularly after she got a few drinks in her. She was right. He had given up on their relationship and allowed marriage to become a convenience. Things had not been right between them for a long time—especially after it became apparent there would never be children. Neal supposed he should be thankful now that his and Barbara's had been a childless marriage. At least their divorce had not caused the heart-wrenching agony of a family being torn apart. He had lived through such an experience once. He had never really gotten over it. He supposed he never would.

A worn and faded reminder of his first failed marriage still resided in Neal's billfold. He would come across it from time to time when searching for a credit card and take it out for a minute to stare at that delightful little face with its smattering of freckles across a button nose, its bright innocent eyes, its eager smile.

Danny. The only child who had ever called him Daddy. The only child who had embraced his neck with plump little arms and fallen asleep in his lap. His little freckle-faced buddy.

For Neal, Danny had been frozen in time. He would always be the little redheaded boy of that photograph even though the boy would now be a teenager. How Neal resented not being able to watch Danny grow up, not being able to continue as a part of the boy's life. It had been over ten years since Neal had held him that one last time before the boy's mother took him away forever. Danny had been her child—the child of another marriage, and all the love he felt for the boy did not give Neal any legal rights to maintain a relationship with him.

So at first, Neal had been relieved by Barbara's lack of interest in a family. Having no children was certainly easier on one's emotions. But after a time, he began to wonder if they were wrong to forgo parenthood. He began to think about a family, about children—his and Barbara's children. He decided he would be willing to risk fatherhood again if the children were his own. But Barbara had not been convinced, and Neal thought of Danny and the pain that could come with children. He did not push the issue.

Now he often wondered if he should have tried harder to change Barbara's mind. If they had children, maybe their marriage would not have become so hollow and meaningless, and Neal would not have turned more and more to his work for fulfillment.

As their relationship continued to deteriorate, he had become increasingly involved in his work at the National Tornado Project—an affiliate agency of the National Severe Storms Laboratory. There was a fascination and a built-in excitement that came with the study of severe weather that was easy to get caught up in—especially when one's personal life was on the wane. He had tried to content himself with professional advancement and promotions. Barbara had tried to do the same with her clubs and charities.

If only Barbara had been interested in a career of her own, he often thought, it might have made her more content. Instead, she had devoted herself to a constantly changing circuit of women's clubs and pet causes, although she always seemed dissatisfied because Neal didn't make enough money for her really to play what she considered a significant role in the city's social circles.

Personally, Neal would have liked to live in the town of Norman, located thirty miles south of Oklahoma City, in order to be near his work at the lab. But Barbara considered a university town dreary and insisted that if they had to live in such a "godforsaken place as Oklahoma," they at least had to live in Oklahoma City, where she could be involved in the symphony and ballet societies and other activities sophisticated enough for her tastes.

Neal loved Oklahoma, with its Indian traditions, western flavor and varied weather, and he especially liked Norman with the hustle and bustle of college life and the thrill of University of Oklahoma athletic events. There was even an occasional opera put on by the O.U. School of Music to gladden his half-Italian heart. But he felt some guilt over pulling Barbara away from her beloved New Orleans and by way of compensation agreed to live in Oklahoma City. He thought it was more important for her to be a part of the big-city community, and he really didn't mind commuting. The daily drives gave him time to think, except that, of late, what he thought about most was how lonesome he was. He realized now that he and Barbara might not have had a lot going for them, but at least it had not been as lonely when she was still around. In the first years of their marriage, they had shared some great times together, but apparently they didn't have what it took to share a lifetime. That was sad.

Maybe he should start dating. He had taken one of the secretaries at the lab to coffee last month, but she was so young. She didn't even know who Audrey Hepburn was.

And his buddy Phil seemed to be husband hunting for his widowed sister—"wonderful woman, fabulous cook, three wonderful kids." Phil kept trying to get him to go for Sunday dinner at Sis's house, but Neal wasn't interested in stepping into another man's shoes. He'd tried that once. He wanted children of his own and not the job of raising some other man's.

His gaze traveled from the glowing embers of his burned-out fire to the blank screen of his television. He wondered if Sally Storm liked children. But it was a passing thought; his mind soon traveled on to others concerning Channel Eight's weather reporter.

After a time, however, he gave up and climbed the stairs to bed. He was tired of pointless daydreams and fantasy women. He was tired of being alone. He wasn't about to have Sunday dinner with Phil's sister and all those kids, but maybe he could invite that secretary over to watch an old Audrey Hepburn film on television.

Chapter Two

Neal looked over the application form perfunctorily. He was running late, as usual, and his secretary had already let him know the applicant had arrived and was waiting to see him.

The man Neal interviewed yesterday had impressed him. He was young and not as experienced as Neal would have liked but was a graduate of the University of Oklahoma's fine meteorological program and currently involved in graduate work there. The young man had an excellent college transcript and superior recommendations from several of the O.U. professors Neal had worked with on research projects from time to time.

If the final choice were left up to him, Neal realized he had already picked the O.U. grad. He thought the man would fit in the lab's research team quite well and eventually be quite an asset to their program. But filling the position would be a decision by committee—although Neal, as head of this particular research team, would have the right to overrule a committee recommendation—and there were several other applicants, including the one sitting in his outer office.

Neal buzzed Nellie, his secretary, on the intercom and told her to send the woman in.

A woman. No women meteorologists worked for the National Tornado Project or at the National Severe Storms Laboratory. In fact, he couldn't remember a woman meteorologist even applying at either lab in the past. Of course, there were some female meteorologists working in other National Oceanic and Atmospheric Administration facilities throughout the country, but the Oklahoma storm labs had thus far remained an all-male domain.

He checked his watch. This interview would have to be quick if he was going to finish going through the computer printouts scattered across his desk and still meet Jerry for handball at six.

When the slender young woman entered the room, Neal thought at first there was some mistake. Had Nellie gotten his appointments mixed up? Nothing had been said about an interview with a media representative. He periodically did that as part of the public-relations effort at the lab, offering a scientific analysis of some recent weather phenomena to visiting reporters. But this afternoon he thought he was supposed to be interviewing an applicant for the research job—a woman named... Neal checked the application form. A woman named Hampton. Sally Jo Hampton. And not Sally Storm, of all people!

But that's who was standing in front of him, her hand extended, the small smile on her lips slowly fading as she took in his puzzled reaction. Sally Storm. In person! Neal was stunned.

He hastily tried to recover his composure and stood up to accept the cool, slender hand. Sally Storm's hand—he was actually touching the woman who had been captivating him during his evening television viewing! Somehow it shocked him that she was a flesh-

and-blood person and not just a lovely daydream he conjured up. He felt as if he had awakened only to find his dream was still with him. It was disconcerting, yet he found himself wanting to linger over her hand, to stroke it and relish the feel of it in his own.

"Dr. Parker, I'm Sally Hampton," she said in that familiar voice. How often he had tuned out the words and listened to that lovely voice.

"Ah, yes, of course, Miss *Hampton*. I've seen you on television. Won't you have a seat?" he said, gesturing to one of the two chairs facing his desk.

He watched as she seated herself, put her purse on the corner of his desk, leaned back, crossed her legs and then looked at him expectantly. Her eyes looked more green than blue, but maybe that was because she was wearing green. It was a soft mint green, and the color was certainly becoming to her. She looked lovely—every bit as good as she did on his television screen. More so, perhaps.

Neal couldn't quite believe she was here sitting in his office. Was she really applying for a job at the lab? But she was a television meteorologist. He couldn't imagine her in any other capacity. Here she was, however, and her application was on his desk. He would have to deal with her somehow.

With a start, Neal realized he was still standing and hastily reseated himself. "I must confess I am quite surprised to discover that applicant Sally Jo Hampton and local television celebrity Sally Storm are the same woman," he began.

"I believe I made my identity clear on my application," Sally said evenly, leaning forward to indicate the form in the open folder on his desk. "Right there on page one: 'Present position and place of employment,' are stated as, 'television meteorologist with Channel Eight News, Oklahoma City,' with my professional name given in parentheses."

She had him, Neal thought. He hadn't even bothered to look at her application or her résumé, and he was obviously unprepared for this interview. He felt completely unnerved, and he didn't like it one bit.

"Yes. Well, ah, most applicants we get here use only one name," he blundered on. "I confess I hadn't noticed your 'professional' name on your application. Yes, here it is. Sally Storm. Is that your maiden name, Miss Storm, ah . . . er, Hampton, or is it a made-up one? Catchy for someone doing television weather. Storm. Knew a Comanche once named Thunder. Billy Thunder. That would be a good name for a television weatherperson, too, don't you think?" Even as he was talking, Neal realized he was sounding dumb—really dumb. He forced himself to shut up and try to gather his thoughts.

"Actually, Storm was my married name," Sally explained, not responding to his Billy Thunder query. "I used that name in Shreveport when I was in television there. When I came to Oklahoma City, it was put in my contract that I continue to use the name even though by that time I had legally regained my maiden name for myself and my daughters."

"I see," Neal said inanely. "Well, I must admit I'm surprised to see *the* Sally Storm applying for this type of position. Why would you want to give up your television work?"

"I worked for the National Weather Service in Kansas City for three years after I graduated from the University of Kansas—that information is also on my application—and I really enjoyed the work there. It was never my intention to get into television work, but that was the only meteorological work I could find in Shreveport when I moved there with my husband. I accepted the Oklahoma City position after my divorce because it allowed me to work in the evenings and spend my days with my two young daughters. But now they're approaching school age, and I'd like to get back into the National Weather Service. I've been aware of the exciting work done here at the Norman facility and felt I was qualified for the position you advertised in the professional meteorological journals—so I wrote for an application."

"I see," Neal heard himself saying again. Surely he could think of a more intelligent-sounding response. "Well, now—qualifications. Television meteorology is important, to be sure, but what we do here is an entirely different brand of weather work."

"I'm aware of that, Dr. Parker. If you'll notice on my résumé, my bachelor's degree is in meteorology, and as my transcript reflects, I've done over twenty hours of graduate-level work at K.U. I'd love to finish a master's degree at O.U. if I should happen to get this job. I understand the lab has a close affiliation with the university. And some of the work I did in Kansas City was in the National Severe Storms Forecast Center, so I am somewhat familiar with the type of work that's done in that field. I worked for almost two years with Dr. Stanley Foster interpreting satellite data on severe weather."

"Dr. Foster?" Neal responded. "Ah, yes. Fine researcher. So, you worked with him?"

"I understood that Dr. Foster was going to write you a letter of recommendation that would explain the type of work I did with him. Didn't you receive the letter?"

Neal fumbled through the papers in the open folder resting among the stack of computer printouts. "Ah, yes. Here it is. My secretary must have filed it here with these other letters of recommendation. Foster. Fine meteorologist. Well, let's see..." Neal made a show of quickly reading the letter as he reached up to tighten the knot on his necktie, but he didn't have on a tie. Damn! It was tossed over the hat stand in the corner—along with the jacket to his suit. He couldn't believe he was conducting an interview tieless and in his shirt sleeves—especially with the interviewee being *her*!

He was feeling too chagrined to concentrate on the rather long letter of recommendation. Its tone did seem to be positive, however. "Enthusiastic" and "highly intelligent" were two of the phrases that jumped out at him.

"Yes, well, ah, he certainly does seem to write highly of you," Neal said after he thought a likely amount of time had passed for him to have digested the letter. "I'll have to look these letters over more closely later, and I'll need to take a closer look at some of this other information. Everything does seem to be in order, however."

Neal felt like a fool. He supposed that no man ever wanted to feel foolish in front of an attractive woman. She was that—attractive. And she looked so composed in her mint-green suit and white blouse with its soft bow at her throat. He'd seen her wear that outfit on the air. When was it? Two nights ago? Her hair was darker than he had thought but just as shiny. And her eyes looked even larger. Her arms were resting easily on the arms of the chair, and she did not appear to be nervous. But she did look quite serious. No bright smile decorated her face, and no lively gestures accompanied her words. He wasn't used to a serious Sally Storm. He was used to her constant smile and lilting laughter. He was used to the way she moved and gestured so freely in front of her maps and charts. Now she didn't quite seem like the same person. He would have known what to say to the Sally Storm of his television set and his late-night reveries. He wasn't doing very well with Sally Hampton.

She was perhaps older than he would have guessed from watching her on television—not in her early twenties as he had supposed. But then, he had her age right there in front of him on her résumé. He glanced down. Twenty-nine. Divorced. Mother of two daughters.

Divorced. She never wore rings on the air. He'd wondered about that. She didn't have any on now. He had noticed that right away. Only a pale pink fingernail polish decorated her hands.

Neal wondered what Miss Storm-Hampton would think if she knew he'd indulged in a few nighttime fantasies about her. He was glad his tanned complexion didn't show a blush, for he felt a flush of embarrassment at the thought. There had been times when he gave a great deal of thought to having this particular lady actually in his presence—in the flesh, so to speak. But now that he had her, he didn't know what to do with her. He was totally at a loss. In a way, he felt as if he knew her after watching her night after night while drinking his beer in his empty living room. But Sally Hampton didn't know him at all and probably thought he was a total numskull. He couldn't ask her to dinner. He couldn't ask her if she fooled around with lonely weathermen. He couldn't think of anything to ask her, and he was supposed to be in charge! He was the project *director*!

He shuffled the papers about a bit more, cleared his throat and said formally, "Well, Miss Hampton, the position for which you're applying is quite a bit different from what you did in Kansas City. We're involved in on-site observation of severe storms—not just thunderstorms but tornadoes and hurricanes. Often when severe storms hit, we chase them down in a plane or in our mobile lab. We're sometimes away from home for days at a time. It's grueling work—and physically demanding. We've never had a woman even apply for such a position before. And if you'll excuse me for saying so, I'm not sure it's work a woman would enjoy or that a woman meteorologist would fit in around here."

"So when you saw that a woman had filled out that application, you didn't bother to read the rest of it?" Sally said, her large eyes more sad than angry. "You decided that because I was a woman, this was not an application you had to take seriously. But how do you know a woman couldn't do this job if one's never tried before?"

"Miss Storm—ah, Hampton—I've seen what you do on Channel Eight. It's very appealing to some, I suppose, but it in no way relates to what's going on at a highly professional research facility such as the National Tornado Project. I think that fact would be more of a hindrance to your getting this job than your sex."

"Why do you think I'm applying for this job, Dr. Parker?" she said, leaning forward in her chair, her eyes full of challenge. "Because I like the work I'm doing now? People usually make a change when they are dissatisfied. I fully realize that the antics on Channel Eight are not up to the professional standards of most meteorologists. But then, it's usually considered professional to at least read an application and interview the applicant before passing judgment on him or *her*."

"I can assure you, Miss Hampton, that your application will get every consideration," Neal said formally, stinging from the truth in her words. "We'll let you know what our decision is sometime within the next two weeks," he said by way of dismissal.

"Oh?" Sally said wearily. "*I* will get every consideration? But I don't get shown around the facility. I don't get a chance to show my familiarity with your equipment or visit with your colleagues. Tell me, Dr. Parker, is that the procedure you have followed when male applicants came for their interviews?"

Stunned, Neal sat there dumbly and watched her retrieve her purse from the corner of his desk and leave his office. She was right. He had taken other applicants on a tour of the facility and given them an opportunity to visit with other staff members.

He tried to be angry at her and tell himself that *she* was out of line. He tried to reason that she had no comprehension of the work done here and of the qualifications necessary for such a job. He tried to shake off the depression that was settling over him like a low front over Death Valley.

He stared at where she'd been sitting, desperately wishing he could replay the whole scenario. Never had he mishandled an interview so completely.

Was that his imagination or did her fragrance still linger in the air? It was clean and sweet—not heavy perfume like Barbara wore, but a light cologne. He knew if a man were to bury his face in her hair, he could fill himself with that fragrance.

But such thoughts! Talk about unprofessional! After all, the woman was here to be interviewed for a job—an interview he had horribly bungled.

Old man, you take the cake! A lady straight from your fantasies walks in here and you run her away. What's the matter? Is she safer in your daydreams? Couldn't handle having her around all the time if she got the job? She scares you to death, doesn't she?

NEAL STOOD IN AN ALCOVE near the back of the spectators' area, not wanting Sally to notice him just yet. He knew she would be busy with last-minute preparations for the evening weather report and decided he should wait until after the show to approach her. He could see her through the glass panels that formed the walls of the area designated the forecast center. She was bending over a computer, apparently sequencing the graphics for her show, judging by the colored maps and captioned cartoons appearing on the row of monitors. He was vaguely aware that the large colored maps with their moving fronts and clouds and other graphics used on weather shows were electronically reproduced and were not actually being screened behind the weather reporter, but he did not realize that Sally herself would be responsible for organizing them into each show's format.

A discernible tension filled the air as the countdown for the show began. Sally and the sportscaster joined the two news anchors on the set at the news desk, and all four waited expectantly for the on-the-air signal. A sandy-haired guy in a plaid sports coat asked Sally to take off her camel-colored blazer, but she gave him a dirty look. "Come on, Sal," he said pleadingly. "That turtleneck knit you have on would look great by itself."

Sally ignored the young man, adjusted the jacket to her beige suit, checked her microphone and was smiling in the direction of the camera when the on-the-air signal came.

All that was required of Sally at the top of the show was the smile, a good evening and a hint of the forecast to come later in the show. Then the camera panned back to the anchors, and Sally went back to the forecast center. The sandy-haired man followed her but soon left wearing a worried frown.

When time for Sally's segment approached, she came onto the set and stood in front of a large green wall. She had an electronic switch in her hand. The news show went to a commercial.

"Let's have the first graphic up," the show's director told her. Sally punched her switch, then turned to look at the monitor. She was there on the screen, but so was the green background. There was no weather map.

"Problem, Frank," Sally said. "The switch isn't bringing the graphics up."

She hurried back to the computer in the forecast center, punched on it for a few seconds, then returned to the set. "It's in the switch," she said. "See if the engineers can come up with another one."

"No time, honey," the director yelled. "Try the switch again."

Sally punched. Nothing.

"Damn," the director said. "Sally, you'll have to wing it."

"Can you cut back my time?" she asked.

"No way. Sorry. Thirty seconds till air time."

"Debbie," Sally called to one of the assistants, "get that Oklahoma map in there—it's on top of the computer. Frank, get a camera on the map so I'll at least have something to use for locating the fronts and temperature lines."

"Ten seconds."

The young woman came racing out with the map of the state that showed only the outline of the counties and no cities. A cameraman pushed in a camera and instantly the monitors on the set showed Sally standing in front of a much-enlarged version of the same map. It was stationary, with no colorful moving graphics provided by a clever computer, but at least it was better than a blank wall.

"Five, four, three, two—" The director pointed to Sally. She was on the air.

Amazed, Neal watched as Sally calmly discussed the nation's weather picture, including her assessment of a low that was forming over the Gulf of Mexico; then turning her attention to the state's weather, she used the map that now appeared to be behind her to discuss what was happening in the state. Standing sideways, she could judge from her monitor where to gesture on the wall behind her and appeared to be gesturing at the map appearing on the television screen.

Anyone familiar with the show might wonder where the usual graphics were tonight. But just by watching Sally herself, no one would guess the show had not been planned that way from the beginning. She was smooth—no, more like elegant, Neal decided—in her presentation. He realized he was watching a real broadcasting professional.

Her weather was more in-depth tonight. Without the benefit of the usual gimmickry, she had more time to fill. She gave a brief and quite marvelous explanation of how Oklahoma's highly variable weather was influenced by its relationship to the Rocky Mountains and by its flat prairies. She finished her segment with a fire warning. "With these high winds and our current drought conditions," she said, looking straight into the near camera, "there's a high risk of grass fires. Be sure to take proper precautions if you burn trash, and you drivers, use your ashtrays for cigarette stubs and matches. And now back to Linda and Mike."

Neal was impressed. Very impressed. Being here with all the tensions and pressures of a live performance gave him a whole different perspective on television meteorology—even the Channel Eight variety. And he realized it did take more than a smattering of meteorological knowledge to put together the show he had witnessed tonight. Somehow he had the notion that copy was put in Sally Storm's hands, and in her pretty fashion, she repeated it for viewers. He now realized how incorrect that notion was.

In some parts of the country where the weather is monotonously the same, it might do for an amateur merely to read the National Weather Service report straight from the teletype. But with Oklahoma's rapidly changing and sometimes dangerous weather, viewers had come to expect an expert delivering their televised weather report. And Neal knew from experience that local meteorologists were often more accurate and up-to-the-minute than the National Weather Service forecast, and in the case of severe weather—especially tornadoes—local forecasters could beat the weather service forecast by as much as ten or fifteen minutes. Sometimes that edge could mean the difference in life and death for viewers in the path of a tornado.

Sally returned once more to the news set following the sportscast and news wrap-up for the weather wrap-up and a good night. By then, an engineer had located the trouble with the switching device, and Sally appeared on screen with a bright graphic representing a raging grass fire and reiterated her fire warning.

The news director gave a thumbs-up sign as Sally unplugged her microphone and stepped from the set for the last time. "Great job, Sal," he said as she passed by. "You covered beautifully. A real pro."

Sally smiled her thanks to the man and headed for the weather center. She was glad that was over. The tension of live television was exhausting enough without equipment failure. As many times as she'd been on the air, she had never completely gotten over her before-broadcast jitters, and she supposed what happened tonight was one of the reasons why. A live broadcast had such potential for disaster, and just about everything bad that could happen during her broadcasts had happened at least once in her year's stint in Shreveport and her four years in Oklahoma City television. Her segments had been disrupted by fainting camera operators, falling maps, upside-down maps, incorrect maps, missing graphics. A streaker had once raced across her set. And she had forgotten what day it was, forgotten the forecast, called the newscasters by the wrong name, mispronounced the names of cities, gotten mixed up on her geography, forgotten to hook up her microphone, and popped the buttons off the front of her blouse while locating a Canadian cool front on her map.

But after five years, Sally could at least *appear* unruffled. She had discovered that was half the battle.

She did take pride in the broadcasting skills she had acquired. Television meteorology could be exciting and challenging. It could serve viewers well if done professionally. Yes, it could be quite satisfying, she supposed, if a meteorologist worked for a station with higher ethical standards than Channel Eight. But she was burned out. She'd like to get back to a more basic form of meteorology—one without computerized cartoons for each kind of forecast. She unclipped her microphone from her blazer jacket, wondering how much longer before the issue of her continuing to wear suits and blazers came to a head. She didn't even look to see whose footsteps were coming across the set. Sally really didn't want to socialize with one of the camera operators or to deal with Barry again. All she was interested in was checking the instruments and printouts one last time and getting out of this large windowless building. She wanted to see the weather, not talk about it. She wanted fresh air and a breeze against her skin, and she wanted a drink.

Something alcoholic would be nice for a change—especially after tonight's fiasco. Too bad she wasn't still seeing Stan. He often used to meet her someplace after the late news, or even come to the station to take her out for a late dinner.

As Sally switched off the lights in the cubicle that held the teletype and Weather Service International scanner, she realized a man was standing in the opening to the forecast center. She turned around, expecting to see Barry's dejected face.

It wasn't Barry.

"Dr. Parker!" Sally said, not quite believing her eyes. She certainly never expected to see him again, especially so soon after that disastrous interview. She suppressed an urge to ask him what in the world he was doing at the Channel Eight studios at 10:30 P.M., but instead asked, "Did you want to see me? Is there something I can help you with?"

"May I come in?" he asked.

"Of course," Sally said.

But he stood for a minute, looking around the area at the maps, the computer, the monitors.

Sally turned to face him in the small rectangle of space in front of the bank of monitors. He looked different than he had at their first meeting. His dark hair was carefully combed, and he was wearing a suit and tie. Standing so close to him, Sally realized he was taller than she had at first supposed—tall and lanky. He seemed all arms and legs like a young Abe Lincoln, only he really wasn't so young. There was a faint showing of gray at his temples and light furrows across his wide brow. She guessed he was at least thirty-five—probably older—but there was a boyish awkwardness about him she had not noticed the other day. He had been so irritated, even flustered, at being caught unprepared for her interview and at his failure to give her application a fair consideration. Sally suspected he didn't get flustered too often. One didn't become one of the leading research meteorologists in the country by getting flustered in professional situations.

Why in the world was he here, she wondered. And what in the world was she supposed to do with him?

"Would you like to sit down?" she asked.

He nodded. She indicated the chair in front of the monitors and seated herself in front of the computer, swinging the chair around to face him.

"Was there something you wanted to see me about?" she asked, crossing her legs and placing her elbows on the arms of her chair. She took pleasure in the fact that *she* was in charge here, and he was the petitioner. The tables seemed to be turned. He was on her turf.

"Yes," he said with a deep breath. "I've been trying to write you a letter for three days now, Miss Hampton, and couldn't come up with anything that satisfied me. So, rather on an impulse, I decided to come and see you face-to-face. I got here in time to watch your broadcast. You handled all the miscues quite well. I never realized all that went into an on-the-air presentation, and I think you're right about the low over the gulf. It *does* bear watching. That's very perceptive of you."

"Dr. Parker, a third-year meteorological student could have picked that up from the satellite maps and the reports from the weather balloons," she said, finding his remark rather condescending. "But thank you for your kind words about the broadcast. It usually goes a little more smoothly than that, but Murphy's law always applies in live television. Anything that can go

wrong usually will—sometimes all at the same time—
but one develops a certain degree of adaptability after
five years."

"Yes, I suppose so." Neal absently ran a hand
through his hair, removing all traces of its careful
combing. 'Look, Miss Hampton," he began all in a
rush, "what I came here for was to apologize. I realize
my behavior the other day was unprofessional, chau-
vinistic and unfair. I *had* already discounted your application because you were a woman and regarded your
interview as a mere formality. I was totally out of line in
doing that, and well... I'm sorry. I want you to know
that I've withdrawn myself from the selection process
for the position you've applied for. I'm sure the others
on the selection committee will be more open-minded
than I was and will give your application the fair consideration it deserves—provided, of course, you are still
interested in the job."

Neal allowed himself a deep breath, obviously grateful to have his little speech over with.

Sally sat quietly for a minute, staring at the earnest
expression on Neal Parker's face, at his dark, heavily
browed eyes regarding her with such intensity. It was a
rather wonderful face—too craggy to be conventionally
handsome but one that managed to convey strength of
character along with intelligence and sensitivity. However, he certainly hadn't been too sensitive during her
interview, Sally reminded herself. But then that was apparently why he was here. She had a sense of how difficult this conversation was for him. He was more of a
man than she had at first supposed—not only to admit
he was wrong but to feel the need to try and make
amends in person rather than with an impersonal letter.
She still resented his initial response to the idea of having a woman on his research team. He had discredited

her on the basis of her sex, and no one was more distasteful to her than the sort of man who reacted that way. But at least he had enough sensitivity to rethink his position and admit he was wrong.

Did she want to work for a man like Neal Parker, who, even though he was trying to overcome them, apparently had some long-standing prejudices against women working in traditionally male fields?

But then she thought of the man she now worked for. Vinson. The jerk! William Vinson would never rethink his position concerning her place in his organization. He didn't mind having women on the news team provided they were attractive enough to suit his—and marketing's—tastes. He thought her bosom more of an asset to his station than her professional qualifications.

"Of course," Neal was saying, the earnestness of his expression bringing two vertical creases between his dark brows, "I can't make any promises. There are several other fine applicants. But if you'd still like your name in the hat..."

"Yes, I'd still like to be considered for the position," Sally said softly.

Neal sank back in his chair, obviously relieved. Sally realized just how nervous he had been. It surprised her. A man with his credentials and in his position—apprehensive about talking to *her*!

She watched as he reached into the inside pocket of his suit coat. He extended his open hand to her. On it rested one tiny crystal figurine—a pig. "Peace offering from a reformed male chauvinist pig?" he queried tentatively. His hand was trembling—just a little, but trembling nonetheless. Sally's heart melted a bit. Maybe there was some hope for Dr. Neal Parker after all.

She smiled and reached for the figurine. It was small but exquisitely worked. A collector's piece. "It's adorable," she said, cradling the tiny creature in her hand. "Thank you. I'll take it home and put it near a window where it can catch the sunlight."

Now another awkward moment seemed upon them. The man's business with her was concluded. It was time for him to leave. Already the camera crew had turned out the lights on the set and vacated the premises, but he shifted his weight in the chair, crossed and uncrossed his long legs. Sally wondered if he was waiting for her to dismiss him like a schoolmarm who was finished chastising an errant boy, or if perhaps he had something more he had wanted to say. But what erupted from his mouth was obviously unplanned.

"Ah, do you eat now? I mean, have you had dinner? Or is it too late to ask you to have something to eat, or a drink? Could I buy you a drink? Oh, hell," he said in exasperation, and began again in a mock-formal tone. "Miss Hampton, I wonder if you would join me for a late-night repast."

A man of surprises, Neal Parker, Sally marveled as her fingers closed over the tiny crystal pig. "That would be lovely," she said.

Chapter Three

They went to Joe Kelly's, a seafood restaurant and bar only a short distance from the television station.

The hostess recognized Sally as the "Channel Eight weather lady" and seated them at a choice table by a bank of windows overlooking a small lake complete with resident swans dutifully paddling around even at this late hour.

"Must be a special variety of nocturnal swans bred just to populate restaurant lakes for the pleasure of late-night diners," Neal joked as they watched the graceful birds.

"It's probably all the lights they have strung around," Sally offered. "Keeps them up. They're pretty, aren't they?"

"Yes, very pretty," Neal agreed, but he was looking at her face when he said the words. Sally pretended not to notice.

Neither one of them wanted a full dinner, ordering instead some boiled shrimp to go with their margaritas. The waitress told Sally she always watched Channel Eight news and weather.

When the waitress left, silence settled over the table. Sally made a show of sipping her drink and watching the swans while searching her brain for a topic of conversation.

"Are you—" But Neal had started to say something at the exact instant Sally spoke. "Go ahead," she told him.

"Oh, no," he said. "You go ahead."

"No, that's okay. I interrupted you."

"Well, I was just going to talk about the weather," he said lamely.

"Me, too." Sally laughed. "You'd think we were a couple of meteorologists."

"How dull," Neal said merrily. An array of small smile lines fanned from his eyes. They were very dark eyes—almost black. And he had a good smile. It was a genuine smile, Sally thought, pleased that the ice seemed to have been broken.

Then there was a wealth of subjects to talk about. By the time the second round of margaritas arrived, Sally had discovered that he was recently divorced and had no children. He played handball for exercise, missed his cat and lived in a sixty-year-old house on the edge of the Heritage Hills area. The house had the potential for being restored as a showplace, but he discovered he was terrible with a hammer and nails.

"And I couldn't afford to hire much done," Neal said. "I think my ex-wife and I were victims of a *Better Homes and Gardens* propaganda compaign—you know, the joys of remodeling. We thought fulfillment was to be found with a paint can and brush. It wasn't."

Sally could read between the lines. He still hurt. She wondered if his wife left him or vice versa—or if it was a mutual parting—but she didn't ask. It was too soon for that, she thought, realizing she was already counting on another time with this man.

She offered no details as to her own situation other than to say she had been divorced since her daughters were babies and to mention that her mother was the guardian angel who kept her life together. She answered his questions about life at Channel Eight and shared with him her frustrations over the lack of professionalism at the station.

Sally declined a third drink, ordering coffee instead. By that time, they had gotten back to the weather and were deeply engrossed in a wonderful conversation about advances in forecasting and the glories of Doppler radar. Stan and the other men she had dated didn't even know what a Doppler was, Sally thought, and didn't want to find out. Yet how many hours of her and Stan's dates had she listened to him discussing the stock market—cattle futures, selling long, the Dow Jones—interesting in small doses, she supposed, but this was better. After all, as she explained to Neal, she was a meteorologist because the field fascinated her more than any other and always had—ever since she spent her summers with her grandparents and experienced the life-or-death hold the weather had over Kansas wheat farmers. Her grandmother especially had taught her how to "read" the clouds and the winds. And from the time she was eight years old, she had maintained a backyard weather station complete with rain gauge, thermometer and wind gauge.

No, Sally realized she would never mind "talking shop" with another meteorologist. She had missed the camaraderie since leaving the weather service in Kansas City. Television weather reporters worked in shifts—one was leaving when the other was arriving, and there never seemed to be time for lengthy discussions on meteorological theory. And not all television-station weather people were trained meteorologist. In

Shreveport, she was the only one employed at the station. But in weather-conscious Oklahoma City, the stations liked to have several trained meteorologists on their staffs.

Neal spoke enthusiastically about his work for the National Tornado Project, where he headed an investigative team that was attempting to learn more about severe weather—especially tornadoes, the most feared weather phenomenon in this part of the country. Neal explained to Sally that the frequency of tornadoes and other violent weather in the Sooner state was one of the main reasons the National Tornado Project and its affiliate agency, the National Severe Storms Laboratory, had been located in Norman—that and the benefits derived from being affiliated with a respected university-based meteorological program such as existed at O.U.

Neal explained how his research team investigated historical records and carefully recorded all data about past and present-day tornadoes in an attempt to learn how better to predict them, how people can best protect themselves from tornadic winds, what sorts of structures best withstand tornadoes and anything else that pertained to the dreaded cyclones. His team investigated the damage after tornadoes and even observed actual tornadoes. It was the observing part that had brought them a great deal of notoriety as "tornado chasers."

"When we see that one's in the neighborhood—meaning within a two-hundred-and-fifty-mile radius, we take off," Neal told her.

"Isn't it dangerous?" Sally wanted to know, wondering if a single parent should be seriously considering this type of employment.

"We don't get *that* close. Oh, we get blown about a bit," Neal admitted, "but as long as you have sturdy vehicles and understand about the patterns and paths of such storms, it's no big feat to stay out of their actual path—or to get out of the way of a funnel after we've set up our instrument packages. There's more danger from lightning than from the tornadoes. We don't chase after dark, and you can see the tornadoes out in the open spaces where we're chasing. Believe me, nobody respects the power of those things more than we do. We know to stay safely out of their way. Of course, I'll admit that the first time I got close to one of those big fellows, my heart was in my throat. That was back when we just started doing this sort of activity, and no one really knew what to expect."

"That must have taken a great deal of courage," Sally commented.

"I guess it did," Neal said, "but not nearly as much courage as it took for me to approach you tonight. I do believe that was the most courageous thing I've ever done in my life."

Sally laughed and shook her head. "Am I more fearsome than a tornado?"

"You are not fearsome at all, but the prospect of seeing you again and apologizing—that was fearsome. I still can't believe I'm sitting here with you having a drink and chatting like this."

"Well, here's to courage," Sally said, lifting her coffee cup in a toast.

Neal responded with his glass and added a toast of his own. "And here's to the nicest evening I've spent in... well, in a very long time. And here's to the very special woman who made it that way."

Their eyes met and held. *Why, he'd like to kiss me,* Sally realized. *If there weren't a table between us, he would be touching me, kissing me.*

She knew that wasn't going to happen—not tonight

anyway. It was too soon. But suddenly she hoped there would be other nights with this man, and then he could kiss her. Yes, that would be nice—his lips on hers. He had a nice mouth—strong and full. He would be passionate, she decided. She suspected he hadn't been passionate in a long time, but he would be with her.

Her lips parted ever so slightly as her mind played out that passionate first kiss. But quickly she averted her eyes from a gaze that had become as intimate as the kiss they were both thinking about. She took a sip of her coffee, hoping her thoughts weren't as visibly displayed on her face as his were.

As he drove Sally back to her car in the Channel Eight parking lot, Neal asked when he could see her again.

HE TOOK HER to an O.U. basketball game the next Saturday evening. Top Daug—dressed in his red-and-white O.U. basketball suit—teased the referees, danced with the cheerleaders and chased the Kansas mascot—a jayhawk—around the floor. The O.U. mascot recognized Sally and climbed over the wall that separated the spectators from the floor. Before she realized what was happening, Top Daug was sitting in her lap, much to the delight of the crowd.

Sally enjoyed the game. She loved basketball. Neal obviously did, too, and this was a particularly exciting game. The Sooners had a most impressive center, and the red-and-blue-clad Jayhawks were blessed with two incredible guards. Neal was a graduate of O.U., and Sally was, of course, a loyal Jayhawk, having graduated from the University of Kansas. They chided each other throughout the game as one team or the other would take the lead, but it was such a seesaw battle that neither could be boastful for very long.

"How about a bet?" Neal asked midway in the first half. "How confident are you about Jayhawk power?"

"With those two guards? Are you kidding?" Sally responded. "What do you want to bet? Your house? Your car? Dinner?"

"How about if the loser cooks dinner for the winner?" Neal suggested.

"Cook?" Sally wrinkled her nose. "I don't cook much. My specialties are grilled cheese and frozen pizza, I'm afraid. And I negotiate drive-through windows at fast-food restaurants with a real flair."

"No confidence, eh?" Neal teased. "Trying to back out of the bet?"

"Oh, all right. Dinner. I like chicken or fish, please. I don't eat much red meat," she announced before returning her attention to the game and cheering as much as she dared for her team while sitting among so many Sooner fans. She'd already decided that if the Jayhawks did lose, she'd make curry. She did like to cook occasionally—for special people. Usually, though, she didn't have the time or the inclination.

Throughout the game, Sally found herself suffused with excitement from two different sources. There was the thrill of watching her beloved Jayhawks playing so well on an "enemy" court—the kind of delight that she always felt when she watched talented athletes in a closely matched contest. And on another level, there was the excitement of being with the lean, powerful man sitting next to her. Not only was she terribly aware of him—of his muscular jeans-clad thighs, of his large hands resting on them, of his shoulder brushing against hers—but she also found herself terribly aware of her own body. For some reason she seemed to fit inside her skin better tonight. Her skin felt *good*. All of her felt good—her breasts as they rubbed against her blouse, and her waist, her stomach, her hips. But the part of her she was most aware of was her left thigh, for it resided only a few inches from Neal's right one. The place on her thigh that would touch his should he move his leg ever so slightly began to warm, and that warmth radiated up through her leg and throughout her body. It was a silly, delicious feeling. Sally wanted to stroke her own arms and enjoy the smooth alivenenss of her flesh. She wondered if Neal would think her flesh felt good if he were to stroke it. Somehow, she felt reasonably confident that he would.

She had thought about him a great deal in the past few days—nothing specific, however. She would not allow herself specific thoughts. After all, she had just met the man. But she had such a sense of anticipation—first for the call she knew would come, then for the evening they would spend together. She could not remember the last time she had felt such anticipation. The time they had been together at Joe Kelly's restaurant was good. They had a lot in common and were attracted to each other. She was aware of that attraction now every time their elbows touched on the chair arm separating their two seats. There was an electricity about touching him that quickened her pulse, and when he looked at her, she knew it was with admiration. That was nice. She could almost *feel* her eyes sparkle and her skin glow. She hadn't felt this good in a long time. She didn't try to analyze why she felt this way, or worry that it wouldn't last, or wonder if he was really divorced or just feeding her a line. She just wanted to enjoy the gift of this evening and this man.

It was only in the last thirty seconds that Kansas put the game away. Sally didn't dare cheer while the rest of the crowd stood in stunned silence, but she gave Neal a smug look. "Want to borrow a cookbook?" she asked sweetly.

"Actually, dinner should be cooking right now," he

said, checking his watch, "provided, of course, the automatic timer on my oven is working correctly."

"What do you mean?" Sally asked. "You've already cooked dinner? You have a crystal ball or something?"

"No, but if the Sooners had won, I was going to be a gracious winner and not hold you to your bet. *My* specialty is anything Italian. Now let's get out of here and see if we can beat some of this crowd to the parking lot."

They raced to the car. Sally beat him.

"I forgot to tell you I was Big Eight champion at the eight hundred meters," she told Neal when he arrived at the car.

He leaned against the car, his chest heaving, his breath making white vapor in the chilly night air. "Geez!" he said breathlessly. "Do I ever know how to pick a date! She can't cook and beats the socks off me in a foot race! I suppose you play handball, too."

"Furiously."

"I was afraid of that," Neal said as he unlocked the car. "Geez!"

THE WONDERFUL AROMA of basil and oregano greeted them as Neal opened the front door of his house.

"Oh, wow!" Sally said appreciatively. "Your oven timer obviously works."

The table was already set—a card table in the dining room complete with candles, flowers and wineglasses.

"Sorry about the plastic dishes," Neal apologized. "They're all I have. Guess I should have bought some others."

"Plastic is fine," Sally assured him. "The table looks lovely."

Neal installed her on his kitchen stool with a glass of Chablis while he bustled around preparing the pasta and a wilted spinach salad and warming the bread. This was nice, Sally thought, trying to remember the last time a man went to so much trouble for her. It made her feel special—very special indeed.

Neal's chicken Alfredo was heavenly, as was everything else about the meal. Sally was impressed and told him so. "Parker doesn't sound very Italian, but this tastes authentic."

"My mother's maiden name is Vittorini," he explained. "I got her brown eyes and her love of anything cooked with oregano and mozzarella. The ability to eat pasta and not get fat I can thank my father for. Mom's been trying to fatten him up for forty years. I think she considers it an affront to her culinary prowess that he's still built like a rail."

"I'd say you got the best from both parents," Sally said. "And my compliments to the chef's mother for being liberated enough to teach her son to cook. This was a delightlful meal."

"Oh, but it's not over yet. Wait till you taste my zabaglione!"

They finished their meal with the sherry-flavored custard and coffee. Sally pushed her chair back and patted her tummy. "I'm going to have to run miles and miles to counteract all that, but it was worth it. I can't tell you how much I enjoyed myself."

"Well, I can't tell you how much I enjoyed preparing it. I haven't cooked—*really* cooked—in a long time. It was wonderful—weeping over the chopped onion, singing opera in my horrible baritone, and thinking about the lovely woman who would be gracing my table, even if it was only a card table set with kitchen dishes. She would make it seem like burled mahogany set with crystal and china. I can't thank you enough, Sally Hampton, for allowing me this pleasure."

The candles burned low as they lingered over brandy. The room was dark but for the pool of flickering candlelight. His eyes reflected the flame. Such wonderful eyes—so dark, they looked black. They were deep-set, expressive and set off by a perfect arch of heavy brows. Sally loved their warmth, the way their corners crinkled when he smiled, the way they made her feel when he looked at her.

And how did they make her feel? As if she were slowly melting inside, Sally decided. Like a woman who wanted a man very much. It was so wonderful to feel like this!

It seemed only natural that they carry a second glass of brandy into his bare living room and light a fire in his fireplace. He brought a couple of pillows from his bed and tossed them on the Oriental rug he confessed he had bought just for the occasion.

"That's why I didn't get around to buying dishes. The stores were closing last night by the time I had decided which rug to buy. I hope you don't mind about the lack of furniture," he said, suddenly seeming insecure as he looked around the barren room with its bean-bag chair, television and lonely coffee table. I guess I should have bought a sofa first, but I've wanted a rug for a long time. It was so empty-sounding in here with no rug. I hated it."

"The rug is beautiful," Sally assured him.

Neal pulled over the coffee table to use as a backrest, and Sally seated herself on a pillow. She slipped off her shoes and toasted her toes by the fire as she allowed herself to become mesmerized by its dancing flames. The wine and brandy had mellowed her, but the effect of Neal's presence was headier than any wine. She felt as though she were floating on a cloud—or perhaps a magic carpet, she thought as she stroked the lovely rug.

He was looking at her as she watched the fire. She could feel the warmth of his gaze mingling with the warmth of the flames. Sally wanted to remember this moment, so she lingered over it, allowing the anticipation to seep through her body. Yes, she wanted to be able to recall how it felt at this moment before they first kissed. It was so sweet, it brought a moistness to her eyes.

They talked for a time, wandering through varied topics—favorite books, music, cities. While they explored each other's minds, they were exploring the experience of being together in a private place and of having their hands touch. An exquisite tension was building between them like a symphonic movement building toward a crescendo.

At last the tension became like another presence in the room, stealing their words and leaving them dumb.

Sally was wise enough not to tamper with the purity of the mood. It mattered not that their relationship was undefined. Perhaps there was only to be this one time for them, or perhaps it was a beginning. There was no way to tell. But she understood they had been presented the gift of an innocent, unfettered moment in their lifetimes. She would have no more turned away from it than she would have denied one of her children a kiss. Strange that she felt this way with this man, whom, at their first meeting, she had disliked so much. Yet she had never felt quite so right about being with anyone before. It was almost as though it was predestined that she be here in this empty house on this night with him. She accepted the judgment of whatever forces had brought them together—and thanked them.

Sally knew all it would take would be for her to turn her face and look at him. Then he would kiss her. In her mind, she had not yet thought past the mystery of his first kiss, but she realized her body had its own longings.

She closed her eyes for an instant and inhaled deeply, drinking in all the sensations she was experiencing. Then, slowly, she turned her face to him. Softly, ever so softly, she touched his lips first with her fingers then with her own lips.

A moan erupted deep inside of him, and he took her in his arms. His kiss was hungry and invasive. He took possession of her mouth with a passion that thrilled her and pushed her yearning to a deeper level.

"Ah, Sally, Sally," he said as he moved his mouth over her face and throat. "I've thought about nothing but you for three days—for weeks, for months. You've been driving me crazy. I want you so. I can't stand it I want you so. I've been watching you on that dumb television for months, then the other night—being with you, it was too much. You're too much. I want to make love to you, but I know it's too soon. I shouldn't be saying this...."

She took his face in her hands and forced him to look in her eyes. "I want you, too," she said. "Make love to me."

He kissed her again and again. Their bodies crumpled onto the mound of pillows. He buried his face against her throat, against her breasts. His fingers were at the front of her blouse.

She was so eager for him to touch her breasts, she almost pushed his hands out of the way and unbuttoned her blouse herself. But she forced herself to wait as he fumbled first with the buttons, then pushed the fabric of her bra aside. That wasn't enough, however. Sally didn't want anything in his way. She wriggled out of her blouse and unfastened her bra herself. The look of naked yearning on his face as he stared at her exposed torso brought a murmur of pleasure to her lips. First his hands, then an appreciative mouth gloried in her breasts. She allowed herself to be vain, allowed herself to be delighted that her breasts were full and firm and tantalized him so.

She unbuttoned his shirt and pushed him on his back so she could feel the erotic delight of flesh against flesh—of her breasts rubbing against his firm hair-covered chest. Then she leaned over him, allowing her breasts to achieve their fullest contours as he took first one nipple then another into his mouth, licking them and delicately tugging at them with his teeth before sucking deeply, so deeply she felt it all the way to her womb.

Sally closed her eyes to shut out everything but his mouth and her breasts. She was so dizzy with sensation she hardly noticed his hand at her waist, unfastening her slacks.

When his hand slid down her belly and between her legs, she gasped with pleasurable shock.

"Oh, yes," she gasped. "Yes." And she began pulling at his belt.

"I want you naked," he told her. "I want to see and feel all of you."

She arched her back so he could peel away the rest of her clothing and watched as he pulled off his clothes. The firelight flickered across his lean, firm body.

Sally touched him, tentatively at first, then with greater assurance as her ministrations brought moans of pleasure from his lips. Then her hands on him were not enough. She wanted to do more for him. Such delight she took in pleasuring this visible proof of his desire for her! He had said she was driving him crazy. She liked that. She would drive him even crazier. She would nurse him to even greater pleasure.

When he buried his hands in her hair and pulled her on top of him, she knew she could bear it no longer. Sally watched the look on his face as their bodies joined. She wanted to see as well as feel his desire. They watched each other as she rocked back and forth on him, as his hands fondled her breasts and stroked her sides and thighs and buttocks.

Then she leaned forward to kiss him, her hair falling in a curtain around their faces.

Her eyes closed now. She was through with being the aggressor. Instinctively, he rolled her off him and, without leaving her body, covered her with his.

With legs wrapped around his thighs, Sally felt her body rising on a tidal wave of sensation. Falling, rising, drowning. Again and again. Each cresting bringing her closer and closer to that ultimate white-hot place of total surrender.

AFTERWARD, AS SHE LAY CRADLED in his arms, Sally wondered if she would ever be quite the same again. She had given away part of herself. She wondered what he would do with her offering. It frightened her. But even as she experienced the feeling of vulnerability their lovemaking had brought her, she also experienced a feeling of peace.

She was covered with his shirt. She didn't remember him doing that. Had she drifted away for a bit? Perhaps. She snuggled closer to him. How natural it felt to be there in his arms.

He kissed her forehead. "I want to say something wonderful and profound," he said into her hair, "but I'm totally at a loss for words."

"Me, too," she murmured. "You don't have to say a thing."

A log broke on the fire and erupted in a series of

loud cracklings, sending an agitated series of shadows across the ceiling. Suddenly the pool of warmth from the fire was inadequate, and an involuntary shiver shook her body.

Neal left her long enough to get a blanket. He covered her, then slipped under the blanket with her. "Now we can do without this," he said as he pulled his shirt away from her and once again their naked flesh touched.

As they lay there, they talked. What had just happened between them was too new, too delicate to examine, so they set it aside in favor of simple things. She told him about the fireplace in her grandparents' farmhouse. He told her about his house and all the plans for this room and others that would never materialize. "I'm going to move," he announced. "I just decided. End of chapter. New domicile. It's time for a change."

Sally wondered where she fit in. Was she at the end of the last chapter or the beginning of the next? She almost dared to ask, but now he was telling her about sitting in this room watching her program.

"Night after night, five nights a week," he was saying. "I sat there in that dumb, uncomfortable chair and watched you like some adolescent voyeur. I don't like Channel Eight. I don't like gimmicky weather shows, but I was smitten by Sally Storm. This isn't the first time you've been here in front of my fireplace. In my fantasies, you've made several visits. But I shouldn't be telling you this, should I? Sounds so damned foolish! I still have this feeling of unreality. You aren't really here beside me. It's just another lonesome bachelor dream, isn't it?"

"Well, yes and no," she said, playing with the hairs on his chest. "Sally Storm may have been a fantasy creature, but Sally Hampton is quite real, thank you."

"The fantasy pales beside the real woman," he said with his lips against her ear. "Sally Storm has more than met her match."

His hand had moved from her waist to her breast, and Sally could feel him stirring against her thigh. A smile tugged at her lips. *Good for you, Sally Hampton,* she thought smugly.

So slowly they went the second time, completely enjoying the sweet agony of their mutual arousal, relishing each touch, each kiss, like two misers counting and recounting their fortunes. It was a wondrous thing, their lovemaking, each greedily wanting to experience every nuance of their shared pleasure.

"You can't be real," he said at last, cradling her once again in his arms and enjoying the afterglow.

He wanted her to spend the night, but she kissed him lightly and said, "I must get back to reality, wonderful man. I have responsibilities out there in the real world."

"But I want you to stay with me. I want to wake in my bed tomorrow morning with you there. I want to wake you with a cup of hot tea, then make love to you again."

She sighed. "A lovely thought, but I can't."

Begrudgingly, he allowed her to leave his arms and with regret watched her dress. "I like you better naked."

"Bird'll come along and sit on your lip." She laughed and touched his pouting lower lip. "Funny, that usually works with my girls when they pout, but I'm not sure how to cure big-boy pouting."

"By staying with me," he said, tugging at her arm. "Can't you call and tell them you're staying with a sick friend?"

"I'd scare my mother to death if the phone rang at this hour," she said firmly. "She's staying over with my girls, and I think it's best for now if I'm in my accustomed place in the morning. I should warn them ahead of time if I'm not going to be there. We always go to the Pancake House on Sunday morning. Would you like to join us?"

"No, thanks anyway," he answered hurriedly. "I've got some measurements I have to make at the lab." He got up and pulled on his clothes.

Sally padded over to him, her blouse still unbuttoned, her hair rumpled. Already he wanted her again. Would he ever get over wanting her?

"Hey, you're not mad, are you?" she asked, her face concerned.

"No," he said, "not really. I'm just being selfish. I understand you have to go. Really I do."

"If you can't make it for pancakes, how about Sunday dinner? My mother would be delighted, and you could meet my daughters."

"Sure, that would be great," he said, hoping his voice sounded convincing.

Chapter Four

It started to sprinkle as he drove home from Sally's house. How nice if the drops turned into something, Neal thought, but he knew the large wet spots disturbing the dust on his car probably would be all there was to the shower. It was just a teaser—enough to make people look heavenward and hope the end had come at last to their long moistureless winter.

Well, the rains would come soon enough now. In Oklahoma, one could be sure of that. Conditions could go from drought to floods within hours. A yellowing cartoon on the bulletin board at the lab showed a farmer rowing a boat down his flooded drive to pick up his drought-relief check from his nearly submerged mailbox.

But there would be no flooding today, only a depressingly gray sky and spotted cars.

And it wasn't just his car bearing spots, Neal thought grimly. He had a spotted necktie and angry red welts spotting the backs of his hands and his neck. He glanced down at the gravy stain on his maroon tie and scratched first at one hand and then the other before attacking the itching skin on his midsection under his white shirt where more of the welts resided. Somehow ruined neckties and hives seemed appropriate.

The Sunday dinner at Sally's house had not gone well.

He had felt acutely uncomfortable sitting there at her table with her family.

Sally's mother, Margie, who lived across the street, was an older version of her daughter. Her brown hair was liberally salted with gray, but she was slim like Sally and had the same charming, one-dimpled smile and greenish-blue eyes.

Neither of the little girls resembled their mother appreciably. They must have gotten their blond hair and vividly blue eyes from their father, Neal decided. He wondered if Sally was reminded of her former husband every time she looked at his children.

Neal hadn't wanted to go to her house in the first place—not yet anyway. The whole Sunday dinner bit with ready-made family in assigned seats was something he had always intended to avoid. After last night, however, it would have been very hard for him to deny Sally Hampton anything. The evening with her had been the most extraordinary he had ever spent. It was like something out of a book, something so perfectly beautiful that it could only happen to made-up people and not in real life. Neal was smitten. He even wondered if he was in love. Never before had there been a woman like Sally Hampton. Never. He wanted to be with her again and again. He wanted to be with her as much as possible—but not in the bosom of her family. A month at hard labor would have been easier than the past couple of hours.

From the minute he arrived and was ceremoniously led to an easy chair in the living room by his three-generation welcoming committee, Neal had been painfully uncomfortable. He wondered if he were sitting in *his* chair—the chair where the man who had been married to Sally and fathered the two blond children used to sit on Sunday afternoon reading his paper while the chicken was being fried and the potatoes mashed.

If he had to be there, Neal would have rather been helping in the kitchen. He never understood the careful division of labor that kept women in and men out of kitchens. In his family, everyone had helped. They had a huge kitchen, and fixing the meal with all the accompanying tasting and anticipation was as much fun as the gathering around the big round table in the dining room.

He'd already read the paper. He wasn't interested in the professional football game that was playing on the television. But when he wandered to the kitchen, Neal was assured "everything was under control, and dinner would be ready shortly."

And indeed, shortly after, they all gathered around the table in Sally's dining room. Neal was given the head of the table—the "daddy seat," he thought to himself.

Sally looked radiant and was obviously pleased to have him there with her daughters and her mother. She was wearing a pink-and-white-striped shirtwaist with a ruffled front and a full skirt—a much more feminine look than she presented for her televised weathercasts—and appeared as refreshing as a piece of peppermint candy. Neal couldn't take his eyes off her. She was so vibrant and lovely! He longed to be with just her—alone, without her watching family. He would rather have been anyplace but where he was. Sunday dinner was a family time. *They* were a family. He envied them but knew he did not belong.

Neal was very aware of not belonging as he watched Sally with her girls. She was the head of this household. Their relationships and traditions had already been established. The way they served the meal, the sharing of chores in their household—all that was long established as, he was sure, the way they celebrated birthdays, Christmas and other holidays, and spent their leisure time. The girls always set the table, Sally explained. The china had been her grandmother's. The recipe for the green-bean casserole was her aunt's. Margie had made her special apple strudel for dessert—a longtime family favorite.

The little girls—Vicky and Amy—were pretty and well-behaved. He sensed the easy, loving relationship they had with their mother. She corrected them not with sharp words but with pointed looks—and not too many of those. Sally obviously adored her children, and Neal had no trouble seeing why. Who wouldn't like being the parent of two cute little girls? He wondered about their father. Did they see him often? Did he like to hold them in his lap and take pleasure in the feel and aroma of their childish bodies? Did he enjoy their bright eyes and constant questions? Did he miss them when he couldn't be with them?

Neal thought of the picture in his billfold of the small child he had once shared with a woman. No, not really shared, for Danny was borrowed. Danny had never really been his.

Neal made a few stabs at conversation with the girls, asking their ages, if they watched their mother on television, if they went to school. But he was uncomfortable with the idea of becoming friends with them. Oh, he would have liked to take them out and swing them in the tire swing he could see through the dining-room window and get down on the floor to help them with their puzzles and games as he used to do with Danny. He even found himself wondering if little girls liked to wrestle or play catch.

But these little girls weren't just any little girls. They were *her* children—Sally's children. That complicated his response to them. He liked their mother too much. Neal felt as if he were falling down a deep well of emotions—out of control. Sally was exactly the kind of woman he promised himself he would never get involved with. She was a woman with children. Neal didn't want to borrow children again. He wanted ones who would be permanently his, so he did not respond readily to Vicky's and Amy's shy smiles and childish overtures of friendship. He did not push them in their swing or work puzzles with them. He did not show an interest in their new coloring books. And the hurtful look in their very blue eyes made him quite uncomfortable. He didn't belong here. They knew it. He knew it.

The problem with the green beans somehow seemed symbolic of the whole uncomfortable afternoon. They were cooked in a cheese sauce with mushrooms and pimientos. Pimientos were the one foodstuff in the world to which he was allergic. They gave him hives. Carefully, and he hoped unobtrusively, he picked the pimientos from the beans and pushed them to one side on his plate, trying to hide them under a lump of uneaten mashed potatoes. That was after gravy dripped down the side of the gravy boat and onto his tie. Sally had wanted him to take the tie off so she could use some spot remover, but Neal insisted he had a fine dry cleaner who would make the tie like new.

His discomfort must have been apparent to the two women, for they began trying too hard in their efforts to converse. The entire mealtime conversation was forced, and the girls sat solemnly watching their elders struggle to be very friendly.

The itching began after dinner. Neal was helping

Sally clean up the kitchen while Margie played cards with the girls in the living room. Delighted finally to have Sally to himself, he was trying to recapture some of the closeness they had shared the night before. He wanted them to do the damned dishes, then get her out of there. They could take in a movie or go back to Joe Kelly's—anything except stay in this house with those two truly charming little girls and Sally's hovering mother watching them. When the itching started, he tried to ignore it. *No, surely not,* he thought desperately. He had been careful not to eat any of the disgusting red things, but the itching would not be denied. It distracted him. He was having a hard time concentrating on his and Sally's conversation. Even to himself, his request that just the two of them hurry up and leave sounded rather rude.

He had tried not to scratch and desperately hoped the blotches popping out on his neck weren't as red as the ones on the back of his hands.

"It's the pimientos, isn't it?" Sally asked, however. "I noticed you were trying not to eat them."

"Yes," Neal admitted miserably. "I thought I picked them all out, but I guess their close association with the green beans was enough to do the trick. I'll be okay as soon as I get home and take some antihistamine. We can stop by on the way to a movie or wherever."

Sally stood in the middle of her kitchen, twisting a dishcloth in her hands. She wore a green apron over her dress. The apron looked new. By her own admission, she didn't cook a whole lot, but she had gone to a great deal of trouble just for him. Neal was touched by her effort. He understood she had wanted him to feel at home, to get to know her family. But he hadn't—couldn't. The look in her eyes was sad.

"Not tonight," she said firmly. "I need to catch up

on laundry and other chores. Monday morning will be here before we know it.''

''Yes, I know how it is,'' Neal had said, his disappointment bringing a sullen tone to his voice. He ached to be with her again—to explore her lively mind, to watch her lips while she talked, to touch her. Oh, how he ached.

But the afternoon had ended. He said good-bye to Margie Hampton and the two girls, awkwardly patting them on the head and trying to remember which was which.

Neal stopped for the stoplight at Classen and Northwest Twenty-third. He used the time to unbutton his shirt and claw at his belly. He hoped the antihistamine would work fast. He was miserable—inside and out. Why did everything have to be so complicated, he thought as he turned the car down his street. The absolutely most delightful woman in the world had come into his life, but she didn't come alone. Neal groaned. She had children—two of them and they looked just like their father.

He felt as though some sort of vicious cycle was starting all over again. Love. Temporary fatherhood. Loss.

No, damn it, he swore silently as he gripped the steering wheel more tightly. The next children he got involved with were going to be his own. When he got married again, he wanted to have children, but he wanted his wife and he to be new parents together. Sally Hampton obviously wasn't *that* woman. The question was could he come to terms with that knowledge. Neal felt as though he was being pulled apart.

But he'd known her such a short time, he reminded himself. *Quit jumping the gun. Just date her, and don't be thinking about lifelong commitments already.* After all, he hadn't been divorced very long. Maybe his falling so hard for Sally was just one of those rebound things that happened to people when they were freshly divorced and terribly vulnerable.

He took some antihistamine for his hives, vowing never to get in the same room with a pimiento again, and took two aspirin for the headache that was starting to invade his forehead.

He carried a pile of reports he hadn't had time to fill out at the office to the dining room and spread them out on the card table. It was just as well he hadn't made plans for the evening, Neal rationalized. He really needed to tackle this mess.

But from his vantage point at the vinyl-covered table, he could see the Oriental rug in front of the fireplace. The ashes from last night's fire formed a mound beneath the grate. The empty brandy glasses still rested on the hearth. His moan echoed in the empty house.

He changed chairs and faced the kitchen, but then he could see the high kitchen stool where she had sat and sipped her wine while he finished up dinner. He could close his eyes and see her sitting there, her eyes vivid, her smile endearing.

He gave up on the reports and went for a walk. The weak front that had brought the scanty rainfall had already passed over. The sky was almost clear with very little cloud cover—just a few scud clouds left over from the front and turned pink by the sunset. The first stars twinkled merrily in the eastern sky, but they didn't cheer him.

Perhaps they could just be lovers, Neal thought as he wandered aimlessly around his neighborhood. His and Sally's relationship didn't have to be more than that. Such an arrangement would probably be temporary—a dead end, but they could share their lives for a time. It might be heaven for a while, but regardless, it was the best solution he could come up with. He just knew that he wanted Sally Hampton in his house, across his table, in his bed, in his arms—even if it meant opening himself up for a greater pain later on.

SALLY HAD INDEED DONE LAUNDRY after Neal left—and cleaned the oven, swept the garage, cleaned out the girls' closet. That evening, she took the girls to a neighborhood park and pushed their swings and the merry-go-round with a vengeance while trying to substitute physical activity for thought.

But now, the girls had been driven through McDonald's, read to and were tucked in bed, and Sally was too tired to tackle another job. As she sank into a kitchen chair with a cup of coffee and a package of Fig Newtons, the disappointment of the day swept over her like a suffocating fog. She was grateful when she heard the tap at her back door.

"Hi, Mom," she said as she opened the door for her blue-jeans-clad mother.

"You seemed a little down," Margie said. "Would you like some company?"

"You bet. Care for some leftover coffee?"

"I brought my own," Margie said, holding up a packet of decaffeinated. She quickly heated a cup of hot water in the microwave and soon was seated across from her daughter at the white metal table. "Dr. Parker seemed nice," Margie said tentatively as she poured the powdered decaffeinated coffee into her hot water.

"Yes, he is," Sally agreed, "but he seemed very uncomfortable around the girls."

"I noticed. Well, maybe after he gets to know them..."

"No, I don't think so," Sally said, absently rubbing a

finger around the rim of her cup. "I think he's petrified of them."

Sally helped herself to a Fig Newton and pushed the pack toward her mother. Margie shook her head no.

"Funny, I had such good feelings about him," Sally continued after a tentative nibble on her cookie. "I will admit I was on a trip with all the floor waxing and cooking Sunday dinner. Can you believe I actually cooked a chicken and didn't go buy one at the Colonel's? And made Aunt Lura's green beans? If I'd had more warning, I'd probably have baked bread and washed all the windows. Kind of dishonest of me, wasn't it? Little starched aprons and fried chicken—that's not me. And relating to two little girls obviously isn't him."

"Maybe you did go overboard a bit," Margie acknowledged. "Perhaps it's time to back up and lay some groundwork for a more honest friendship if you think you want to see him again. He probably rushed you a bit."

"Mom, I was the one moving too fast. My gosh, I've known him less than a week, and I'm throwing myself at him." Sally closed her eyes and shook her head as she recalled just how quickly she had allowed their relationship to proceed. She who had always been so wary had really tossed caution to the wind. But, oh, what a wonderful night they had shared! She didn't regret it. She was so very sorry, however, that it seemed to be both the beginning and the end with them.

"There I was rattling pots and pans," Sally continued berating herself, "and parading my dressed-up little girls in front of him. Look here, a ready-made family up for grabs. See how sweet and darling we all are. But the night before I hadn't been acting so maternal and domestic. I'd been indicating something else altogether to him. Poor man. Talk about crossed signals! He probably felt as if he'd been run over by a freight train."

"You really fell for him, didn't you?" Margie said with a sympathetic pat on her daughter's arm. "It's the first time I've seen you care so much since..."

Margie's voice trailed off, but Sally knew what her mother was thinking. This was the first time she had cared so much since Michael—and Michael broke her heart.

Sally could not meet her mother's gaze. She took a quick sip of her coffee and willed away the stinging tears that threatened to well up in her eyes. She could still remember the pain. She supposed she always would.

"Well, Michael was not the man for me, and apparently neither is Dr. Neal Parker," Sally said defiantly.

"Isn't it a little soon to be making that judgment?" Margie challenged.

"What's the point of even thinking about it, Mom? I'm not alone in the world. I have Vicky and Amy. It's an all-or-nothing proposition. The girls and I are a package deal."

"I don't recall Stan's ever having much to do with the girls," Margie offered, "and you went with Stan for quite a while."

"Yeah," Sally said with a shrug, "but Stan was just someone to go out with—someone to date."

"And Neal?" Margie prodded.

"He's different," Sally said evasively.

Ah, yes—different, she thought after her mother had left. Neal was more than just someone to date. He was the kind of man you fell in love with.

But she would not love him. No way. She wasn't going to love a man who couldn't love her *and* her children.

IT HAD BEEN almost two weeks since Barry had discussed a change in Sally's on-the-air image with her, and she dared hope the whole matter had been put to rest. But when she received a summons to Mr. Vinson's office, she had a pretty good idea the subject was about to be raised again.

Barry was there, perched on one of the two armchairs facing the station manager's huge leather-topped desk. Sally slipped into the other.

"Barry tells me you aren't agreeable to some of the proposed changes in the weather presentations," Vinson began, absently toying with a rather ominous-looking jade-handled letter opener. His manicure appeared fresh.

"As a professional meteorologist, I find it insulting to be asked to wear 'sexy' clothing and do some of the stunts I'm hearing about," Sally said. "Barry tells me there is even a contest being planned with the winner to have a date with me."

"Yes," Vinson agreed, offering a small nod of his carefully coiffed head with its mane of snowy-white hair. "Sounds like a wonderful idea. Barry and I were just discussing it. Win a date with the sultry Miss Storm—or something like that. Should really help our ratings."

"Yeah," Barry said, avoiding Sally's eyes, "Mr. Vinson thought you could interview the finalists on the air—sort of a local 'Dating Game.'"

"Please understand my position on this, Mr. Vinson," Sally pleaded. "I was hired to do the weather on this station because I happen to be a trained meteorologist. I would be embarrassed to be a part of the things you are suggesting and would appreciate the station's adopting a more businesslike approach to its weather news. I wish Channel Eight would quit trying to out-gimmick the competition."

"Miss Hampton," Vinson said evenly, his hooded eyes glaring at her, "I could hire some other good-looking broad to read the wire-service report—someone *younger*—and pay her half of what I pay you."

"I'm aware of that," Sally said. "I'm also aware of what the people in this region of the country expect out of television meteorology. They have come to rely on stations as more than weather reporters. They expect forecasting ability. They turn to their television sets when severe weather threatens. The viewers expect each station to operate a forecasting center *and* have trained meteorologists operating it. If you put a chorus girl in front of the camera merely to read the weather, I don't think the viewers will have much confidence in the station's weather news. They would realize there was no up-to-the-minute forecasting being done. I doubt if they would turn to Channel Eight during weather alerts."

"So, we'll turn our 'trained meteorologist' into a chorus girl and kill two birds with one stone," Vinson said. "Take it or leave it, Miss Hampton."

"WHAT NOW?" Barry asked Sally as they left the luxurious administrative wing of the building and headed for the station snack bar. "Going to go along with Vinson or quit? What's the status of that job in Norman?"

"I was interviewed by the other members of the search committee," Sally said. "And I talked to the head of the meteorology school at O.U. about finishing up my master's degree if I get the job—but I'm not optimistic, and I'm not sure whether I should take the job even if it is offered."

"How come? I thought you really liked the guy you'd be working under."

"I did—I mean I do. I have a lot of respect for him.

He's a world-class meteorologist if there ever was one. It's just that we..." Her voice trailed off as they entered the deserted room with its bank of vending machines and coffee bar.

"Your date with him didn't go too well, I take it," Barry said as he fed two quarters into the Coke machine and Sally helped herself to a cup of coffee.

"More like it went too well," Sally admitted. "So I invited him over to dinner and to meet the family. I really rushed the poor guy."

"And?" Barry asked as they seated themselves in a booth. "What's the problem?"

"Well, let's just say relations are now strained. It would really cloud my decision about the job if it should happen to be offered, but..."

"Yes?" Barry prodded.

"Oh, I'm kidding myself, Barry. I have no choice. I'd do anything to be able to walk out of here. If that job in Norman is offered to me, I have to accept. I'll take it and hope Dr. Parker and I can do better on a professional level than we did on a personal one. The job at the tornado project is my only salvation right now. If it doesn't work out, I'm going to have to start contacting other stations. That would probably mean leaving the Oklahoma City area. And with my mother having her home here—well, I couldn't ask her to move, but we all depend on one another so much. Moving would be hard on us, but I have to find some way out of here," she said with a sweep of her hand indicating the building they were in—the domain of Channel Eight.

NEAL WAS THERE when she finished the ten o'clock news. She walked off the set, and he appeared by the door of the forecast center.

She stopped and they stared at each other over the

maze of electrical cables that occupied the expanse of floor. He tilted his head to one side and shrugged his shoulders as if to say, "I'm sorry—I just couldn't stay away."

Sally's heart took a disconcerting leap to her throat. How wonderful he looked—all tweedy and groomed, so dark and powerful and fine. She watched as he picked his way across the cables, his hands thrust in his jacket pockets, his shoulders hunched forward. There was an endearing awkwardness about the lanky man.

The careful wall she had been building around her emotions began to crumble. She leaned against the back of her chair, suddenly feeling the need for support while her heart leaped and spun about in her chest.

"How do you keep getting in here?" she asked as he drew near, trying to keep the quiver from her voice. "I thought we had security that kept out unauthorized personnel."

"I told them I was an official inspector from the National Weather Service—that the station's up for its five-year certification on its weather programming," Neal said, his eyes revealing the hesitancy. Sally realized he was unsure of what her reaction would be to his coming.

"And they believed you—twice?" she asked. "No one checked and found out there was no such thing?"

"Nope. I showed them some pretty official-looking cards from my billfold, and I've got the sort of face no one ever questions."

"I see. Well, Inspector Parker, how can I be of assistance to you?"

"I'd like you to have a drink with me at Joe Kelly's," he said. "There are some things we need to talk about."

His voice was firm, his jaw set, but his eyes questioned. Sally wanted to throw her arms around him, but she answered with a small nod of her head instead.

It was only after she was in his car and heading up Kelly Avenue that the nagging doubts began eating at her. Why was she doing this? She didn't need entanglement with another confirmed bachelor. She'd had that before. Before, however, such uncommitted relationships suited her. The desire "not to get too involved" had always been mutual. But she did not feel that sort of distance with Neal Parker. He was a man she could care too much for—and get hurt.

She had tried to be angry with him for not taking to her girls. Indeed, she had tried to dislike him for it. He had rejected a part of her, but in a way, she understood. If the tables were turned, she might very well be the one with deep-seated reservations about getting involved with a man who wanted her to love his children, too. And if she had no children, she might very well want to find a man to start a family with—not a man who already had one. She had certainly seen the complications that children sometimes brought to relationships.

Intellectually, she had always known her daughters might be a problem when she was ready to settle down with another man—if she ever did reach that stage again. But she had never really felt it at such a gut level until that ill-fated Sunday afternoon. The realization had frightened her. She had never felt so alone as she had since that day. She had fought the feeling. After all, she had her children, and she had her mother. But the part of her that needed a lover and a friend was alone. The aloneness struck her at odd, unexpected times throughout her days and overwhelmed her at night.

It troubled her that she could have fallen for a man

who wanted no part of her children. It made her feel
disloyal to them. But there was no mistaking the emo-
tion she experienced when she saw him standing there
in the studio. She was glad he had come—glad, glad,
glad!

And now? How did she feel now that she was with
him again and the lights of Joe Kelly's lay ahead.

She felt terribly confused.

Ironically, they were led to the very same table, with
its excellent view, they had occupied during their first
visit. The lighted lake was still quite lovely—perhaps
not quite so fairyland-looking as before, but nice. The
swans, however, seemed to prefer huddling near the
bank rather than gracefully swimming about the lake.
The margaritas were quite good. Sally was certain they
only seemed better the first night they came here.

The small talk was forced—as it had been at Sunday
dinner, and when their knees accidentally touched
under the table, Sally jumped as if she'd been shot.

"Oh, I'm sorry," she said miserably. "I'm kind of
nervous."

"Me, too," Neal admitted. "Look, Sally, I want us
to start all over again." He leaned forward, the intense
gaze from his thick-lashed eyes holding her own.

"Start all over and do what?" she asked.

"Get to know each other," he said, reaching for her
hand. His eyes were imploring. "Let's back up and quit
rushing into things. I know I was a real jerk at your
house. I just haven't been around kids much lately.
Couldn't we see each other on neutral turf for a while
and be friends?"

"I'd like to be your friend," Sally said softly, staring
past his shoulder at the lighted lake through the broad
window. The water was down, leaving an exposed
muddy shoreline. Had it been like that the other night

or was she just seeing things more clearly tonight? She did not understand where this man fit into her life and what was being offered to her. What sort of friendship did he have in mind for them? Or did he even know? Was he like her and simply had a need not to end it—at least not yet?

They didn't stay long. No second round of drinks was ordered that night. It was as though they both felt one round was all their tenuous relationship could stand.

He pulled up beside her car in the Channel Eight parking lot and turned to face her. "I've missed you, Sally," he said simply. For an instant, Sally thought he would kiss her. But instead, he lifted her hand and buried his lips in her cupped palm. She leaned forward and touched her forehead to his hair—just for an instant—then left him there without a spoken good night. She did not trust herself to speak.

Later, when she was lying in her bed staring at a moonlit ceiling, she thought of the night two weeks earlier when she had come home from their first visit to Joe Kelly's. She had lain here spinning the most bizarre assortment of fantasies involving Neal Parker—jumping from passionate lovemaking to trips to the zoo with the girls. In her mind's eye, she could see him being her lover one instant and walking hand in hand with her daughters the next.

Her night dreams and daydreams had accelerated after he called her and asked her out. The night after they made love, she had come home and lain here gloriously reliving it all, luxuriously planning the next time they would be in each other's arms—and deciding what the girls should wear when they met him.

Her mother had said to give the man time. Maybe he would be more comfortable after he got to know Vicky and Amy, but Sally wondered if he'd ever give himself the chance. She wondered if he would ever come back to her house. She would give him time, however, and see what happened. So desperately she wanted to believe there was a chance for them.

But it was hard to foresee any real future in store for her and Neal. Perhaps she was just putting off the inevitable by agreeing to see him again, but she had to find out for sure.

Chapter Five

It was midafternoon two days later when Neal called. Sally had just showered after her afternoon jog and was preparing to leave for the station.

His voice was deep and wonderfully male. "I just got the report from the search committee," he told her.

"The job is yours if you want it. Conditionally. You would be expected to finish your master's degree in a year."

"Do you think I should accept?" Sally asked.

"Why shouldn't you?" he demanded.

"I don't want you to be uncomfortable," Sally said. "If having me work at the severe-storms lab would bother you, I can certainly stay on at Channel Eight."

"Oh, it will bother me, but not in the way you mean," Neal said, his voice teasing, then taking on a serious note as he continued, "and it would bother me a whole lot more for you to stay at that television station. I can tell you're not happy there."

"You don't know the half of it," Sally admitted, picking up the tiny crystal pig that now resided on the small desk in her bedroom. "The work at the lab sounds so challenging, and I would have a chance to grow professionally—something I haven't had much opportunity to do since leaving Kansas City. But I do have reservations about working for you, Neal. What if..." She paused, searching for a way to finish her question. How could she express her fear that their personal problems would carry over into the workplace?

Neal tried to finish it for her. "What if we see each other for a while and things don't work out between us? Then what happens on the job?"

"Something like that," Sally acknowledged, holding the pig so it intercepted a sunbeam and cast a rainbow on the opposite wall of her bedroom.

"I don't want that to happen, but if it did, don't you think we could be adult about it?" he asked.

"I don't know," Sally admitted, cradling the crystal figure in her hand. "There have been times when I never wanted to see a man again."

"I hope I am never put on that list," Neal said. "Give it a try, Sally. If it doesn't work out, I can help you get a transfer to another N.O.A.A. facility."

"Thanks. That helps—although I would hate to have to move from Oklahoma City. But if I hadn't gotten the severe-storms job, I was going to have to anyway."

"Then you accept?" His voice was eager. He really did want her to. Oh, that wonderful voice!

"Yes," she said with a small laugh. "I accept. What do I call you now. Boss? Sir? Your directorship?"

"A simple 'your majesty' will do," he said, teasing, "and my first command is that you go out with me Saturday night for a celebration. I've discovered a wonderful new restaurant. Its chef is right off the boat from Milan and prepares the most incredible pasta. And there's a strolling violin player. The waiters even burst into an occasional aria. How about it? I might even sing along. You haven't lived until you've heard my *La Traviata*!"

He sounded so enthusiastic, so eager for her to say yes.

"Oh, Neal, I'm sorry. Vicky's school is having a carnival Saturday night. I'm signed on as a fortune-teller."

"Well, what about Sunday night?"

"Sure, if I can get a sitter. Mother's out of town for the weekend and won't be back until Monday. Can I call you back? Or if I can't make it for dinner, maybe you'd like to drop by here late Sunday evening. The girls usually go to bed about nine or nine-thirty."

"Why don't we just make it Monday night. Same table at Joe Kelly's," he offered, but the enthusiasm had gone out of his voice.

NEAL WAS WAITING for her after the news again on Monday night. Sally had cleared him with security so he wouldn't have to continue with his inspector charade. She introduced him to Barry, and the three of them visited for a while.

Sally told Barry about her job offer.

"I'm happy for you if that's what you want," Barry said, "but it's sure not going to be the same around here with you gone."

"Oh, I don't know. Just think of what my replacement is bound to look like," Sally teased. "Younger, dishier, tighter sweaters."

"On second thought, when do you leave?" Barry said with a grin before turning the conversation to basketball. The three of them chatted awhile about the Sooners' chances in the Big Eight postseason tournament before saying good night.

As Neal and Sally started down the long hallway toward the parking-lot exit, Barry called out, "Hey, Sally, I almost forgot. Tell Vicky I have a special surprise for her birthday. He's named Clyde."

Sally stopped in her tracks and turned. "Not something alive?"

"Yes, but very small."

"Barry, don't you dare..."

But he had already ducked into the men's room.

"I wonder what that overgrown boy is up to this time," Sally said with good-natured exasperation. "He's crazy about those two girls. Vicky's birthday is next Saturday," she explained. "We're going out for pizza and then have cake and ice cream at Mother's, and we'd love to have you join us."

Sally was sorry she had said it before the words were out of her mouth.

"I don't think so," he said, rather tight-lipped. "I'm sure Vicky would rather have just family and friends around on her birthday."

Sally let it drop. She was pushing again. But damn! How would he ever get to like her children if he was never around them? She sensed, however, that Neal was going to avoid all contact with her daughters for the time being.

At Sally's suggestion, they didn't pay a return visit to Joe Kelly's and its swans but instead headed for a small nightclub on Memorial Road. The nightclub wasn't much, but Sally had heard two of the cameramen discussing the singer who was currently appearing there. And the woman was good—surprisingly so. The young singer sat on a high stool under a small spotlight and sang of the joys and agonies of love. The songs made Sally melancholy, but they spared her the need of making conversation with Neal. That suited her right now. She wanted to be with him, but she wasn't sure what they should be saying to each other.

By intermission, however, she had relaxed enough to tell him the trials of being Channel Eight's Safety

First Weather Lady. "So you see, I really was in need of another job," she concluded as the singer picked up her guitar and perched herself once again under the smoky beam of light. "I'd reached the point where I really was going to have to quit."

"Somehow I knew you couldn't be in sympathy with all that went on at Channel Eight," Neal said. "Their whole weather format just infuriates me. It has for months."

"Then why did you watch?" Sally asked.

He had to whisper his answer. The singer had started her next number—a song about "takin' love where you find it." "Because," Neal said softly in her ear, "I wanted to see *you*. You may have just met me a couple of weeks ago, but I've had my eye on you for a long time."

At midnight, the singer departed and a disc jockey took requests for dance tunes. The first number was Willy Nelson's "Always on My Mind." Neal grabbed her hand as he stood up.

"Come dance with me, Sally," he said as he drew her to her feet. They eased their way among the half-dozen or so other couples on the small dance floor.

Sally wondered if this was why she suggested they come here. She knew there would be dancing. Then she could be in Neal's arms without having to get involved with more lovemaking—not that she didn't think about lovemaking with Neal. But this was safer for now.

Or was it? He held her close. Her arms automatically reached up around his neck. She could feel his face in her hair, feel the movement of his thighs against hers. Her body responded.

They didn't bother to sit down between numbers. Their drinks grew watery on the table as they danced to one song after another. The lyrics spoke to Sally. The music cast its magic over her. She was spellbound by it and Neal's closeness, and she knew it was the same for him.

His hands were tantalizingly low on the small of her back. Her breasts were pressed against his chest. He was physically aroused by her nearness, but she didn't draw away. That was a part of the magic.

Sally lost all sense of time. It was as though she was enveloped with this man in a time capsule—just him and her. There was no need to think about or respond to any other stimuli. Their bodies melted against each other. Sally felt no tension—only awareness of him.

The past was not important. The future was not a concern. All that mattered was right now and floating to music with this man whose body complemented her own desire. She wanted to make love with him again. So much she wanted it! Such wonderful sweet agony overtook her body.

But the music ended, and the lights were turned up. The mood was broken. Sally stood for a minute in the circle of his arms as a sense of time and place returned to her.

Without the protective veil of darkness, the club looked seedy and old. The tables were littered with the debris of the evening. The chairs were all askew, and the air suddenly smelled stale and close. The few people who remained were scurrying around them, hastening to leave the now-inhospitable room.

Sally retrieved her coat and purse, and very quickly they were making their way across the parking lot toward Neal's car. She clasped her jacket close to her body, seeking protection against the biting wind.

It was warmer in the car. The tires crunched on the gravel as Neal backed out of his slot.

There was tension between them. It was a third presence in the car. Sally had fully realized the extent of his arousal only minutes before, just as she was sure he had been aware of hers. But now, there was awkwardness. What should she do? Did one discuss it or ignore it?

Ignoring seemed best. She commented on the chill, on the full moon. Neal commented on nothing.

When he pulled up beside her car in the Channel Eight parking lot—a now familiar pattern—he reached for her and held her, his face buried in her hair. Sally clung to him for a time, not with desire but with another sort of need. When he kissed her, she felt as though their souls had touched.

Then he held her for a minute, whispering her name over and over. She touched her fingers to his lips, then left him, not trusting herself to stay any longer.

Sally slid behind the wheel of her car, fighting down an urge to cry, but she knew Neal would sit in his car watching to make sure she got safely on her way. Crying was dumb anyway—and unproductive. She'd found that out a long time ago. And what did she have to cry about anyway? She'd just spent a lovely evening with a lovely man. There would be other evenings with him. Days, too. And she had a new job to look forward to.

The prospect of her new job was exciting. She forced herself to think of that on the way home. She was going to be a real meteorologist again and working with a research team involved in one of the most exciting aspects of meteorology—the study of severe weather phenomena as they related to tornadoes. And she would have the opportunity to finish a graduate degree in her chosen field. She was damned lucky!

Of course, she was going to have to readjust her and the girls' lives. Working eight to five would be difficult, but Vicky would be in school most of the day next fall and Amy half a day. And her mother had agreed to continue helping out.

Sally planned her and her daughters' new life as she drove through the darkened city. She would not allow other thoughts to intrude.

But when her head hit the pillow of her bed, the dumb irrational unproductive tears she had talked herself out of earlier began to flow. He was just another man, she tried to tell herself. But she knew that was not so. Neal Parker was not just a man to date or have a casual affair with. A relationship with him would be much more complicated. She felt about him the way she would want to feel about a man she was planning to marry—a man she would share her children with. And it seemed that was not to be.

She swore softly into her damp pillow. It didn't help. The tears still came, accompanied by muffled sobs. *Damn,* she thought, *don't do this to yourself.*

She hadn't cried over a man in a long time—not since Michael.

THE THRILL OF HER NEW JOB was good therapy. Sally threw herself into learning all about the National Tornado Project and its sponsoring agency, the National Severe Storms Laboratory. Over the next few days, she became acquainted with the various activities that went on in the one-story precast concrete building adjoining the building that housed the severe-storms lab. The two research facilities were located on the University of Oklahoma's north campus along with a cluster of other research organizations.

During her first days on the job, Neal was busy meeting with a visiting team from the tornado project's parent organization, the National Oceanic and Atmospheric Administration, and Sally felt a stab of disappointment when she realized he would not take charge of her orientation. Instead, he turned that job over to his second-in-command, Phil Rankin. Sally tried hard to rationalize that the arrangement was better. She would not be distracted by Neal's presence and could turn her entire attention to learning about her new job.

Sally learned from the genial Phil that he was recovering from a heart attack that had sidelined him for almost two months. He patted his rotund belly and told Sally, "This may look big to you now, but you should have seen me before I started my diet. I've lost twenty pounds. Of course, I have forty more to go. No wonder the old ticker was having a hard go of it."

Phil showed her pictures of his brand-new grandbaby—his first. "I plan to be around to see this young lady grow up," he announced firmly. "I'm going to start taking care of myself. The doctor says as soon as I lose ten more pounds, I can start a real exercise program and do more than take long walks. You know, I'm actually looking forward to it—me, who never did anything more strenuous than pushing a pencil around a bunch of weather charts!"

Sally liked the portly meteorologist and appreciated the care he took to introduce her to everyone of the seventy or more people who worked in the severe-storms lab and the tornado project, including other meteorologists, engineers, physicists and clerical personnel. Sally was impressed with what she saw and heard. She had not realized the extent of the research that went on in the twin N.O.A.A. facilities or the number of people employed there.

Phil informed Sally that the National Severe Storms Laboratory had been established in 1964 to study severe thunderstorms and attendant phenomena such as tornadoes, hurricanes, hail, damaging winds, flash floods and lightning. The lab was continually striving to improve methods for detection and prediction of tornadoes and other severe weather phenomena and to discover ways to enhance aircraft safety within and near severe storms.

Phil explained that the severe-storms lab and its auxiliary organization, the National Tornado Project, had become an internationally recognized leader in severe-storm research and attracted visiting scientists from around the world. The facilities contained networks of weather and storm electricity sensors and a state-of-the-art Doppler radar and instrumentation. Studies conducted at the labs had already led to a greater understanding of severe-storm structure and evolution, which had led to more accurate and timely warnings of tornadoes and other storms.

The National Tornado Project had been established about ten years earlier to intensify this country's investigation of tornadic winds and the type of thunderstorm systems that fostered them. The project was also entrusted with improving the tornado-warning system throughout the midsection of the country known as Tornado Alley, where most tornadic activity occurred, and with studying the effect of tornadoes on different kinds of structures in order to determine safer ways to construct buildings in the future. And the tornado lab served as a clearinghouse for the research findings of other public and private research investigations into tornadic winds, including research efforts of various universities.

Both meteorological laboratories had been built in Oklahoma because the state had the dubious honor of being located squarely in the middle of Tornado Alley. Each spring the state was plagued by a rash of severe thunderstorms that produced a higher percentage of tornadoes per ten-thousand-square-mile measure than any other state in the nation, making the state an ideal site for the study of severe weather.

Sally learned that although the meteorologists spent a portion of each spring chasing tornadoes—primarily across western Oklahoma and the Texas Panhandle—the odds of actually chasing down a twister and getting close enough to take useful measurements and photographs were slim.

"If we have luck photographing two twisters a year out there, it's a bumper crop," Phil told her with a gesture at the large expanse of sky revealed by the wall of windows in his office. "We chase them around all right, but we either don't get there in time, or it's already dark or raining so hard we can't get pictures. But every so often we get a storm we can really document. And if we're really lucky, we can measure and photograph one that's in the range of our two Doppler radars. Then we have so much data, it takes us years to study that one storm. Our team's still working on one that went through here in 1973, and we got so much data on a 1978 storm, it will be years before we finish with that study. Now we've got a fantastic new instrument package we'd like to drop right in a twister's path. If we could ever pull that off, it'd sure fill up some holes in our knowledge of cyclonic winds. Would it ever!"

Sally certainly understood why Neal felt her strong math background was a factor in her being awarded the job. Most of the meteorological work done at the lab had nothing to do with forecasting per se or chasing storms about the countryside but, rather, with the mathematical analysis of the data that had been collected on various thunderstorm systems that had passed through the region. She was grateful her early affinity for math had led her to continue studying it in college. She always had taken more advanced math than her meteorological major required.

In addition to Neal, the other senior member of the meteorological research team was Jerry Baldwin, whom Sally recognized immediately as a dedicated ladies' man by his rather blatant head-to-toe surveillance of her when they were introduced.

"Hey, sweetheart," he said, casually flipping the ashes off his cigarette, "where have you been keeping yourself?"

"Busy," she answered flatly, then turned her attention to the slide he had projected into a desk-top viewer. "Those are certainly impressive wall clouds. Do you have corresponding data to go with the photograph? What is the rate of rotation? What is their altitude?"

Seemingly disarmed by her professionalism, Jerry dropped his flirtatious routine and filled Sally in on the set of slides he was studying. They had been taken last spring of a four-and-a-half-mile bank of rain-free low-hanging accessory clouds to a cumulonimbus base. The series of slides documented a rapidly changing formation that showed marked rotations but never developed into a funnel.

"It showed every indication of developing into a twister," Jerry explained, "but it didn't. Damned if I can figure out why some of these babies do and some don't, but I'm workin' on it."

"Were the clouds southwest of the precipitation shaft?" Sally asked, wanting to know if the storm followed usual patterns.

"More west that southwest," Jerry explained as he showed Sally the computer printout of data they had accumulated on this particular storm system.

Sally was intrigued. She could well understand why this facility had so advanced the frontiers of knowledge of severe weather. And she experienced a thrill of delight to think she was now part of the National Severe Storms Laboratory meteorological team involved in the National Tornado Project. It was frightening in a way. There was so very much to learn. But it made her feel positively heady to realize she would now face intellectual challenges rather than the petty power plays of a television station manager who had about as much class as a garbage truck.

She relished the idea of her first tornado chase. Now that was something television meteorologists never got to do! When she got to chase, she would really feel like a full-fledged member of the research team.

During the afternoon of her third day on the job, Jerry and a visiting meteorologist from London took off in one of the lab vans to observe a front forming over Roger Mills and Beckham counties in the westernmost part of the state. They were accompanied by two students from O.U.

And in the weeks that followed, most of the other meteorologists except Sally were involved in at least one chase—some in several. She assumed that Neal did not believe she was adequately indoctrinated in laboratory procedures to be included in a storm chase, but Sally worried that the tornado season would pass without her first tornado chase.

She saw Neal most days at the lab. She was terribly aware of his presence in the building and could not stop herself from looking up anytime someone walked by her small office. The sound of his voice in the hallway would steal away her powers of concentration. They would share an occasional cup of coffee or lunch at the small airport café that served the nearby university air-

field. Their conversations were friendly and neutral—
shoptalk mostly, but Sally always felt emotionally
drained after being with him. An unspoken morato-
rium on their dating seemed to be in effect during her
first days on the job.

At the end of her second week, however, a discussion over coffee of a current movie they had been hearing about did lead to their going to a movie together.
They sat side by side in the darkened theater, shoulders
occasionally touching. Sally was so aware of the man
beside her, she found it difficult to concentrate on the
screen.

They had a beer afterward and talked about the lab.
When he walked her to her dark front porch, he
roughly pulled her to him and kissed her—a deep,
searching kiss that left her weak. Sally responded with a
surge of need that left her breathless and aroused.

Her girls were across the street spending the night
with her mother. Sally felt Neal's searching tongue and
thought of her empty house, of her waiting bed upstairs. She had dreamed so often about him loving her
there. *Yes,* she thought, *I want him in my bed. Oh, how I
want him!*

She leaned into his body, her arms entwined about
his neck, her breasts crushed against his chest. She
begged him with her mouth, with her hungry body.
Her message was clear. But when she unlocked her
door and stepped inside, he didn't follow her. It was as
though there were some invisible barrier over her door
he could not or would not step through.

THE PATIENCE her mother had counseled did not seem to
be working, Sally thought as she closed the door behind
her and tried to quell her frustration. While she understood that children certainly could complicate a rela-

tionship, she was beginning to resent Neal's obvious reluctance to have anything to do with her children or her home. What did he expect her to do? Pretend they didn't exist?

Well, she wasn't going to do that. And as though to reinforce her decision, Sally brought her mother and daughters to work with her on Monday morning to show them around her new place of business and to establish herself among her new colleagues as a single working mother. As a part of the tour, she took her family by Neal's office.

"You remember my mother, Margie, and my daughters, Vicky and Amy," Sally said formally.

Neal shook hands with Margie and smiled at the girls, but Sally did not think he seemed at all glad to see her family. He did not invite them to sit down or seem prepared to extend their visit in any way. Sally felt her cheeks heat with a mother's anger. *You'd think my children were monsters,* she thought. If only he would take the time to get to know them, surely he would see that they were two perfectly normal and unusually delightful children. But once again, she tried to tell herself that perhaps he just was unaccustomed to being around children, and that was the reason for his reticent behavior toward her daughters. But just as she was asking Neal to join them for a Coke, his secretary announced that Washington was on the line. The look on Neal's face as he reached for the phone was one of profound relief.

Sally felt her anger heighten as she marched her family from his paneled office. Damn him anyway! He probably didn't like dogs, either. Some people were insufferable. Neal Parker was one of them.

As her first month on the job ended, Sally was starting to feel a growing uneasiness when more and more of the public-relations functions for the meteorological labs began to be shunted in her direction. Neal seemed to feel that since she was well known in the community because of her television work, she was a natural for public-relations duties. In its two-decade history, the activities of the severe-storms lab had become well known throughout the state. And now the National Tornado Project had captured the fancy of Oklahomans, who were intrigued by anyone who would actually go out and chase the legendary tornadoes—or cyclones, as some of the old-timers preferred to call them. Such work had an aura of derring-do about it to people who preferred their storm cellars—or "fraidie holes" as they were often called when severe weather threatened to sweep across the prairies. Consequently, there was a great demand at local civic clubs and other organizations to have the storm chasers as speakers. Television stations liked to avail themselves of their expertise. Magazines and newspapers often ran articles about them. And teachers frequently brought schoolchildren on tours of their facility. It wasn't long before Sally began to wonder if she had been hired because of her broadcasting background and because she was an old pro at meeting the public. Even though she enjoyed such activities from time to time, she certainly hadn't quit her television job to play tour guide to schoolchildren.

But as soon as she was well enough versed in the operation of the two research facilities, Neal started sending her out to fill speaking engagements and to meet with reporters. She even had the unique experience of appearing on Channel Eight's Safety First Weather with her replacement. Sally was interviewed about tornado safety and what tornado-project studies had revealed about which types of buildings could best withstand tornadic winds.

The new Channel Eight evening weather reporter had flaming red hair and a large bust that was prominently displayed in a hot-pink sweater. The young woman had been a broadcasting major in college but had taken a few meteorology courses in order to prepare herself for just the sort of job she now had. Sally had noted the woman was referred to as a "university-trained meteorologist" in the newspaper announcement of her addition to the Channel Eight news team.

"Any regrets?" Barry asked her as she had a cup of coffee with him after the six o'clock news. "You miss the old shop?"

"Just you and a few others," Sally told him. "But the station itself—no way."

"Then what about those dark circles that makeup doesn't quite cover up?" the sandy-haired public-relations director asked as he leaned forward and softly touched the skin under her eyes. "Is it the job or the man?"

"A little of both," Sally confessed. "Actually, it's a lot of both. You would be better qualified for the job they seemed to have designed for me. As for the man—well, the man and I just weren't meant to be. It hurts."

Sally was glad when two of the secretaries from the front office stopped to say hello and spared her from having to explain further to Barry. She was afraid the tears that always seemed lurking just below the surface would well up in her eyes if she continued their conversation.

Even her daughters seemed to have noticed the change in their mother. In their childish way, they became very solicitous, doing small favors, drawing her special pictures with their crayons and picking her bouquets of dandelions from the healthy crop that was

emerging in their backyard. Sally resolved to shake off
the depression that had overtaken her and get her life
in order again. She had to come to terms with the feelings of loneliness and isolation that had taken such a
hold over her emotions of late, and she had to deal with
her growing frustration over yet another job that promised professionalism but in effect denied it. On both
counts, Neal Parker was the man at the root of things.
It was time they talked—really talked.

He had asked her to his house for dinner the Sunday
after Vicky's birthday. Sally refused. When he asked
again, she accepted the dinner invitation but declined
to go to his house. After all, he didn't seem inclined to
make a return visit to her house. Why should she return to his? Neal didn't try to dissuade her, but he did
reach out and touch her arm. The look on his face was
one of aching need. *He's as lonely as I am,* Sally
thought. She cared so for this man it hurt—actually
hurt.

"Pick me up at eight," she instructed.

Neal looked as though he would have liked to offer
another suggestion. Sally realized with a start that he
didn't even like the idea of coming to her house to pick
her up for a date. Did he find her children that hard to
take?

She deliberately had the girls in attendance when he
arrived. They were dressed in denim overalls and had
their hair in ponytails. Sally thought they were the two
prettiest, sweetest-looking children in the entire world.

She had coached them. Amy asked Neal if he knew
anything about planting a garden and took him to see
the one she and Vicky were attempting to start in their
backyard. Sally hoped Neal would volunteer to come
back and spade the hard earth for them. He did not.
Vicky was to ask him if he'd like to see the gerbil that

Barry had given her for her birthday, but she had a sudden attack of tied tongue. Sally didn't blame her. Neal was obviously anxious to be on his way.

They went to Sullivan's, a popular restaurant on Reno Street, first visiting the restaurant's bar for cocktails. Sally waited until the waitress had taken their order before she confronted him.

"We don't have a future, do we?" she asked.

"Don't say that," he said, his voice almost angry. "I want us to have a future—a long one."

"Based on what?" Sally challenged.

"Mutual respect. A shared profession. Friendship. Love." His voice emphasized the latter word. Sally's heart turned over.

"In a way, I wish we'd never made love that night," she said.

Neal look startled. It was the first time either of them had directly mentioned the intimacy they had shared in front of his fireplace.

"I'm sorry you feel that way," he said. "It was the most wonderful night of my life. I've wanted to tell you that. I've wanted to be with you again so badly. I can't think about anything but you, Sally—day and night. I keep wanting to hunt for you at work and find excuses to be in the same room with you. I get jealous when you go out to lunch with someone else. I dream of taking you places. I want to take you skiing, canoeing, to the beach, on all sorts of trips."

"And where are my children in these daydreams?" Sally asked softly. "I'm not alone, you know."

"I know," he said miserably. "I know you realize that I've got a real problem with your children. I like children, but I'm not sure I could ever feel comfortable with your family. When I'm at your house, I feel like a trespasser. I keep wondering if the girls look like their father. I wondered if I was sitting in his chair in your living room or at his place at the table. Oh, Sally, more than anything else I want you to be a part of my life, but I'm not sure I could ever be a father to some other man's children. I can't help it. I'm trying to deal with it—really I am. It's just that I want any children I raise to be my own.''

Sally barely contained her fury while the waitress placed their drinks in front of them. She waited until the woman was out of earshot before she spoke.

''Those are not 'some other man's children'!'' she said vehemently, struggling to keep her voice low. ''Those are *my* children. The man who fathered them forfeited his right to them years ago. He abandoned us! He couldn't take two babies, one of them sick all the time, always in and out of the hospital. He walked out one day leaving me and the babies and the debts. I've never seen him or heard from him since. So don't talk to me, Neal Parker, about *some other man's children*! Those children are mine. Mine alone! I've earned them. I've scrimped and worked and taken more hell than you've ever dreamed of to be their parent—their only parent!''

She was trembling as she pushed her drink away. ''I don't want this,'' she said as she grabbed her purse.

He reached for her hand. She pulled it from his reach. ''Sally, I'm sorry. I didn't know.''

''Please, Neal, just take me home.''

The short ride to her house passed in stony silence. Sally quickly opened the door and left him without a farewell.

Neal felt physically ill. He realized the nerve he had touched went deep. Sally was angry and hurt, and she had every right to be. Obviously, she had dreamed of him loving her children and wanting them as well as her in his life. She had wanted him to feel joy at the prospect of becoming their stepfather.

But could he ever feel like a father to those two girls? He was so desperately in love with their mother—with the angry, hurt woman who had just exited from his car, not waiting or wanting him to walk her to her door.

A feeling of despair washed over him. He wanted her so much, so very much, but now he feared she was lost to him forever.

Chapter Six

Sally threw herself into her work. No facet of the lab's operation escaped her attention, and spongelike, she tried to absorb everything she could learn about the lab's work—past and present. She observed and asked questions. She studied the projects in progress and undertook her own analysis of a storm system that had produced three small tornadoes in Comanche County three years ago. She took the lab's published findings home with her and every night fell asleep reading and learning about the lab's research achievements.

By driving herself, she hoped to accomplish two things: to master her new job and to subdue her confused thoughts about Neal. And her thoughts about Neal were very confused indeed. She was hurt and angry over his admission that he didn't want to raise children who were not his own. Yet she could not stop wanting him. Her heart would pound when she walked by his office, and catching sight of him in the hallway left her breathless. And when their duties at work brought them into the same room, Sally sometimes felt as if she were suffocating, so great was her need to touch his cheek, to bury her face against his chest.

It was hard for her to concentrate on his words during the meteorological staff's frequent meetings, which were an integral part of the work at the lab. She had to force herself to listen for the content of his words and stop thinking about other times when his words were not about meteorological concerns and were just for her.

Yet she wanted to learn from his words and from her association with him and the other meteorologists. With sheer force of will she would compel the lovesick part of her to sublimate itself to the part striving to be a professional career woman. She believed people who were professional about their work somehow managed to get a job done regardless of personal problems. So Sally concentrated intently when Neal led discussions about the lab's current projects and past research. She was determined to become a contributing member of the meteorological research team as quickly as possible.

She could well understand why Neal was in a position of authority at the severe-storms lab, why his work was cited in study after study in the professional journals she had been reading. He was internationally known in his field, a world-class authority on severe weather. As her hopes for their personal relationship faltered, her respect for Neal as a professional meteorologist grew. He was at the top of his field and had managed to gather together an excellent meteorological team at the Norman facility to do original research in tornadic storms. Some of the men—like Phil and Jerry—were also well established in their field, while others were promising newcomers. Sally was honored to have been made a part of their group and to have been handed this fine opportunity to grow as a professional meteorologist. There was so much she could learn from this job and from all of these men—especially from Neal. Sally could sense the respect that all of the men had for Neal as an administrator and as a learned scientist.

Sally wanted very much to stay on at the lab permanently and take advantage of the professional growth the job offered. There were times, however, when she seriously wondered if she would be able to remain. What if the ambiguousness in her and Neal's relationship was never resolved? She wondered if her presence in his workday was as difficult for him as his was in hers.

When he had first told her she had been selected for the job, Neal had said he would help her get a transfer to another National Oceanic and Atmospheric Administration facility if the two of them had difficulty working together. Perhaps it would come to that.

But she wanted to stay in Oklahoma and be part of this exciting work. And as long as she was here, there was always the hope that things would work out between her and Neal.

Of course, after their disastrous last date, she told herself she wanted nothing more to do with Neal Parker on a personal level. *Ever.* She was thoroughly disillusioned and terribly angry.

At first her anger was therapeutic. She didn't have to love someone she hated—or thought she hated. To hear him call Amy and Vicky "some other man's children" had almost driven her wild. She still trembled when she thought of his words. Her daughters were not "some other man's"! They were hers alone.

To think that since her divorce, the one man with whom she had ever thought of sharing Vicky and Amy didn't want them because he still considered them as belonging to a man who had cared so little for them he had abandoned them! Sally would never forgive her former husband for what he had done. Even if Michael wanted out of their marriage, he did not have to cut his daughters out of his life and totally renege on his responsibilities to them. And now she wondered if she would ever forgive Neal for his lack of understanding, for his unwillingness even to get to know her children as unique and special individuals who had no control over the circumstances of their birth.

Her daughters were a fact of her life. Someone had to have fathered them, but there was a vast difference between "fathering" and being a father to a child. Neal, it seemed, would not consider being a parent to children he had not fathered, and his unwillingness to accept their place in Sally's life was almost like his saying he wished they had never been born. That thought brought rage to a mother's heart.

As the days went by, however, Sally's anger softened to sadness. While she could not bring herself to forgive Neal for feeling the way he did, she did come to understand part of the reason he had spoken as he did about her daughters. He had not known about Michael. Neal was still reacting jealously toward a man for whom she had long since stopped caring—a man Vicky and Amy wouldn't recognize if he walked in the front door. Neal didn't understand the circumstances surrounding her marriage and its demise. How could he? She had never told him. He could not have guessed the grief that "other man" had caused her. He did not know there had not been any contact between Michael and the girls since the day he exited from their lives.

Michael had left her and the girls without so much as a farewell. He just took his clothes, the car, cleaned out their savings account and vanished.

Sally was left alone in a strange city with two babies and no money. Her life had been a nightmare. Vicky was in and out of the hospital. The utilities in their tiny house were turned off when she couldn't pay the bills. The furniture was repossessed. More than once, she hid when bill collectors came to her door. Her parents had helped her some, but they were people of modest means. Sally never let them know how truly awful things were with her during that dreadful time.

Gradually, however, Sally rebuilt her life. She obtained a divorce and took back her maiden name. She worked hard at polishing her broadcasting skills, studying videotapes of herself and performances of accomplished television professionals by the hour. Her television presentations steadily improved. She gained poise and popularity and pay raises. By scrimping and cutting every corner imaginable, she was able to reestablish her credit rating and get her financial affairs in order.

Sally later learned that Michael was living on the West Coast, but she made no attempt to contact him or to force payment of the child support to which the court had said she was entitled. She feared doing so would give him a future entrée into their lives, and she didn't want that. Michael had forfeited any right to those children. She never wanted to see him again. Neither she nor the girls had ever heard from him again—not on the girls' birthdays, not at Christmas. Never.

Michael had always been irresponsible. Sally knew that before she married him. He never seemed to keep a job for very long. He often was late for dates, and sometimes he wouldn't show up at all, but she had been young and blindly in love with the charming, fun-loving young Adonis with the laughing blue eyes and sun-streaked hair. Life was a delightful party when Michael was around. Together they laughed and played and didn't think much about the future. Planning a big wedding with a festive reception was a game for them with very little thought of what came after the "I do's" and the honeymoon.

And they were happy as newlyweds. The sex was exciting, decorating their new apartment was fun, and they went out a lot. Sally supposed they really had been still playing at life, but at the time she was sure Michael's love for her was genuine and enduring. And he had seemed so delighted with Vicky when she was born. He spent money they could not afford on very expensive cigars to give to his friends in honor of his daughter's birth.

But it soon became apparent that Vicky was asthmatic and would take much special care. Michael's enchantment with fatherhood began to fade. By that time, Sally was already pregnant again. There were no cigars to herald Amy's birth.

Michael grew more and more resentful of the girls. He complained they took all of Sally's time. He complained when they cried. He complained about the medical bills. He complained about the soiled diapers in the bathroom and the toys in the living room. He complained about spilled food and spit-up milk. He complained about the apartment looking like a "goddamned nursery."

Then he left. At least there had been no more complaints, but Sally was overwhelmed by a sense of loneliness and hopelessness—and failure.

For several years, Sally told herself she would never again marry. No way was she ever going to allow some man to hurt her like that again! But gradually the bitterness left her. Her parents had a fine marriage, and other people did also. All men should not be condemned for Michael's behavior, and surely there would be a wonderful man someday who would love her and her children.

Sally had dared to dream that wonderful man was Neal. Even after she came to realize he had reservations about getting involved with a woman who had children she dared to hope he would come to terms with those reservations.

But so much for romantic daydreams, she told herself firmly after that hurtful scene at Sullivan's restaurant. She seemed to have a knack for falling in love with men who caused her pain.

The dream refused to die, however. In spite of the buffer she tried to build around her emotions, hope kept creeping back to tease her. She rationalized. After all, Neal now knew about Michael. Perhaps when he considered that the man to whom she had once been married no longer played a part in her or her daughters' lives and hadn't for the past five years, Neal would realize how foolish his reservations had been and could perhaps come to terms with them. After all, he seemed to be a sensitive individual. Hadn't he readily admitted he was wrong to discredit her job application because of her sex and sincerely tried to make amends?

Maybe Neal would try to make amends for his initial negative reaction to the girls. After he had thought about it for a time, he might come to realize a future with her family might not be so bad after all.

Sally wished she could simply put her emotions on hold and adopt a calm wait-and-see policy, but she could not control her tormented thoughts. Her work brought only limited relief. Each night, after a few hours of sleep, she would awaken to thoughts of Neal. Her memory of their night of love haunted her, and he kept flitting in and out of her mind while she was reading research reports and attempting to solve lengthy mathematical equations. Concentration was difficult at best, but her job and her responsibility to her daughters were all that kept her from going crazy.

She tried to take one day at a time—to do her job, to

take care of her children and her home. And as those days passed by, she had less and less hope that Neal would ever be a part of her life. The more time that went by, the greater the distance between Neal and her seemed to become.

The irony of it! After all these years, she had finally fallen in love again. Sally had planned to be so careful next time. She was only going to allow herself to fall in love with someone who not only would make her happy but would be a suitable father for her children. What a joke! She had fallen in love with a man with whom she could not share her life. There were moments when it was more than she could bear, when she wanted to sink to the floor in a heap and not get up. But she had responsibilities, including two children to support. One did what one had to do.

She began trying to avoid contact with Neal as much as possible at the lab. She had been assigned to work mostly with Jerry Baldwin and Phil Rankin. Sometimes a day or even two would go by without her seeing Neal. When their paths did cross, they were cordial to each other. In spite of her besieged emotions, she was able to maintain a calm facade when he was around. But when he left her presence, her hands would start to shake and her knees would tremble. It would take her several minutes to calm herself and get back to work. Her involvement in her work was her salvation. If she had stayed on at Channel Eight, there would have been little to buffer her pain.

At night, however, there was nothing to stand in pain's way. She wanted a man she could not have. Desperately, she tried to fall out of love with him. If only she could hate him, but that, she suspected, would be impossible.

And even her work was becoming a source of frus-

tration for Sally. The month of April had come and
gone without her ever being included on a storm chase,
and now May was in its closing days. She knew most
severe storms occurred during the spring and early
summer months, and if she did not go on a chase soon,
it might be several months or even next year before
another opportunity arose.

Of course, not all the meteorologists chased storms.
Phil did not because of his health. Two of the older
men no longer were involved in what was considered
the province of younger meteorologists, and a couple
of the men were simply no longer interested in such
pursuits and were content to stay behind at the lab. But
seven of the men rotated chase duties. Sally could see
no reason why she was not included in the chase group.

Jerry Baldwin agreed with Sally. He encouraged her
to pursue her case and insist on her right to be included
in storm-chase activities.

Jerry had become her best friend at the lab in spite of
his flirtatious behavior her first day on the job. Sally
had grown to understand that under Jerry's playboy ex-
terior was a genuinely nice man who had adopted his
womanizing ways because he had difficulty dealing
with women on any other level. He confessed to Sally
that she was the first woman he had ever worked with
in an other than secretary-boss relationship.

At first Jerry had not known how to treat Sally as a
colleague. Their every conversation seemed laden with
sexual innuendo. He couldn't relax and accept her as
just another meteorologist.

Sally became very irritated with Jerry from time to
time. On occasion she snapped at his sexist remarks.
"No, Jerry," she would say sarcastically, "I'm not a
damned good *female* mathematician. I'm a damned
good mathematician. Period."

She would remind him, not too gently at times, that her name was Sally and not Sally Honey or Sally Babe. Gradually, however, his attitude toward her changed and a genuine friendship developed.

Jerry told her of his disastrous marriage, which had ended in divorce, and how much he missed his son, who now lived with his mother in Canada. Sally came to understand that much of his carefree bachelor demeanor was simply a protective mechanism. He was afraid to deal with women on a friendship level. His life since his divorce had consisted of one sexual encounter after another. He confessed his motto since his divorce was "Love 'em and leave 'em."

"That way you don't get hurt," the handsome meteorologist explained as he and Sally worked at sorting through the slides that had been taken by the last chase expedition. There were no photographs of tornadoes, but there were some really remarkable photographs of mammatus and other cloud formations associated with severe thunderstorms.

"I know what you mean," Sally confessed. "I've had a few pretty superficial relationships myself since my divorce. I never really wanted to get close to anyone. It was safer just to date and not get too involved. Then you don't open yourself up to pain."

But it happened anyway, Sally thought to herself. The pain. It was a part of her now like her lungs and her heart.

As Jerry came to realize Sally could be his friend, they spent more and more time together. She recognized that he was a human being in need of a friend and confidant, and she enjoyed his company. He was lively and funny and bright. They would be serious one minute and play practical jokes on each other the next.

When Jerry invited her and her daughters to accompany him to nearby Lake Thunderbird for an afternoon on his boat, she accepted. They had a marvelous time. He had a lovely natural way with children. After a short while, Vicky and Amy were clambering all over him and calling him Captain Jerry. *Why couldn't it have been this way with Neal,* Sally could not help but think. *Why couldn't it be Neal holding Amy on his lap and his hat on Vicky's blond head? Why does life have to be so damned complicated?*

His friendship with Sally seemed to precipitate Jerry into a more liberated way of thinking, and he chafed at the unfairness when Sally's name was continually being left off the chase teams.

"Why don't you call old Parker on it?" Jerry asked Sally on several occasions. "I don't see any reason why he should leave you out. And while you're at it, tell him you're sick and tired of making speeches to the Lions' Club, or ask him how he expects you to represent the lab at all these speaking engagements when you're left out of the activity the public finds most fascinating. I'd love to take you along on a chase, Sally. Even if we don't spot a twister, the chases are exciting and you do get to see a lot of weather, really glorious weather, I may not have grown up in Oklahoma, but I love this state. It's got fantastic weather and great football. What more could a man ask for?"

Jerry's attitude concerning her right to be on a chase team helped reinforce her decision that the time had come to confront Neal, but she dreaded a confrontation and kept putting it off. By this time, her and Neal's relationship had deteriorated to stiff formality. As her friendship with Jerry and the other people at the lab grew, the distance between her and Neal seemed to widen. Sally felt as though they stood on opposite sides of an unbridgeable gulf. Even a seemingly casual good morning between them was a hurtful experience for Sally. She began to doubt once again the wisdom of her having taken the job at the severe-storms lab in the first place. A nagging voice told her with growing frequency that she should move on. But if she left, she might never see Neal again. She wasn't brave enough for that, not yet. Maybe she would never be. What a mess her life was in!

Perhaps it would one day come to that—moving on. But in the meantime, as long as she was with the tornado project, she was going to learn as much as she could and gain as much experience as the job allowed. And that meant storm chasing.

No matter how difficult or painful it was going to be, Sally knew she would have to challenge Neal on the chase issue.

"Am I or am I not a full-fledged member of the team?" Sally finally asked over a cup of coffee at the airport café.

"What do you mean?" Neal asked, his dark eyes troubled. "Of course you are. Your work has been quite good, and we'll expect even more out of you after you get some more graduate work under your belt. I understand you're enrolled in a class for the summer semester."

He was thinner, Sally realized, and tired-looking. There was no sparkle in his eyes when he looked at her. She longed for that other Neal, the one who looked at her with love.

"Yes, I'll be taking atmospheric energetics under Dr. Goldstein," Sally said. "I'm looking forward to it. And I'm delighted you consider my work good, but what about the tornado chases? Why have I been left out of that particular facet of the lab's work?"

"There's really no need for you to go along on those," Neal said. "The others are experienced; they know what to look for and how to stay out of trouble. After all, those are *tornadoes* we're chasing."

"I'm well aware of the weather phenomenon you are investigating," Sally said dryly, "and I'm well aware of the necessity for caution. After all, I've been intensely studying the storms for almost two months now. I've seen slides and films of them in action and of the devastation they leave behind. I've read the reports. I have no desire to take risks that might impair my ability to look after my children or to leave them orphaned. But you yourself pointed out there have never been any close calls to chase-team members, that there are rigid safety policies concerning the chases."

Sally paused while a pink-clad waitress refilled her cup. Neal waved her away and pushed his half-empty cup to one side.

"You say I can't go along because I'm inexperienced," she continued, "but how does one get experience in chasing storms if one is not allowed to participate in the chases? Inexperience doesn't seem to prevent you from taking along undergraduate meteorological students from the university. But of course only male students go chasing. It makes me wonder, Neal, if that's what this is all about, if you don't want me to go along because I'm female."

"Well, damn it, Sally, it does seem wrong somehow," Neal admitted. "Sometimes the chase teams are gone overnight. They go without sleep and baths and meals. They camp out in a van, and the only 'rest rooms' are behind a bush. They live on coffee and candy bars. They get rained on and hailed on and blown around. There's no privacy, and they often strip off wet clothes in the back of the van. It can really get tough."

"I'm not a pansy, Neal. If you don't think I'm willing to put up with a little lack of privacy, inconvenience and loss of sleep, you're wrong."

"Am I wrong to want to protect you from physical discomfort?" he asked with a shake of his head. "I may have really screwed things up with you, Sally, but I still have such feelings for you, I can't think straight."

"You do?" Sally said in amazement. "I mean you can't. You mean you..." Her voice trailed off. She diverted her gaze to the window and watched a small single-engine plane land on the nearby airstrip, using her observation of the landing as a reason not to finish her sentence or to look at Neal's eyes. She was too confused to make sense.

He said he had "such feelings" for her. He was bothered by thoughts of her, and her heart gladdened to know he still cared. Oh, how it gladdened! She wanted to ask him to say it again and again. She wanted to tell him how much she cared.

But if he cared, why did he seem uninterested in continuing their relationship? Or had he been waiting for some sort of sign from her that it was okay? She wondered if she dared risk opening the Pandora's box of her emotions again by responding to the question in his eyes.

"I've missed you, Sally," he said softly. "Couldn't we try again? Couldn't we just start all over again?"

"Oh, Neal," she said, her voice catching. "I want to. But I can't help thinking it would just mean more heartache in the long run. I wonder if it isn't best to leave things as they are now."

But that's not what her heart wanted. Even as she said the words, Sally hoped he would be able to say something to dissuade her. *Oh, please let him have the right words and make it all right for us to be together again!*

"I'm going to Kansas City, Missouri, the end of next week for a conference. I have to give a speech and present a research paper," he announced all in a rush. "Come with me. You'd meet a lot of the N.O.A.A. folks and be able to attend some interesting meetings. You'll probably run into some of your former colleagues from the National Weather Service. And we could be together. We'd go sight-seeing and out to dinner. How about it, Sally? It'd be good for us to get away from here and have some time together, just the two of us. We could have separate rooms if you like. I'll accept any terms you want."

"Oh, Neal, I don't know. The girls..." She didn't finish. It always came back to the girls. Neal's face stiffened.

"Couldn't you ask your mother to take care of them while you're gone? After all, you were just telling me you want to chase storms. Sometimes you'd have to leave your daughters overnight to do that. They're not babies, Sally, and I'm only talking about three days away from home." He reached for her hand. "Go with me, Sally. We owe it to ourselves to get away and try to figure things out between us."

His touch sent a shock wave through her body. She watched, mesmerized, as he turned her palm upward and gently stroked the sensitive skin on the underside of the wrist. Did he have any idea of what that did to her? How could she think when he was touching her like that? She fought the urge to close her eyes to better relish the sensations that were traveling up her arm and bringing a flush of warmth to her breasts and throat. She knew if there hadn't been a table separating them, she would be in his arms. It was as though a magnetic force were drawing her toward him.

"Well, what about it, Sally?" he implored, his fingers drawing feather-soft circles on her wrist.

What about what, she thought through the fog of her desire. *Oh, yes—the trip to Kansas City.* She thought what that could mean. Intimate dinners in fine restaurants with candlelight reflecting in crystal goblets. A moonlight walk around Country Club Plaza. Drinks at the Alameda Plaza. Lovemaking in a hotel room between crisp, ironed sheets. Her eyes did close. She wanted the vision to become reality. She wanted it with a painful intensity, actual pain that filled her chest and stifled her breathing. How could this have happened to her? How had she changed from a self-contained woman who enjoyed the company of an occasional man to one who wanted this one man so much she was in pain? She felt out of control of her own emotions.

Suddenly Sally was frightened, sensing that she was at the final turning point with Neal. Either they worked something out now, or they would have to give up on each other. People couldn't continue to live their lives with such continual emotional upheaval. Survival entered in at some point.

"I can't think now, Neal," she said, begging him with her eyes not to make her give him an answer now. "Let me see what I can work out."

They drove the short distance back to the lab in silence. It was only as they approached the front entrance to the building that Sally realized Neal had not dealt with her request to be a part of a chase team.

But she couldn't think about that now. She didn't trust herself even to discuss the time of day with Neal at this point. All she wanted to do was seek out the privacy of her office and calm herself. She was not going to cry. She absolutely was not going to cry.

Chapter Seven

The invitation to the high-school reunion had come several weeks before. Margie mentioned it at the time but didn't seem inclined to go.

"That was all so long ago," Margie said with a wave of her hand. "I haven't kept up with any of those people. In fact, I haven't been back to Springfield in over thirty years. No, I won't go. It'd just make me feel old. Imagine, forty years since I graduated from high school. I really didn't need to be reminded of that!"

Sally thought the high-school reunion might be good for her mother. She often worried about her mother's limited existence. Although Margie seemed to enjoy caring for her granddaughters and working part-time at the branch library, Sally thought she should have more friends and get out more. Sally made suggestions from time to time: church singles groups, special-interest clubs and the like. She worried that her mother's life was empty in a way that a grown daughter and grandchildren could not fill, but she understood that Margie still grieved for her husband and was unaccustomed to facing the world as a woman alone. Taking a trip by herself to Springfield, for example, to attend a high-school reunion unescorted was not something she would be comfortable doing. Sally pushed a bit but accepted her mother's decision not to journey back to the city of her youth.

But when Sally stopped by Margie's house after work to pick up her daughters, she was aware the minute she walked into her mother's kitchen that something special had happened that day. Sally herself wanted to discuss Neal's invitation to accompany him to Kansas City, but the radiant look on Margie's face gave her pause. She decided to put that discussion on hold and find out what was going on in her mother's life.

"Okay, let's have it," she said. "You won the Irish Sweepstakes? You have Robert Redford hiding in the closet? You've discovered a diamond mine in the cellar?"

Margie laughed and actually blushed. Sally couldn't remember the last time she'd seen her mother blush!

"Don't be silly. I'm just pleased at the way my pie turned out. Isn't it a nice one?" Margie indicated an apple pie sitting on the table.

"It looks splendid," Sally said, "but every pie you ever made looked splendid. No, I think it must be Robert Redford in the closet."

Sally opened the door to the broom closet, then checked the pantry. "Robert, you can come out now," she called down the basement steps. "I know you're here someplace."

But the only forms who materialized were those of two small girls carrying large purses and wearing their grandmother's old high-heeled shoes.

After giving her mother a welcoming hug, Vicky asked, "Who's Robert?" She looked around the kitchen in search of the mysterious male, glancing with curiosity at the open door to the basement.

"Oh, he's a very handsome movie star, but your grandmother and I were just playing a joke. He's not really here, I don't think—unless she has been holding out on me," Sally said as she sat down and clasped her daughters to her. "My, aren't we big ladies today! I've got a sack of tacos from Mexican Fiesta over in our kitchen, but I'm afraid such fancy ladies wouldn't want that ordinary food."

Vicky and Amy quickly returned the shoes and purses to their grandmother's closet and hurried home with their mother to indulge in one of their favorite meals. It was later in the evening when they returned to Margie's for a piece of pie that Sally learned about her mother's phone call.

The girls were watching television in the living room. Margie and Sally were enjoying a second cup of coffee at the kitchen table. Sally found herself staring at her mother, who, through some magic, looked ten years younger than she had this morning. Something was definitely going on.

"How long are you going to keep me in the dark?" Sally said. "You're dying to tell me but just a little embarrassed. Right? Must be a man?"

"Just an old friend," Margie admitted as she nervously stirred her coffee for a second time, "someone I knew back in high school."

"An old high-school friend was hiding in the closet?" Sally teased.

"No one was hiding in the closet," Margie said in mock irritation. "He called. That's all. Just a phone call."

"Ah, it is a *he*! Very interesting. And this mysterious man is here in town?" Sally asked.

"No," Margie said, ignoring her daughter's teasing. "He lives in Dallas. He had talked to the people who were organizing that reunion next week in Springfield. You know, I told you about it a couple of weeks ago.

Anyway, whoever he talked to must have told him about your father and let him know where I lived. Well, he just called to say hello and ask if I was going.''

Sally found herself staring at her mother. There seemed less middle-aged sag to her cheeks, more sparkle in her eyes, more tilt to her chin. Margie looked almost girlish. Sally didn't need to ask if the man who called was an old beau. She knew that already by the soft faraway look in her mother's eyes.

For an instant, Sally felt an irrational stab of anger that her mother would look like that for someone other than Ernie Hampton. Sally was jealous for her father's memory. Somehow her mother's thinking of another man seemed to violate that memory.

But her father was dead, Sally reasoned, and her mother was not. Her mother was alive and happier at this moment than she'd been in a very long time because a man she had once cared about called her on the phone. Sally realized she should be grateful to that man, whoever he was. She reasoned that her mother's response to this man's call probably did not diminish the love she had shared with her husband of many years. Nothing could alter what had already been. It was just that the prospect of another man in her mother's life seemed to push her father even further out of Sally's mind. And her father's memory was very dear to her. *But that's* my *problem, however,* Sally told herself firmly. She was not going to let her hang-ups stand in the way of her mother's revitalizing her life with a gentleman friend—if it came to that.

"What's his name?" Sally asked.

"Casey," Margie said softly. "Casey Tinsley. We dated all through high school—until I started going with your father."

"And is Mr. Tinsley married?"

For the second time in one evening, Sally saw her mother blush. "No," Margie admitted. "Casey's been alone for a number of years."

The blush decided it for Sally. Her mother was going to that high-school reunion no matter what.

They talked clothes then. Margie would have to buy a new dress for the dance—something blue, Sally insisted. Her mother looked lovely in blue. And she would borrow Sally's navy suit in case they went out to dinner. Her own red slacks with her white cotton sweater would do for the picnic on Sunday. She'd need to take her navy dress shoes to the shoe shop.

"My hair is a disaster!" Margie moaned, running her hands through her sensible hairdo. "Maybe I should get a permanent. Yes. I want curls, and a manicure. But what about the gray? Should I color the gray hair? Maybe just a rinse to soften it a bit."

Sally could not get over how happy and excited her mother was. How long had it been since Margie had cared, really cared, about her clothes and her hair? Too long, Sally realized. She just hoped Casey Tinsley didn't turn out to be a big disappointment. After all, it had been so many years since he and her mother had known each other. Could torches be rekindled after all that time?

Sally pondered that thought later, after she had tucked her girls into bed. She sat curled in the big easy chair in her living room with an open book in her lap and wondered if she were not to see Neal for many years how she would feel were they to meet again. Would they still be special to each other?

With a sigh that sounded loud in the quiet room, she realized there would always be such feelings in her heart for Neal no matter how many years went by. He was a part of her now and would always be tucked away in her heart. Maybe meeting again in the autumn of their lives would be the only hope she and Neal had of getting together, but there was small comfort for Sally in the thought. It made her sad. She didn't want to wait half a lifetime for the man she loved. She wanted him now.

Sally wanted to feel as excited and happy as her mother felt. She wanted to think of the future with warm promise and high hope.

Suddenly the tears she had not allowed herself to shed at the office welled up in her eyes and spilled over. *Damn you, Neal Parker,* she thought. *Why aren't you here with me now? I need you. I'm so confused and lonely. Why can't you love me and my little girls? Why, damn it! Why?*

Through a mist of tears, she stared at the phone on the table beside her chair. Would Neal be at home? Maybe he was out with someone.

But if he wasn't out, she could at least hear his voice—if she dared.

NEAL WAS WATCHING an old Gary Cooper western on television when Sally called. She had never called him before. Her voice sounded a little shaky and nervous.

"Is it hopeless with us?" she asked after the briefest of preliminaries.

"Oh, God, I hope not," Neal said.

"I want to go on that trip with you," Sally said, her voice stronger now. She had a wonderful voice—soft, but rich and clear. He'd always loved her voice from that first day he heard her give Channel Eight's Safety First Weather.

"My mother's going to a high-school class reunion," she was saying, "but I could probably hire a sitter."

"Do it, Sally. Please."

"I have to know first if there's any hope for us. I'd go if I thought we could talk and maybe work something out, but you seem so unreceptive to my children, Neal. I'm their mother, and I have to plan my life around them."

"I know," Neal said, gripping the phone so tightly his knuckles grew white. He loved her so. Oh, how he loved her, and because he loved her, he had to be completely honest. He didn't want to mess up both their lives with another failed marriage. And if he couldn't manage with her children, he knew that was what they would end up with. A divorce. His third, her second. And so much heartbreak. She would end up hating him, and he couldn't stand that.

Maybe he should try again with those children. It might make a difference if he got to know them better. But what about the family *he* had always wanted to have? He would like to have his own children. He was a twice-married man pushing forty, and it was high time he got his life straightened out. But Sally already had a family and was dedicated to a career. Maybe she didn't want more children. What if he and Sally and her two children were not able to meld together into a workable family? He understood better than most how easily that could happen. Then he would have caused them all so much pain—himself included. What if he allowed himself to love those little girls and lost them? His free hand strayed to the pocket that held his billfold and its picture of Danny. He started to pull it out, to look at the picture.

"You haven't really tried with the girls," Sally was saying. Her voice was accusing. They really did need to talk, Neal realized. He now knew about her past, about her marriage and how her husband had walked out on her and her daughters. It was time he told Sally about his marital failures, about Danny and why he had such doubts about ready-made families. Then maybe she would understand why they had to be just lovers and friends for a while longer anyway, while he was trying to come to terms with things.

"Go away with me," he said. "We'll talk about it—really talk. I need to tell you some things about myself, and I'd like to make love with you, Sally. I want you so, more than you'll ever know. I've never wanted a woman like I want you."

But then he remembered his promise about the trip. *Her* terms would apply. "Of course, if you'd rather keep it platonic, that's okay, too. I'll get one room, two rooms—whatever you say. Just come with me. I want to be with you on any terms."

"One room will be fine," she said in a small voice.

Neal closed his eyes and silently thanked whatever lucky star was shining up there in the heavens that night. Two weeks from tomorrow night, he would be with her again. Unless she'd come over here now—but no. He wouldn't ask her. Best go easy. He must not do anything to jeopardize the precarious balance of their relationship. He could wait. Somehow, he would wait.

He replaced the receiver on the phone and stared at it for a while. He was going to Kansas City with Sally! His triumphant whoop echoed in his empty house.

He would have to make reservations tomorrow. The Alameda Plaza—*one* room. Airplane reservations—first-class. Rental car—maybe a sporty two-seater. Yeah, why not?

Then, to keep from pacing about his house like a lion in his cave, he went out to run. He ran much farther than usual. He was so exhilarated, he felt that he could have run to the moon and back. When he came home, he wrote letters and tried to concentrate on an article in a professional journal about grant-proposal writing, but his thoughts kept wandering from the world of meteorology to a hotel room in Kansas City.

When he finally got around to going to bed, he lay for a long time in that cozy place between deep sleep and wakefulness.

Neal wondered if Sally was thinking of him. Would her thoughts be as erotic as his? He hoped she was remembering the night they made love and was wanting it all to happen again. They had been so right together, so very right. He still couldn't get over it. Never one to believe in destiny, Neal found himself thinking there was a preordained quality about their togetherness, as though it was meant to be. He felt sorry for all the world's other mortals who had never experienced the completeness he had felt that night. He wondered, however, if making love to Sally had ruined him for any other woman. If he and Sally did not make a go of it, would he constantly compare any other woman who might come into his life to her?

Other women—he had spent no small amount of time thinking about other women in the months following his divorce. He had mentally auditioned several for a role in his bed and his life, but now he thought only of Sally. She had the starring role in all his fantasies, from erotic to companionable.

It was the erotic, however, that colored his dream that night. He floated finally into sleep, leaving the real world for one choreographed by his subconscious mind.

As he came to awareness in his dreamworld, he found himself dressed in a long dark robe and standing alone atop a small hill. He was watching a crowd over in the distance—dozens, maybe hundreds, of people milling around in the basin of a small, lushly green valley.

Everyone in the crowd was a blur but for one dark-haired woman dressed in filmy white. Only Sally stood out. An aura of light surrounded her and separated her from the others. He watched for a time as she wandered aimlessly through the milling throng. He knew she was looking for him and that she would look up soon. Then she would see him.

Sally paused, tilted her head to one side as if she were listening internally. Then, raising her hand to shield her eyes from the bright sky, she looked up and gazed in his direction. *Now she will come to me,* his dreaming mind willed. But she just stood there, her eyes hidden, her face tipped upward.

He willed her to come to him, willed her to separate herself from the vaguer inhabitants of his dream and climb the small incline to where he stood.

She took one step. Then another.

She drew nearer but hesitated at the bottom of the hill, looking up at him. He could see her eyes now. They were the color of a calm sea at eventide. Her gaze met his and reached deep inside of him, touching his heart, his soul, the secret place where his desire waited.

Once again he exerted his will and slowly she began to climb the hill. A breeze played with the gauzy material of her white robe and swirled it about her slim body. Her hair lifted in a dark cloud about her face. A mist began to engulf the valley below and obscure the faceless crowd of people. As she climbed, the mists followed her, closing off the world behind her and leaving a pure white cloud in her wake.

Slowly she climbed, too slowly. He was impatient for

her and tried to hurry her to him by increasing his mental concentration. He wanted her here on this high place with him, isolated and alone with only the winds to keep them company, but she continued to come as though in slow motion. Even the breezes billowing out her white robe seemed to be doing their task ever so slowly.

He reached out to her and finally a slim cool hand touched his extended fingers, and he pulled her the last few steps. And now the mists were all around them. There was no hill, no sky, no valley, no other person anywhere—just he and this dream woman. The whole world was bathed in mist. Even her garment seemed made of the warm damp mist.

He looked into her face. Her expression was serene. Her beauty was otherworldly. He wanted her. With a throbbing painful need, he wanted her.

Slowly her arms opened to him. Her lips offered a small smile. She knew of his longing.

With great ceremony, he began undressing her. He discovered, however, that her body was clothed not in one layer but in many. He would remove one from her delicate form and toss it to the leisurely breeze, which caught hold of it and carried it off into the mists. Then Neal would remove the next and the next, and with each layer, the film covering her body became more sheer. As each layer slowly swirled away into the mists, he would look upon her, relishing the gradual revelation of her womanly body. Breasts with their dusky rose nipples began to show themselves, and hips and thighs with that mysterious darkness in their midst.

He continued unwrapping each sheer layer and pulling it from slim white shoulders. At last, he knew that only one misty thickness separated him from the alabaster body he desired. Sally's eyes fairly glowed with invitation as she stood before him. She swayed ever so slightly in the wind.

Then suddenly she threw up her arms and allowed the breezes to take the last layer. Neal imitated her gesture, raising his own arms and allowing his dark robe to lift from his body. Then they were free of all constraints—a man and a woman in the sanctuary of a misty hilltop with nothing to encumber them, nothing to keep them apart.

He touched the skin on her shoulder. It was moist from the warm mists and silky smooth. So very smooth. He was mesmerized by its smoothness. He wanted to feel all of her smoothness, to feel with his fingers, with his mouth, with his need.

Slowly he drew her down on the soft vapor. It enveloped them with a warm, moist veil. He hovered over the precious woman, holding her face, kissing her eyes, her lips, her throat. Her fingers played across his shoulders and down his back to his buttocks. His skin awoke to tingling sensation as her fingers trailed across his naked flesh. How he wanted her! His body, his will were nothing but a testament to his need of this one perfect woman.

Reverently, like a high priest, he began his ceremony, ministering to their mutual desire, celebrating the landmarks of her body, partaking of her sweetness, performing his ritual of love.

Their merging was a natural progression of the ritual. He entered her. Cradled in the mists, they wrapped themselves in each other's bodies and became one.

Forever, he thought. *Let me stay here forever.* But the feeling was too intense to last forever.

It came to an end with a violent shudder that expelled him from the misty dreamworld and brought him to abrupt wakefulness in his own damp bed in his own darkened bedroom.

His breathing came in ragged gasps. His body was wet with his perspiration and his dreaming.

Neal grabbed his pillow and buried his face in it, muffling his voice as he said her name over and over again.

WHEN SLEEP TOOK NEAL AGAIN, it was dark and dreamless, with a distorting effect on his sense of time. When the thunder awoke him at two-thirty, he felt as if he'd been unconscious for days. He stared at the ceiling of his room, orienting himself.

The thunder came from the southwest, and lightning momentarily lit the sky outside his window. He had seen the front on the satellite map before he left the office. Nothing more than a few local thunderstorms was indicated, certainly nothing worth chasing. There wouldn't be anything they could photograph since all the activity was going to occur after nightfall, he had decided before he closed up shop for the night.

He listened to the thunder and thought about his dream that had drained him emotionally and propelled him into the comalike sleep. He felt as though he had been drugged. He was a goner, Neal realized with grim certainty. He was gone on Sally Hampton. He felt as if he'd just survived one tidal wave and was hanging on to a tree trunk waiting for the next one.

What was a man to do? Part of him said do whatever was necessary to make the lady his. *Rob. Lie. Cheat. Anything. Take the risk.* Tell her he was crazy about the kids. Sure he'd be their father, anything. Just come live with him, and sleep with him, and never leave him.

But if it didn't work? What if he changed her love to hate?

IT WAS SALLY'S TURN to fuss about clothes. She and her mother spent the week in a flurry of activity, trying on clothes, adjusting hems, shopping for a party dress for Margie. There were trips to the beauty shop, the cleaners, the shoe-repair shop, and Sally helped her mother update her makeup to the delight of Vicky and Amy, who critiqued the whole operation and insisted on their turn.

Sally was able to secure the services of a competent sitter who had helped her out a few times before when Margie was out of town. Sally found herself still harboring doubts about the wisdom of going to Kansas City with Neal but pushed them aside. She wanted the trip too much to be rational about it.

She longed for the trip to be a turning point for her and Neal, a time of coming to terms with their situation and deciding once and for all what the future held for them. She realized she was being carried along on a romantic daydream of three glorious days alone with Neal. She refused to think of the possibility that they might not get along or that they might try to discuss the future but be unable to formulate a plan for sharing their lives.

Neal had indicated there were some things about himself he wanted to tell her, things she needed to know. That worried her. Perhaps there were insurmountable obstacles to their being together. Maybe he still hadn't emotionally accepted his divorce. Maybe his former wife wanted to come back, or he was going off to do meteorological research at the South Pole. A small voice warned that this weekend might be the end for her and the man she had come to love, but she chose not to listen to it. She would have this time with him no matter what! If it was an ending to their relationship, she would go out in a blaze of glory.

The entire week before the trip, Sally was giddy with anticipation. When she and Neal saw each other at work, Sally could not control the muscles in her face that insisted on smiling at him constantly. She found herself humming most of the time, and her skin had developed a disconcerting habit of tingling whenever she thought of him. She felt foolish and happy, and a little embarrassed that the others who worked on the tornado project were starting to notice the smiles, the hovering, the inane excuses she and Neal found to go by each other's offices and confer with each other.

"Correct me if I'm wrong," Jerry said teasingly, "but first I find out you're going to the conference in Kansas City with Dr. Director, then I start noticing silly grins on his face every time you walk by—and a few on your pretty face, too. Now, my hypothesis is that the Kansas City trip is not going to be purely business."

"Neal just thought I should meet some of the other N.O.A.A. research people," Sally insisted, knowing she probably wasn't putting anything over on Jerry but feeling the need to be circumspect about her relationship with the project director.

The grandfatherly Phil came in on Wednesday morning announcing that Neal had canceled his appearance at the Kansas City meeting and he was to go in Neal's place.

Neal not go to Kansas City! Sally was stunned by Phil's announcement and practically froze in midstep in the center of the hallway—until she heard the stifled laughs from her colleagues. She turned in time to catch the two men with their hands over their mouths, trying to keep from laughing out loud at her.

Chagrined, Sally escaped to her office, but she could still hear them out in the hall.

"She really believed you," Jerry said, his laughter

causing him to gasp for breath. "She actually thought there for a minute that old Neal was going to send a substitute. Doesn't she know there's not a force in the universe that could keep our esteemed director from accompanying our gorgeous colleague on this little junket?"

Sally smiled in spite of herself. What a nice thought. She didn't want any forces in the universe keeping Neal Parker from her. She wanted to be with him, to glory in his company, to pleasure in his body.

A long pensive sigh escaped from her lips as she bent over the wire-service report from the National Weather Service. Would next Thursday ever come?

At least she was busy. Sally was in charge of organizing the tornado project's annual report for N.O.A.A., and she had another television interview coming up— network this time. A special report called "Nature's Wrathful Winds" was scheduled on "Weekend Magazine." The program producers asked for Neal, but they got Sally instead. Neal did not enjoy media interviews. Sally found that she didn't mind them so much anymore. She had come to realize public relations was something she could handle very well, and therefore it was appropriate for her to assume those chores. After all, she certainly had experience along those lines. But she just didn't want to be relegated to that role exclusively. If she were just allowed to go on the storm chases and feel she was a full-fledged member of the tornado project, she actually wouldn't be making public relations a permanent part of her job.

With the upcoming broadcast being a network show, Sally needed to make sure she was well prepared. She took special pains looking over the format of the interview and making sure she had all the answers well under control.

The taping session took all day on Monday. She rode with the broadcasting crew to southwestern Oklahoma's Wichita Mountains, a tiny range of mountains that rise abruptly out of the surrounding tabletop-flat prairie. The site selected for Sally's segment of the broadcast was the peak of Mount Scott, the highest mountain in the state.

A drive up the twisting W.P.A.-built road took the television crew to the top of the 2500-foot-high boulder-strewn mountain. The breathtaking panoramic view of the surrounding prairie brought an ecstatic response from the blue-jeans-clad director. She also expressed delight with the day's weather, which provided both a bright sunlit sky to the southwest and a dark bank of clouds heralding an approaching front to the northeast. The shots from the top of the area's best-known tourist attraction promised to be quite dramatic. To the director's delight, it was even windy, a condition the woman found most appropriate for the taping of a program about weather.

Sally's hair and jacket whipped about her as a handsome young broadcaster introduced her and indicated her affiliation with the National Tornado Project, which he explained was affiliated with the National Severe Storms Laboratory in Norman, Oklahoma.

As the interview began, Sally pointed out the path a tornado had once taken across the countryside just west of the small mountain range.

"In 1951, a small funnel crossed those fields just west of the small community there at the base of the mountain," Sally explained, pointing to the area for her interviewer. "It was about thirty feet wide, and its on-the-ground path covered about one-half mile. The funnel was on the ground about two or three minutes, and its winds were estimated at about one hundred miles per hour. It was strong enough to lift a thirty-by-fifty-foot barn and carry it five hundred feet from its foundation."

Then the crew shifted their cameras to the opposite side of the flat summit. Sally indicated another area of interest to her interviewer.

"And over there lies what's left of the small Indian community of Eagle Nest," Sally said. "Last year, a medium-sized funnel completely flattened forty-seven of the town's seventy-two structures. Nine people were killed. That particular funnel lasted about fifteen minutes and cut a swath over five hundred feet wide and ten miles long."

"You say the Eagle Nest tornado was a medium-sized one. You mean tornadoes get bigger than *that*?" the reporter wanted to know.

The camera moved in for a close-up of Sally as she explained. "Oh, yes. They can be much larger. They might be up to a mile and a half in width and cut a path two hundred miles long. Tornadoes have been known to last for hours, with winds greater than one-hundred-and-fifty miles per hour. The worst tornado in the nation's history struck a tri-state area over Missouri, Illinois and Indiana in 1925. It killed about seven hundred people. Fortunately, however, giant funnels such as that one are rare. Most are like the smaller one over by Mountain View that we described earlier, and since much of the region known as Tornado Alley is rather sparsely populated, most tornadoes that do touch the ground come down in open areas. Of course, there are those that strike cities and towns like the one in 1979 that caused so much death and destruction in Wichita Falls, Texas, a city about fifty miles south of here. Forty-four people died in that storm, and countless others were left homeless."

The reporter asked Sally if the Tornado Alley area of the country was the only section susceptible to tornadoes.

"There have been tornadoes reported in every state in the United States. And although this country has more tornadoes than any other country in the world — an average of over two hundred every year — tornadoes have been reported elsewhere, even in England. And while the spring and summer months are the most common times of the year for tornadoes to strike, they may occur at any time of the year. Afternoon and evening are 'prime time' for twisters, but they have been known to strike at every hour of the day or night. They can hit before the rain, during the rain, after the rain. And though tornadoes are certainly more prevalent out here on our prairies, they have been reported moving across hilly terrain, lakes and even mountains."

Sally went on to explain that the energy expended by tornadic winds can equal that of many Hiroshima-sized atomic bombs *every second*.

The reporter then asked Sally questions about the effectiveness of warning systems and what people can do to protect themselves against the awesome force of the killer winds.

"The ordinary American home cannot withstand a tornado," Sally explained. "Neither will the average school building. Light metal structures such as many motels and shopping centers are particularly vulnerable, and mobile homes are the most dangerous and susceptible structures of all."

"So how do people protect themselves?" the reporter asked.

"Ideally, they should seek shelter in storm cellars, basements, any sort of underground structure. If they don't have access to an underground structure and if there is time, people should seek shelter in public buildings that have been designated as shelter areas. Otherwise, they should seek refuge in the southwest corner of a building away from windows to prevent injury from flying glass and debris and lie flat under a bed or table or crouch in an inside room or closet.

"But of course, the most important factors in tornado safety," Sally explained, "are a good warning system and an enlightened public. We work on both at the National Severe Storms Laboratory and the National Tornado Project. We are trying to develop the best possible warning system. Great strides have already been made due in great part to the application of Doppler, or continuous-wave, radar, which determines the speed of moving objects. For example, an estimated eighteen thousand people were in the damage path of the Wichita Falls tornado. The loss of life would have been much higher without adequate warnings and knowledge of safety rules on the part of citizens. But there is still much that needs to be done to ensure the issuance of warnings prior to every occurrence of a tornadic storm. That's a primary goal of the research going on at the Norman N.O.A.A. facilities."

At the conclusion of the taping, a smiling director congratulated Sally. "I was irritated when Dr. Parker wouldn't do the broadcast," she told Sally. "But you handled it like a real pro. You ought to be doing television meteorology."

"No, thanks," Sally said emphatically. "I'll leave that to you broadcasting types."

"Well, you may get offers after this airs in a few weeks," the woman said. "You're a natural. And you'll probably also hear from people all over the country you'd forgotten you even knew. A network appearance usually digs up lots of long-lost cousins, forgotten friends and former sweethearts.''

All over the country, Sally mused. She hadn't really thought much about that, and she wasn't sure if that prospect pleased her or not.

Chapter Eight

It took longer with the sitter than Sally had planned. She had written out every instruction she could think of but still felt the need to go over everything with the woman.

"My mother's not leaving until this afternoon," Sally explained to the small, gray-haired woman, "so if you think of anything I've forgotten to mention, give her a call. Otherwise, don't hesitate to call me in Kansas City. I've put the telephone number of the hotel by both telephones, along with the phone number of the girls' doctor and my next-door neighbor, who's awfully nice and would help out if you needed anything."

Finally the woman shooed Sally out the door. "The girls and I will be just fine," she assured Sally. "Your daughters are such nice big girls, they'll tell me everything I need to know, won't you, girls?"

Vicky and Amy nodded solemnly to the sitter's query.

"Now, you'd better run along or you'll miss your plane," the grandmotherly woman warned.

Sally hugged her daughters—twice. "I'll be back Sunday afternoon," she assured them, "and so will your grandmother. We'll take her out to dinner, and she and I will tell you about our trips. And who knows, we might even bring you something."

Sally checked the clock on the dashboard as she backed out of the driveway. She was late in getting away and was going to have to hurry.

The midmorning traffic was worse than usual, and Sally soon discovered the reason why. Two lanes of traffic on the interstate were closed for road repairs, and traffic was moving along at a snail's pace. Sally began to get knots in her stomach. What if she missed the plane? Neal was surely wondering where in the world she was. She should have had the sitter come earlier, or not spent so much time giving out all those instructions. But it was harder to leave the girls than she thought it would be. Suddenly three days away from home seemed like a long time, and a sitter wasn't like a grandmother. She'd have felt differently if her mother had been staying with Vicky and Amy.

Sally thought of Neal waiting for her in the airport lobby. He had needed to go to the lab for a couple of hours that morning and planned to meet her at the airport, which was located between Norman and downtown Oklahoma City. She should already be there. They had planned to have a cup of coffee together after they checked in. What must he be thinking? Would he be angry? What if she didn't make it? Surely he would go on to Kansas City since he was scheduled to present a paper at the afternoon session of the conference. Sally wondered if there would be a later flight she could catch if she missed this one.

One at a time, she removed her hands from the steering wheel and wiped her sweaty palms on her skirt. She was going to be a nervous wreck by the time she got to the airport.

In her nervousness, she began to reevaluate her decision to come on the trip in the first place. Suddenly it seemed terribly inappropriate for a woman with the re-

sponsibility of two young daughters to be running off
for a romantic weekend in a city hundreds of miles
away. She and Neal didn't even have any sort of "understanding." The whole trip might turn out to be just
a sexual escapade, and she would come back feeling
used and unhappy.

But, she reasoned, she might come back with a new
lease on life. She might come back with Neal in her
future—if she ever got to take the trip in the first place.
Damn this traffic, she thought impatiently. At this rate,
she was never going to get there, and her stomach
wouldn't be able to take much more of this.

At last, however, the other two lanes of traffic
opened up, and the flow of traffic thinned to normal.
Sally quickly pushed her car to the speed limit—and
then some.

This was better. It was a good thing they had allowed
some extra time for that cup of coffee. That just might
provide her with the leeway she needed. She wasn't
going to get the coffee, but maybe she'd make it to the
airport in time after all, she thought as she glanced at
the dash to check the clock again. But it was the red
warning light that drew her attention.

With alarm, she realized the car engine was overheating. Damn, she muttered aloud. Just what she
needed!

Frantically, Sally tried to decide what to do. She de-
bated whether to stop at a service station or risk driving
the last five or six miles with an overheated engine.

She slowed down. If she stopped, she could not possibly make the plane. But if she continued, she might
ruin the engine in her car, and she certainly couldn't
afford to do that.

If the needle on the temperature gauge moved any
higher, she would stop, Sally decided. She would have

to. Otherwise, she would limp along to the airport and worry about the car when she got home.

She eased her way into the right-hand lane. Cars raced by her as she slowed down to fifty, then forty miles an hour. The needle on the temperature gauge moved ever so slightly upward. She tried thirty-five, constantly checking in her rearview mirror and hoping no one rear-ended her. What a nerve-racking beginning for a trip! She almost felt as if the closed lanes of traffic and the overheating engine were some sort of ominous signs warning her not to take the trip.

Finally the sign announcing Airport Road came into view and she hastened up the exit ramp to the Will Rogers International Airport just ahead.

She took a chance on finding a parking place in the parking garage near the terminal. It cost more, but she didn't want to take the time to hike from the cheaper parking lots.

After finding a spot on the lowest level, she ran to the elevator and rode one level down to the tunnel leading to the terminal building.

She stepped onto the motorized sidewalk but quickly decided it wasn't moving fast enough. She half ran along the moving walkway, her folded garment bag awkwardly swinging from its shoulder strap and slapping against her side. She was thankful she'd brought it, however, instead of a suitcase. At least she could hang it on the plane and wouldn't need to take the time to check luggage.

As she hurried along, Sally tried to remember if she had brought anything for a nervous stomach. Hers felt as if it needed something to soothe its queasiness. Why in the world had she wanted to come on this trip in the first place? The whole thing was starting off like a big disaster.

Neal was waiting for her at the appointed place under the antique aircraft suspended from the high ceiling of the lobby. His worried frown changed instantly to a relieved smile when he saw her. In spite of her haste, Sally paused a minute and stared at him across the lobby.

She would have noticed him standing there even if he had been a stranger. He was impressive-looking, not just because of his above-average height but because of his broad forehead, his intense dark eyes, his determined jaw and strong full mouth. There was about him an air of unpretentious self-assurance. One just knew by looking at him he was special, that he had to be a scholar or a scientist or someone important.

He was wearing a gray summer-weight suit and maroon tie and holding his ever-present battered briefcase. She loved the way he looked—so distinguished, so intelligent. But most of all, she loved the way he looked at her. The gaze that met hers across the lobby said so many things: that he thought she looked wonderful, that he adored her, that he was so very glad she was there.

In an instant, he was at her side. He grabbed her, garment bag, and all, and held her tightly.

"I was so worried," Neal said. "I was afraid you'd changed your mind or had a wreck. I can't tell you how glad I am you're here."

And he kissed her.

With a poignant mixture of gentleness and intense yearning, his mouth held hers. Anything that was left of her heart, he stole away with that kiss.

Sally felt her apprehension melting. She could relax; everything was all right. She was with Neal again—where she wanted to be. It was like arriving home after a long journey. In his arms, she felt safe and protected and warm.

"I'm sorry I'm late," she started to explain. "Everything in the world went wrong. The traffic, my car—"

"It's okay," he interrupted. "You can tell me about it later. You're here now, and that's all that's important."

He wasn't mad, Sally realized. She almost made them miss their plane, but there would be no recriminations from him.

Neal hastily grabbed his bag from a nearby chair. "We'd better hurry," he said. "I've checked us in. The plane's boarding now."

Sally thought of Michael as they went through the security check. Her former husband would have been so angry at her for keeping him waiting. So much of her married life with him had been spent worrying about his temper, about trying not to make him mad. Neal wasn't like that. Neal knew she hadn't been late on purpose, and that was enough. She reached over and squeezed his arm before retrieving her bag and purse from the X-ray machine. He smiled.

"You're gorgeous," he said. The look on his face told Sally that to him, at least, she truly was.

The final call for their plane sounded over the public-address system as they raced down the long corridor toward the boarding gates. They were going to make it, Sally thought gleefully. They were going to fly away together. She was going to have her three days alone with Neal—and three nights.

They weren't the last passengers on the plane—but almost. Their seats were in first class. When Sally questioned this extravagance, Neal said with a grin, "My treat. I supplemented our government travel allowance. This will be a first-class trip all the way, milady."

He hung up their garment bags, and soon they were settled in the roomy seats at the front of the plane.

"I've never flown first-class before," Sally said.

"I didn't want to sit three across with you and someone else, back in tourist class," Neal said. "I wanted to sit just with you. I wanted to be able to touch you and discuss with you in private the way we are going to spend our nights."

By way of reply, Sally slipped her arm through his and rested her head against his shoulder. How wonderful it felt to be able to do that. For a time neither of them moved. Sally wanted to prolong the moment, to imprint it on her memory, for it felt like more than the beginning of a trip. It felt like the beginning of forever.

He fastened her seat belt for her. "I want to do everything for you for the next three days," he said. "I don't want you to lift a finger. I will serve you and bathe you and dress you."

"And what about the undressing?" Sally asked, his attentions making her feel quite bold.

"I had a dream about undressing you," Neal said. "Such a dream! And right now I believe in dreams coming true."

As the plane taxied toward the runway, Sally thought how symbolic it was that in the next few minutes she would be flying high above the earth, for her spirits were already soaring. She was high on Neal! His presence was more intoxicating than any drinks the flight attendant might serve. Glorious anticipation seeped through her body, awakening every fiber and pore. She could not have been more thrilled if she had been flying away to Paris or Rome or London. It was the man and not the destination that thrilled her.

First-class passengers were served first, Sally discovered as the flight attendant put the drinks they had ordered before takeoff in front of them almost the same instant the seat-belt light was turned off.

"How positively decadent, to be drinking before noon," Sally observed as she took the first taste of her Bloody Mary. After a few more sips, she leaned back and closed her eyes. "We are actually on our way," she said with a sigh. "I didn't think this minute would ever come."

"I know what you mean." Neal said, leaning across the armrest rest that separated their seats. Their bodies drew closer together, and his face was very near to hers. "This has been the longest two weeks of my life. If I wasn't actually thinking about you every minute, Sally, thoughts of you were lurking in the wings waiting to come onstage. I had to force myself to work, to get the paper I am to present finished and my speech written for Saturday. When I ate, I planned the meals we would have together. When I tried to sleep, I thought of us together."

She turned her head and met his gaze. Only inches separated their eyes. So brown his were they were almost black, but tiny flecks of gold were there in their rich darkness. His lashes were short and thick. His brows were bold dashes across his broad forehead. She'd seen those eyes looking stern—and troubled, tired, even teasing—but now they were adoring. Sally could not have felt more special if she had been a royal princess.

She raised her glass to him, and Neal returned the gesture. "To us," she said. He responded by leaning even closer and brushing her lips with his.

"Tonight," he whispered.

"What about tonight?" she asked coquettishly.

"Well, for starters, we'll stroll down the hill from the Alameda Plaza, across the bridge to the La Mediterranée for an elegant French dinner."

"French! You mean we aren't dining Italian!" Sally teased.

"Well, tomorrow night I thought we'd go to the Italian Gardens. Saturday night I'm afraid we're stuck with banquet fare, but tonight we will have French wine and *salade canaille*, Dover sole *belle meunière au citron*. And the pastries! I want to see your face when you bite one of the La Mediterranée's napoleons."

"And then?" Sally prodded. She was enjoying herself immensely. He really had planned their whole trip—every minute. The knowledge that he wanted this trip to be special every bit as much as she did thrilled her. The past two weeks had been as delightfully agonizing for him as they had been for her.

"Then back to the Alameda," he continued, his hand caressing her arm. "There's dancing at the Alameda Roof, and I want to dance with you again. I want to hold you in my arms and feel the music with you. I want to put my face against your hair and smell your perfume."

He leaned even closer, his face touching her hair. "I like the feel of your body against me when we dance—your breasts, your thighs moving to the music. I like to put my hand on your waist, then let it drop down to where your hips start to swell. It drives me crazy, but I love it."

"It drives me crazy, too," Sally admitted. "When I know you are wanting me, I get almost dizzy."

"I want you now," he said.

"I know. I want you, too."

"Really want me?" he asked. "Physically?"

Sally laughed. "Oh, yes. *Physically*." She held up a hand and wagged her little finger. "Even this little finger wants you."

Neal bent forward and took her little finger in his mouth. The gesture was so intimate, so sensual, that Sally felt her insides turn over. When next she reached for her drink, her hand was trembling. Neal noticed and shook his head in wonder. "Is that because of me?"

"Oh, yes," she said breathlessly. "You have an incredible effect on me."

"I'm glad." The look on his face was so charmingly smug that Sally had to laugh. They hugged each other and laughed some more.

"What will the flight attendant think?" Sally asked, pulling away from his embrace and straightening her blouse.

Neal put his mouth close to her ear. "She's probably thinking those two people can hardly wait to get into bed together."

"Bed?" Sally said with feigned naiveté. "The last I heard of your plans for the evening, we were still dancing—at the Alameda Roof."

"Ah, yes," Neal said, taking up the tale, "dancing. Well, by that time, I absolutely won't be able to keep my hands off you. We'll sit for a time by the window and enjoy the spectacular nighttime view of Kansas City, and sip an after-dinner drink, then I'll dance with you one last time. We'll both know that when the song ends we'll go to our room, so the dance is special. Our bodies talk to each other."

"And the maid will have turned back our bed," Sally said, taking up the story. "There will be a chocolate mint on each pillow. I will unwrap yours and put it in your mouth." She took up one of the peanuts from the package left by the flight attendant and put it in Neal's mouth in imitation of the promised gesture.

"Will you want champagne in the room?"

"I think not. I'll be ready for that bath you promised."

Neal groaned softly, his face suddenly serious. "Oh, yes, I want that. I want to soap every inch of your wonderful body. Your body is so lovely, Sally—so perfectly lovely. I can't count the times I've thought of how you looked there on the rug in front of my fireplace."

"Oh, Neal," she said, embarrassed, "my body's far from perfect. I've had operations and children. I have scars and stretch marks."

He put his finger over her lips to hush her. "You have lived, and life leaves its marks, but you have the most perfectly proportioned body, and the smoothest, silkiest skin imaginable. I plan to kiss each of those marks life has left. They are a part of you."

Sally stared at his face—his sincere, beautiful face.

"But how can you be so accepting of that part of me and not of the children whose births brought about those scars?" she asked.

Sally knew she had broken the romantic mood with her question, but the words had come out. It would have been dishonest of her not to say them.

For a long minute, Neal said nothing. He looked away, his eyes focused someplace out the window in the clouds. "I'm working on it, Sally," he said softly, earnestly. "I really am. Tomorrow, we're going to talk about all this. I have some explaining to do about myself, and we're going to come to terms. But tonight, let's just feel young and in love."

She nodded her head in agreement, then touched his face and ran her fingers over his cheek and chin to his mouth. He kissed her fingertips. Maybe the mood was not broken after all.

Suddenly Sally no longer cared what the flight attendant thought. She put her arms around his neck and pulled his mouth to hers. With such longing she kissed him, telling him of her love with her lips and tongue, telling him with the soft murmurs that arose from her throat, telling him with her soul. With her kiss she offered him a promise of what was to come. How she would love him that night!

IT WAS EARLY AFTERNOON when the plane touched down at the Kansas City airport. The sports car Neal had ordered was waiting. It was black and flashy and delightfully frivolous, with scarcely enough room for their luggage. The mood in the tiny car was one of gaiety as Neal flitted it skillfully through the noontime traffic. Sally accused him of being a frustrated race-car driver, and he informed her he'd rented the car because he'd heard women really had a "thing" about men in sports cars. Sally could tell he felt as youthful and merry as she. It was a glorious ride, a glorious day.

Even the stately old hotel to which Neal drove the shiny little car looked quite glorious with its Spanish architecture, splashing fountains, marble statuary and hilltop site that offered a panoramic view of the city. Not only were they staying in the Alameda Plaza, but the famous Kansas City landmark was also the site of their conference—the annual meeting of N.A.R.M., the National Association of Research Meteorologists.

Neal left their luggage with the bell captain and hurried Sally to the coffee shop, where they grabbed a quick sandwich before the three o'clock seminar at which Neal was to deliver his paper. Sally would have liked to take time to check in after lunch and use their room to freshen up, but she did not want to miss a minute of Neal's presentation.

Neal went into the meeting room while Sally ducked into a first-floor ladies' room and fussed a minute with her hair and makeup. The face that looked back at her from the mirror was prettier than the one she had seen at home that morning. It was slightly flushed and had a look of wide-eyed anticipation.

Feeling a little silly, Sally smiled at herself. "This love stuff isn't so bad, is it, Sally girl?"

She slid into a chair at the back of the meeting room just as Neal was being introduced, and she listened with interest as the woman gave Neal's truly impressive list of credentials. She knew about all his many publications in scientific journals but was unaware of his work on many influential government committees—and she did not realize he was president-elect of N.A.R.M.

The paper Neal presented on severe-storm structure and evolution as it related to tornado formation was a collaborative work of the tornado project lab, with Neal listed as principal researcher. Sally had already read the paper in one of its earlier drafts, but nevertheless she found Neal's presentation fascinating and the question-and-answer session at the end even more so. Neal had a commanding presence in front of the group and answered their questions concisely and with authority. She still could not quite believe that such a man had actually fallen in love with her. Today, she realized Neal belonged to his fellow scientists, but tonight he would belong just to her. An image of them together came to her with such dizzying clarity, it took her breath away.

There was a welcoming reception immediately following the seminar. Neal firmly took her arm and introduced her to many of the group of well-known meteorologists. "Sally's a comer," Neal promised the current president of the organization. "Her grasp of our project has been impressive, as have been her first studies. We're expecting great things from her."

Sally had never felt so proud in her life. Such praise—and from a man like Neal!

It was nearly six when Sally finally was able to find the time to check into their room. Neal had a few more people he needed to see and sent her along ahead of him. "You go on and get ready for dinner," he said. "It won't take me long to change. Our reservation isn't until eight."

Sally signed both their names on the registration card. The desk clerk checked his computer for the reservation, then said, "Oh, Miss Hampton, I see here we have a message for you."

A message? Immediately Sally thought of the children and her heart took a lurch.

The note was from her sitter. Vicky had been taken to the hospital after suffering an asthma attack.

Sally called home at once. "I wish now I hadn't even called you," the sitter told Sally. "Vicky's doing much better now. I just talked to the doctor again a minute ago, and he says to tell you there's no need for you to come home."

"Are you sure?" Sally asked.

"Here, you talk to Vicky yourself," the woman said.

Vicky still sounded a little wheezy but quite calm. Her calmness helped to reassure Sally. She knew how nervousness and apprehension aggravated an asthma attack. "I did the breathing machine at the hospital, Mommie, and I'm much better," Vicky assured her mother.

Almost mechanically Sally got ready for dinner. She could not help but think of all those asthmatic episodes in the past when she truly feared for Vicky's life. The attacks didn't come very often now, and when they did, they were not so severe as they had formerly been. Sally dared hope that Vicky was outgrowing the worst phase of her disease. She knew that many children did outgrow it, but she still remembered all those other times, racing to the hospital with her daughter turning blue on the seat beside her as she gasped for every breath. Sally still had nightmares about asthma attacks.

The attack today had been Vicky's first in almost six months. *Why did it happen now, of all times,* Sally asked herself, deciding it was probably because the child was a little nervous with both her mother and grandmother out of town. Sally and Margie were often able to head off the attacks by talking the child through the initial stages and encouraging her to relax and take deep breaths, but a sitter wouldn't know about that.

Sally heard Neal's tap at the door. She took a quick glance at herself in the mirror and went to open the door for him. Resolutely, she put a big smile on her face, but it didn't fool him.

"What's wrong?" he said the instant he saw her.

"It shows that much?" she asked. "I was hoping you'd at least notice my dress first."

He put his arms around her and drew her near. "The dress is elegant. I love you in white. You are so beautiful, it makes me ache. But I can tell something is amiss. It shows in those incredible blue-one-minute-green-the-next eyes of yours. What gives?"

"Probably nothing," Sally said, allowing herself to relax enough to appreciate the feel of his lips brushing against her forehead. "I had a message from the sitter. Vicky's asthma is acting up, and she had to take her to the hospital. I called home, and she seems better. But you know us mothers," she said with a shrug, "we do worry."

"Of course you do," Neal said. "You going to be okay now?"

Sally leaned her cheek against his chest. "I think so.

It just shook me up, that's all. Bring on that wonderful French dinner and a glass of wine, and I'll be okay."

The Alameda Plaza overlooked the area known as Country Club Plaza, which was famous for its Spanish architecture, important statuary and fountains, beautiful tree-lined walks, elegant shops and some of the city's finest restaurants. As she and Neal walked hand in hand down the hill to the plaza area, Sally felt as though she were leaving Kansas City behind and entering a bit of old Spain.

It was such a beautiful evening, and she had such a beautiful man at her side. She had wanted this to be one of the most special nights of her life. She had wanted that desperately. She had promised Neal she would be okay, but she was not. She couldn't get Vicky off her mind. What if she had another attack tonight? They were often worse at night.

Well, if that happened, the sitter would just have to take her back to the hospital, she told herself. The woman was competent. She had a car. She could handle it.

Sally worked hard at relaxing. The restaurant was charming with its French Provincial decor, superb service, excellent wine and romantic violin music. Sally drank more wine than usual and forced herself to eat most of the elegant, sauce-laden French cuisine.

Before the pastries were served, she excused herself and called home. Vicky had suffered another small flare-up, but she was now sleeping peacefully. "She's breathing just fine, Miss Hampton," the sitter said reassuringly. "I have her sleeping in bed with me so I can keep an eye on her. You're not to worry, hear? I've taken care of things like this before. Vicky and I will be just fine."

Sally hung up and called the airport, just in case.

There was a late-night flight to Oklahoma City and one early in the morning.

She went to the ladies' room and brushed her hair for a longer time than necessary and carefully reapplied her lipstick. She wanted to look good for Neal. She wanted everything to be as they had planned.

"I ordered you coffee," Neal told her when she returned to the table, "and took the liberty of selecting you a treat from the pastry tray. They were out of napoleons, but I'm told this is a josephine and just as good."

Sally took a bite of the flaky cream-filled pastry. She was sure it would have been sinfully delicious under normal circumstances, but it tasted like cardboard to her. She put down her fork and bowed her head. "I guess I better go home, Neal."

"I was afraid that was coming," he said. "Well, I won't pretend it's okay and that I'm not disappointed, but I understand—I guess. But are you sure you're not overreacting? You said the woman was competent. What can you do at home that the sitter can't?"

"She can't be Vicky's mother, Neal. Those girls are my responsibility, and I have to put them first no matter what. I'm sorry. I'm so very sorry," she said in complete misery.

"I see," Neal said in a voice that indicated he really didn't quite. "Well, in that case, I'll go back with you."

"You can't do that," Sally said firmly. "You're scheduled to address the entire conference, and you have administrative duties with N.A.R.M. This is my problem. If I hurry, I can catch a late-night flight back to Oklahoma City."

Neal insisted on taking her to the airport. The sports car seemed painfully silly as they made the forty-five-minute drive in uncomfortable silence. At first, Sally racked her brain to try to think of something to say to him, then she gave up. She was grateful when Neal turned on the radio. It helped ease the silence.

Her seat on the plane was next to the window. As she stared out into the night, she grieved. Their weekend, their wonderful weekend—lost. She wondered if theirs was a lost love.

A great sadness permeated her entire mind- and body. She felt tired and ill and so lonely.

Chapter Nine

It was after midnight when Sally's flight arrived in Oklahoma City. Not trusting her sickly car, she left it in the airport parking lot to deal with the following day and took a taxi home.

Her older daughter was sleeping peacefully when Sally tiptoed into her room. Vicky's breathing was only slightly wheezy. Sally kissed the sleeping child, marveling as she always did at the softness of her innocently round cheek and the clean sweet aroma of her delicate skin.

Sally pondered the interesting state of motherhood as she smoothed the fine wisps of white-blond hair from her sleeping daughter's brow. Motherhood exposed one to the most heartwarming aspects of life and to the most frustrating—to both ends of life's spectrum—and Sally had experienced both ends in this one day. There had been the frustration from having her dream weekend ruined—and just possibly her entire relationship with a man she cared for very deeply. But sitting on the edge of the bed in the darkened room, and knowing that her child was safe and well, exemplified the heartwarming part. Sally experienced such relief knowing the danger from the asthma had passed, and all those frightening thoughts of what might have been waiting for her when she got home could be put to rest. The profoundness of that relief only served to reinforce her commitment to this child and to the one sleeping in the next room. They were her children, Sally thought vehemently. They were hers to love, to care for. It was a matter of duty, but a duty wrought with such love.

Vicky and Amy would help fill her life for many years to come, and they would continue to be the happy family they were now. Sally was determined to see that was so. At least the mothering part of her would be content. But what of the passionate woman she now knew resided within her? What of the woman who longed to share her life with Neal, who longed for the loving, the companionship, the kind of caring that only a man and a woman who truly love each other can bring to each other's lives?

Her two children would not be hers forever. They would grow up and leave her. That was the way of life. Of course, there would be grandchildren, but they would only be hers to borrow. When Vicky and Amy left home, she would truly be alone, burdened with the kind of aloneness that had inhabited her mother's life since Sally's father died. She thought of how the luster had gone out of Margie's eyes and anticipation for tomorrows had disappeared from her outlook. Even though Margie filled her days with her daughter's family and with her job, her life was lonely and lacking.

Sally wondered if perhaps that loneliness was coming to an end for her mother. It looked as though Margie's old sweetheart would become her new love.

Sally wondered, if she lost Neal, if there would someday be another man in her own life. Part of her hoped there would be, but in her heart of hearts, Sally knew her love would always belong to Neal, to a man who might never be hers. And feeling the way she did about Neal, would it even be fair to enter a relationship with another man? Would companionship and respect be enough to sustain a marriage?

She went to Amy's room and repeated her mothering ritual at the bedside of her younger daughter. So different they were, her girls, one quiet and fragile, the other outgoing and sturdy, and both so incredibly dear. If only Neal could have come to appreciate their dearness.

Sally returned to the entry hall for her garment bag, checked the door locks, then started up the stairs. She was tired, so very tired. The staircase suddenly seemed insurmountable. She was drained, emotionally drained. She felt as though a part of her heart had been gouged away.

Sally sank to her knees on the third step, then collapsed across the stairs. Where would she ever find the strength to get her body up all those stairs? Where would she find the strength to get herself through all the days, weeks, months, years that lay ahead?

She didn't even have the strength to cry.

MARGIE RETURNED FROM HER TRIP as high as Sally was low. If one ever doubted the power of love, a look at Margie Hampton that Sunday evening would have dissolved those doubts. She was radiantly happy. Sally tried to conceal her own depression and let her mother have center stage without putting a damper on her stories of the reunion.

"So many people came," Margie told Sally and the girls over a bowl of stew at a neighborhood restaurant. "I wouldn't have missed it for the world. I swear, some people looked just the same, older, but just the same, and I would have recognized them anywhere. While others didn't look one bit like the kids I spent my growing-up years with. It was only after you talked to them for a while and heard their voices and saw their facial expressions that they became familiar again."

Margie filled Sally in on the lives of people she had told her about over the years. Mary Bell, the one with the Arabian horses, still rode every day. Phillip Rosser, who was always taking cars apart, had invented a thingamabob for airplane engines, and it had made him rich. Joe Kimball, the rowdiest boy in the senior class, was now a priest! Sue Ann Collins, the prettiest girl in the class, was now fat as butter. Ruthie Jones, who almost flunked senior English, was a newspaper editor in Washington state. Mark Robinson, who had been absolutely the handsomest boy in the class, didn't have a hair on his head but he was still incredibly good-looking.

"But what about your friend Casey? Has he changed a lot? Is he fat or bald? Is he a priest?" Sally asked teasingly.

"I knew him the instant I laid eyes on him," Margie said, her eyes getting that faraway look Sally had noticed so often in the past two weeks. "He's a little heavier but not at all fat. He has less hair than before, but most men do at his age. And he will never make the priesthood."

Sally laughed at her mother's last comment. Margie blushed and readjusted the barrette in Amy's hair to cover her embarrassment.

"What does he do?" Sally asked.

"He has a restaurant in Dallas," Margie said with a sigh. "A small place featuring home-style cooking in a nice neighborhood—probably a whole lot like this place," she said, looking around rather wistfully, "a

place with checkered tablecloths that serves homemade
apple pie and where families go a lot. It sounds so wonderful. I always thought I'd love the restaurant business. I am a pretty good cook, you know.''

"Are you moving to Dallas?" Vicky asked, her eyes
large and her lower lip quivering.

"Oh, probably not, honey," Margie said with a reassuring pat on her granddaughter's arm. "If I did, it
wouldn't be anytime soon, probably not until you girls
are older. And Dallas isn't very far. It's just a hop, skip
and jump down the interstate. You and Amy could
come and spend weekends with me, and you know
what's close to Dallas, don't you?''

"Six Flags Over Texas!" both girls chimed in at
once. Margie and Sally had taken them to the famous
amusement park last summer, and they all had a wonderful time.

Later, as Vicky and Amy played in the yard, Margie
and Sally sat on the porch enjoying a cup of coffee in
the twilight. With the girls occupied, Sally was able to
find out more about Casey Tinsley.

Sally realized her mother was falling in love with her
former classmate. "Would you like to marry him and
move to Dallas?" she asked.

"It's too early for talk like that," Margie said. "Oh,
we discussed it some in a roundabout, wouldn't-it-be-
nice-if sort of way, but marrying him and moving away
would be an awfully hard decision to make. I'd worry
about leaving you and the girls. You've been my whole
life since your dad died, and you've really needed me
to help you with those girls. I've liked that—still being
needed. But now I worry about how you'd get along
without me. It would be so hard on you trying to manage with the girls on your own, and it does look as
though you'll still be alone for the time being. I take it

from what Vicky told me that your trip to Kansas City got cut short. She also reports that 'Mommie's sad.'"

Sally nodded. "Vicky had a bad flare-up with her asthma. After I found out about it, I was too worried to relax and enjoy the trip, so I came on home. It's probably just as well, though. I don't think a shared future is in the cards for Neal and me. If he has serious reservations about marrying a woman with two young children, then I'm obviously not the one for him. It's best to find that out before we got any more involved."

"Seems to me you're pretty involved right now," Margie said, "and pretty depressed. Do you think just because you didn't have your wonderful weekend together that Neal isn't going to want to see you again?"

"Not exactly, Mom. It's just that the whole incident graphically demonstrated how confined my life is, how much I belong to those kids. Neal thinks he would always feel like the odd man out, and maybe he would be. It's hard to say how things like that will turn out. Maybe the four of us could become a family. I'm willing to give it a try, but he's apparently not—especially after things turned out this weekend the way they did."

Their conversation was interrupted by shouts of "Watch me" from Amy and Vicky as the two girls swung upside-down from their knees on their jungle gym. Sally sprinted across the yard and showed them that mothers, too, could swing from their knees.

When she got back to the porch and her lukewarm coffee, a thoughtful Margie asked, "Would you consider moving to Dallas if I did? Casey suggested that. Dallas is a wonderful city. If I should get married, I probably wouldn't continue to baby-sit as much as I have in the past, but then Amy will be in school a full day next year and day care won't be quite such a problem. You can probably enroll them in an after-school program someplace, but I could still be your backup pilot. If Casey and I do get together, I'd really like to be a part of his business. Running a restaurant sounds so wonderful, but I know I would miss you and the girls so much! If things continue to go badly for you here, why don't you see about a transfer to a N.O.A.A. facility in Texas? Then we could still all be together, and I'd still be able to help you with the girls. Casey can hardly wait to meet you and Vicky and Amy. His son doesn't have any children, and I think he'd like to be a granddaddy.''

"You two really did talk seriously, didn't you?" Sally asked.

"No promises were made, honey," Margie said, touching her daughter's hand. "Your situation is too unsettled, and I don't have to do anything about Casey for now."

"Go for it, Mom. I'll be okay."

But Margie did not look convinced. Sally turned her attention to her daughters, who were pushing a one-eyed teddy bear in the tire swing. She knew her mother loved her and the girls very much, and Margie had shared the responsibility for their care for over four years now. But she had her own life to lead—especially now. It was as though her mother had been handed a whole new lease on life, and Sally did not want her to miss this chance for future happiness because of the sense of obligation she felt toward her daughter and granddaughters.

The prospect, however, of facing the future as a single parent without the backup of a loving grandmother was frightening. She had managed alone, however, for those first years after Michael left, Sally reminded herself, and she could do it again. But oh, what a shame that she couldn't share the children she loved with the man she loved. What a damned shame!

NEAL WAS NOT at the lab on Monday. Early Sunday morning, a huge storm system over South Dakota had spawned several large tornadoes, one of which had done a great deal of damage to a community in the southwestern corner of that state. Sally learned that Neal had flown from Kansas City to South Dakota Sunday morning to measure the path of the funnel clouds and study the extent of the destruction. Apparently, there were problems with some of the new prefabricated storm shelters that were now being installed by several different manufacturers, and Neal had decided to check into the matter.

Sally sank into the orange canvas-backed chair that occupied a corner of Phil's unbelievably cluttered office.

"When will he be back?" Sally asked, not sure if she was disappointed or relieved by Neal's temporary absence from the lab.

"In a day or two, I suppose," Phil said, making a halfhearted attempt to straighten the stacks of satellite photographs, facsimile maps and teletype reports completely obliterating the surface of his desk. "In the meantime, I'm in charge, and it looks as though the same front that brought havoc to the Dakotas will push a little bad weather down our way."

Pointing to one of the facsimile maps, Phil indicated the two powerful high-pressure masses of cold arctic air forming a dumbbell shape over the northern sectors of the continent. And together he and Sally examined the status of a low-pressure system hovering over Texas and Louisiana and a second system that had dissipated against the western slope of the Rockies and was now forming over New Mexico.

It was a volatile situation illustrated by the weather map. As Sally tried to explain in her civic-club speeches, "When the cold, dry air from the north comes down in a hurry, and the hot, moist air from the south rushes up to meet it—where those two masses meet, there are going to be downdrafts and updrafts and sidedrafts. There're going to be rain, hail, lightning, thunder, some cyclonic rotation of the winds, strong straight winds and just possibly a tornado or sometimes a whole series of tornadoes."

"Looks like the weather's going to come down over our region," Phil said. "We'll monitor this morning. If something develops, would you be available to go out and chase? Jerry's next up on the roster, and he needs a partner."

"Yeah, sure. I'm available," Sally said halfheartedly. Somehow the excitement of anything that had to do with the National Tornado Project had diminished.

" *'Yeah, sure'?* This from the woman who's been champing at the bit since April to chase a storm. Is that all you have to say? *Yeah, sure!* First Neal calls from South Dakota sounding like he's not sure just how he got there or why he's there. I can't figure out why he's there, either, since the N.O.A.A. folks up in Minneapolis are responsible for that area. They're certainly capable of checking into the defective storm shelters and reporting to us. It's weird for Neal to take off and go up there uninvited, almost like he's putting off coming back to Norman, and then you come in with your chin dragging on the ground and acting like you'd just lost your last friend. What gives? The big weekend didn't go too well, I take it."

"It didn't go at all," Sally explained. "I had to come home. Vicky got sick."

"I see," Phil said, giving up on his desk and leaning back in his squeaking swivel chair. "Motherhood came first, and Neal got his nose out of joint."

"Something like that, I guess."

"Look, Sally, if you don't mind an old man butting in where he doesn't belong, just remember if Neal wasn't crazy about you, it wouldn't have mattered so much to him about your having to abort the big romantic weekend. Don't judge him too harshly. I'm crazy about all my kids and always prided myself on being a good father, but there've been times when I was jealous as hell of those kids, times when Edna didn't have any time or energy left over for me. My own kids, mind you! There were times I'd be feeling really amorous, and she had to rock a screaming baby. Or there were times when I got home early and wanted to have a before-dinner drink with her, and she'd have to feed the kids and finish the laundry 'cause there were no more clean diapers or Billy needed his baseball shirt for a game. I gave her some bad times over it all, too. I think I do better now. I kind of grew up and realized we were in this parenting business together, and tried to do a better job of pulling my own weight around the house and being more understanding about her mothering duties."

"But Neal isn't my daughters' parent," Sally explained. "It's different for him."

"I know, Sally. The two of you have a real problem, but just remember Neal isn't the first person who's been hesitant about taking on the responsibility of children who are not his own. That's really a heavy-duty decision, you know—no matter how in love, you happen to be with the kids' mother—or father, whichever the case may be. It happens to women, too. Just put yourself in his shoes. What if he had two kids, and you'd never had a family? Wouldn't it be something to come to terms with before you became his kids' *stepmother*? What if they turned out to hate you? Wouldn't you worry about that happening? What if they prevented Neal from spending much time with you? And what about all the times he'd have to put his kids first? What if you'd been the one left in a lonely hotel room in Kansas City while Neal raced home to his sick kid? Maybe part of you would be understanding, but part of you would feel neglected, disillusioned, hurt and jealous as hell.''

"How'd you get to be so wise?'' Sally insisted with a shake of her head.

"Oh, just wait until you're as old and fat as I am, then you'll have to develop wisdom because it's all you've got going for you,'' he said jokingly before leaning forward in his chair to give her a paternal pat on her hand. "If ever I've seen two people who belong together, it's you and Neal,'' he continued. "But things worth having are seldom easy. You come to each other with a lot of past history that has to be dealt with before you can start building a future. For instance, I suspect Neal still hasn't gotten over Danny—or has he ever told you about Danny?''

"Danny?'' Sally asked. "Who's he?''

"Oh, Neal'll tell you one of these days,'' Phil said evasively. "I suppose I shouldn't have mentioned it, but when he does tell you the Danny story, it'll make things a lot more clear to you.''

Phil sat up straighter in his chair and began shuffling papers again, as though indicating an end to that part of their conversation. He was ready to get back to business. "Now, what about chasing?" he said, unrolling a large weather map.

"Yeah, sure," Sally said again, rising from her chair. "It's about time I did that. I'd better grab the chance while Neal's gone, or he'll pack me off to talk to some garden club instead."

"Great," Phil said enthusiastically. "Take the time to run home at lunch and get some jeans and boots and rain gear. If this storm gets as big as I think it will, you and Jerry should probably head out this afternoon. Can your mom take care of your kids?"

Sally paused at the door. "I think so. She wasn't feeling very well yesterday, but she seemed okay this morning when I called to check on her. I'll call her again to make sure, but I don't think there'll be any problem."

After calling her mother, Sally settled into her morning routine, first checking the satellite photographs for the past twenty-four hours and reading the wire-service reports from the National Weather Service. Then she tackled her ongoing project of classifying the photographic record of the 1979 Wichita Falls tornado. Even though many of the photographs of the actual tornado had been acquired from amateur photographers, they offered an invaluable record of the devastating storm that had killed forty-four people. And there were literally thousands of photographs that had been taken of the storm's aftermath by investigators from the lab.

As Sally viewed slide after slide, she found herself wishing she could get excited about the prospect of a chase, but her heart was too heavy with other things.

She did as Phil asked and used her lunch hour to drive back to Oklahoma City for some appropriate clothing. She packed a small bag and grabbed a peanut-butter sandwich before hurrying back to Norman. She supposed that from now on, she should keep a packed bag in her office for future chases—that is, if there were to be any future opportunities for her to be part of a chase team. Neal had not seen his way clear to allow her to be a part of the important lab activity, and her continuing to work at the lab didn't seem like such a good idea right now. Maybe she should give some thought to her mother's suggestion about moving to Dallas.

By noon, a tornado watch was in effect for most of southwest and central Oklahoma and a part of north-central Texas until nine-thirty that evening. Word came at three-fifteen that the watch had been changed to a warning for the residents of Caddo, northern Comanche, western Washita and Iowa counties in the southwestern part of the state.

The chase was on!

Sally hurriedly changed her clothes. As she headed out the front door, Phil called to her over the upstairs railing. "Radar indicates a possible tornado six miles northwest of Fletcher. It's moving toward the east-northeast at forty miles per hour. Take the truck. Maybe you'll have a chance to place the robot. Get going."

She raced out the door and headed for the parking lot. The sky to the southwest was already growing dark even though Norman was a good sixty miles from the center of the front.

As she hurried down the sidewalk, she was startled to see Neal standing by the truck used to haul the instrumented robot to the storm area. Jerry was standing on the front bumper of the truck, his body halfway under the open hood of the vehicle.

"When did you get back?" Sally asked Neal, not

sure if she should laugh or cry at the sight of him. He
looked tired, disheveled and definitely in need of a
shave, yet she had never felt more drawn to a man,
never wanted to bring pleasure to his eyes and a smile
to his lips more than she did at that minute. Did he in
any way understand how difficult it had been for her to
leave him the other night? Did he begin to realize the
depth of her feelings for him?

"Just drove up," he said, taking in her attire through
narrowed eyes. "What's this?" he asked.

"My storm-chasing clothes," Sally announced. "I'm
going along—finally."

Neal's eyes darted from her to Jerry. Abruptly, he
took her elbow and half pulled her across the parking
lot until they were out of Jerry's earshot. "I'd rather
you didn't go along on this chase."

"But why?"

"Well, because of Jerry, for one thing," Neal said.
"He's a known womanizer, Sally, and you shouldn't be
out alone with him. People might get the wrong idea."

"Neal, I'm not an adolescent girl. I don't need protection from flirtatious men, and anyway, Jerry and I
worked all that out long ago. He is my friend—my very
good friend. Besides, I've gone places with him before."

Neal seemed startled by her answer. "But you don't
know about him."

"I know all about Jerry," Sally said. "He doesn't
'womanize' with females who don't want him to. Give
the man credit for that."

"So you want to go with him?" Neal asked. Even his
voice betrayed his weariness. Sally realized he probably
hadn't gotten any sleep the night before and was overreacting to the situation, but she didn't want to deal
with his silly jealousy. She didn't want to argue with

him. All she wanted to do was touch him and feel the comfort of his embrace—whiskers and all. She wanted to tell him he was foolish to be jealous of another man but found herself resenting the need to explain anything to Neal. After all, she had certainly made no secrets about her feelings for him.

It seemed so foolish for two people who cared about each other to be petty and to deny themselves the comfort of each other's arms. Once again, Sally wondered if she should rethink the terms she had set for their relationship. Should she forget about the future and take what love there was for her now? She could love him now and live for the present. She could take what happiness and joy there were today.

Sally knew, however, there would be no real joy for either of them without the promise of tomorrow. True, they had already known each other sexually, but their physical joining was done with wonderful expectations of what lay ahead for them. Both she and Neal had wanted that first time to be a beginning. Now Sally would always be wondering if each time they were together was the end—especially after the disappointment of their ruined trip to Kansas City. Neal could certainly no longer harbor any illusions about what it would mean to be married to Sally, mother of two.

"I'd rather go with you," Sally explained, "but that does not seem to be an option. So to answer your question, yes, I want to go with him," Sally explained, not even trying to keep the exasperation from her voice. "I told you, Jerry's my friend, and he wants me to go along. Phil says radar shows a possible funnel by Fletcher, so if you'll excuse me, we'd best get going."

"Oh, I'm sure he's looking forward to having you go along with him," Neal said dryly. "He obviously admires you very much. I wasn't aware, however, that the two of you had been seeing each other."

"I have spent some time with him," Sally announced angrily. "He happens to like me *and* my children. But that doesn't have a damn thing to do with his or my work here at this lab. If we're going to have any chance at all of sighting a storm today, he and I need to get going."

"There's a problem with the truck," Neal said. "I think I may cancel the chase."

"If there's trouble with the truck, we can take the van," Sally said. "We can't tote the robot in it, but we can still take pictures and instrument readings. What's going on, Neal? Why are you so against me going on a chase? It's not my reputation that's at issue, is it? Whatever the problem is, your attitude has been robbing me of an opportunity to be a full-fledged member of this research team, and I resent it."

"Wait and go out with me on the next chase," Neal said, grabbing her arm. He was silhouetted by the bank of dark clouds rapidly filling up the sky behind him. So intense, he looked almost fierce. "I wanted your first tornado chase to be with me, Sally—not with Jerry or someone else. I admit that at first I didn't think you should go along at all, that it was no place for a woman. I worried about your comfort and the possible danger, but I was wrong. I see now that your enthusiasm and your intellectual curiosity are all that really matter. And if you're willing to put up with physical demands and inconveniences of storm chases, I shouldn't stand in your way. Then I realized I wanted to be the one who took you out the first time. I wanted that very much. I've loved seeing you grow on this job, Sally, and enjoyed assisting you in becoming a top-flight researcher. I want to be the one who turns you into a storm chaser, but I've been so busy getting ready for the conference—getting my speech ready and that research paper finished up—well, I haven't been going out on any chases myself lately. The very next time, though, I was going to take you along. I wanted to surprise you."

"I'm sorry, Neal. You should have told me what you had in mind instead of letting me continue to think you considered me some sort of second-class citizen around here. I would have liked my first time out to be with you, Neal, but it's too late now. Today may be my last chance ever. The season's about over, and my tenure here may be, too. So unless you plan to fire me here and now, I'm going along with Jerry."

Sally started toward the white truck, then stopped and turned to face Neal once again. His hands were in his jacket pockets, his shoulders hunched over in that familiar lanky posture. His disappointment showed through the scowl on his face.

And the pain was there in his eyes. They kept bringing each other such pain, Sally realized.

"Remember when you said you'd help me get a transfer to another N.O.A.A. agency if it didn't work out for me to be employed here?" she said. "Well, I think the time has come. This is too hard on both of us, trying to work together when our personal lives are such a disaster. We don't function as well as we should. Your personal feelings have prevented me from going on storm chases, and they sent you off on a wild-goose chase to South Dakota. And every day I'm here is such an emotional trauma that I go home at night too drained to be an effective mother to my children."

Sally turned and trotted over to the truck. "Let's go, Jerry," she called. "I want to get to our storm before dark. If the truck's got a problem, let's go in the van. Just hurry! I want to get going."

THE WORD "HORIZON" HAD a different meaning in the
southwestern United States than it did in places where
cities, hills, mountains or forests dominated the landscape. The short grass of western Oklahoma's prairie
did not obstruct one's view. There were no towering
cities of steel and glass. It was church spires and grain
elevators that pinpointed distant towns and aptly sym-
bolized the dominating forces in the lives of the sturdy
folk who tilled the prairie sod and adhered to the God
of their fathers. A small hill would occasionally gentle
its way above the prairie floor, and the Wichita Mountains, a very small, worn and ancient mountain range,
rose abruptly out of the short grass in the southwest
corner of the state. But in western Oklahoma it was not
unusual to see from horizon to horizon.

And across that broad expanse, the winds blew unfettered. They swept in from the north, rushed up from
the south, swooped down from the slopes of the
Rockies, and they blew. And blew. And blew.

Wind was a part of life in Oklahoma—and the
weather brought by those winds. Oklahomans respected weather. It had once made a dust bowl of their state.
They lived inside their weather more than most of the
other inhabitants of the earth. Their brand of weather
was one of extremes: of sizzling summers with arid,
baking winds; of dry, frigid winters with biting winds
that intensified the cold; of storm-ridden springs with
the ever-present threat of that most fearful sort of
wind—tornadic. Only in autumn did the winds calm
themselves into breezes. Each day was such a perfect,
glorious gift that in quite another way, even in the fall
of the year, weather was an ever-present force in their
lives.

Oklahomans understood better than most the good
and the bad of weather. Its caprices dominated their

lives, brought success or failure to their crops, and sometimes weather killed. No place did people know that better than in Oklahoma. They scanned their horizons with a practiced and wary eye.

Between the towns of Verden and Andarko in Grady County, the road climbed to the top of a gentle bluff and offered a view to motorists of an especially broad expanse of sky and prairie. The spot was a watch post for local civil-defense workers entrusted with visually monitoring each severe-storm system that swept across their county. Their job took up where modern meteorology and its forecasting equipment left off. Volunteer spotters watched the black clouds in search of forming tornadoes. Their vigilance often meant the difference between life and death to inhabitants of their communities.

The van topped the bluff, and Jerry eased it off the pavement, stopping next to a spotter's car, with its civil-defense logo painted on the side. Jerry compared notes with the spotter while Sally strode over to the edge of the bluff to survey the tremendous bank of clouds that completely dominated the sky to the west and northwest. From horizon to horizon, an awesome panorama unfolded before her.

Sally had been a meteorologist or studying meteorology for almost twelve years. She had read countless accounts of storms. She had studied scientific monographs about storms. She had plotted them on charts. She had watched them on films. She had been *in* storms before—violent ones. She had been rained on, hailed on, blown about, but basically, she had been an indoor meteorologist performing her forecasting duties inside, often in windowless buildings. She had never witnessed anything like what lay before her. She could not even have imagined such a sight. Behind her was sunshine and blue sky. In front of her was the forward edge of a gigantic storm, a black, churning, violent storm.

"Oh, my God," she said, shaking her head in awe.

"Ain't it the truth?" Jerry said as he came up behind her. "Now that, Sally, my dear, is a storm!"

"I had no idea," Sally said, slowly shaking her head back and forth.

"You can't until you get out here among it," Jerry said. "Sometimes I see something like that and wonder if I've died and gone to a meteorologist's heaven. No book, no photograph can ever convey the power."

It was all there; all the component parts of a thunderstorm were laid out in front of her like a diagram. Closest to her were the marshmallowlike mammatus clouds and the rain-free base. Farther to the west, she could see the main tower, the flanking line towers, the precipitation shaft—all of it. Only it wasn't a diagram. It was real, and no diagram could convey the power, the fearsome power. And Neal wanted to be with her when she first experienced this. Her eyes filled with tears at the thought.

"You see now why this city boy's going to stay put right here in Oklahoma. Where else could you ever see anything like that?" Jerry asked.

"No wonder they built the storm labs out here," Sally said. "I mean, I knew why statistically, but to see all this from horizon to horizon illustrates the reason why pretty dramatically. There it is, a whole big Oklahoma sky filled with that awesome storm. I feel like...like I'm in church, like there should be a thousand-voice choir standing here singing an anthem in praise of the Creator."

"Know what you mean, kid," Jerry agreed. "The-power-and-the-majesty bit. If you can't feel it looking out there, you never will."

They stood a bit longer, silently gazing.

"Well, we'd better hurry," Jerry warned. "We need to take pictures before that front gets to us. When that thing goes over, you'll think the Devil himself has you by the tail."

Chapter Ten

Neal tried to work, but all he succeeded in doing was shuffling papers around his desk. He probably should have gone home after the lecture and his dinner engagement, he told himself, but somehow his car had not wanted to head up the highway to Oklahoma City and insisted instead on returning to the lab.

Going home would be useless, he decided. He wouldn't have been able to sleep for thinking about Sally and Jerry on the chase. His feelings were part chagrin in that he, the project director, hadn't managed to take Sally out on her first chase and part jealousy that she was out there with another man, a man who had quite a reputation with the ladies. And even though he knew Jerry was an experienced storm chaser, Neal couldn't help but worry about Sally. Chasing could be dangerous if the chasers took chances or got careless.

Yes, he thought with such regret, *when I finally figured out the lady could be a storm chaser, I should have somehow rearranged my schedule and taken her myself. Then I would know for sure she had been instructed in proper procedures and precautionary measures. I would have made certain she understood just how dangerous those savage storms could be. I could keep her out of harm's way.*

But things didn't turn out like that. Jerry was doing

the honors for her first storm chase, and although Neal was certain everything would be all right, he wanted to see for himself Sally stepping out of the van safe and sound. As Neal let himself in the deserted lab building, he realized he might be in for a long, lonely vigil while he waited for Jerry and Sally to return.

Neal probably wouldn't have come back from South Dakota until the following day if he hadn't already made plans for the evening—important plans to attend a program on stepparenting that was to be held on the O.U. campus. The program was to consist of a lecture followed by a panel discussion. The lecturer—Larry Behrman, an O.U. human-relations professor—was an old friend and handball opponent of Neal's. After reading about the program in the Norman *Transcript*, Neal had called Larry, told him of his intention to attend and invited him to dinner following the program.

Of course, Neal could have called Larry from Pierre and canceled the dinner invitation, but he hadn't. He knew of Larry's reputation as an expert on child rearing and parental concerns. Neal very much wanted to hear what the man had to say, and he had a few questions he wanted to ask the learned professor. Oh, did he ever have questions. Yes, it was way past time for him to stop wrestling with his problem alone and listen to an expert opinion or two.

Neal was able to catch a return ride on an N.O.A.A. plane and fly back to Oklahoma, reaching home just in time to shower and change before heading down I-35 to check in at the lab and go to the university campus. He realized it had been rather foolish of him to fly to South Dakota in the first place. He'd gone on a whim; an N.O.A.A. plane happened to be going up, and he was worried about what was going to occur between him and Sally when he returned to Norman.

Putting off his return home had seemed attractive

when one of the N.O.A.A. officials invited him to go on the trip, but Neal regretted accepting the invitation almost as soon as the plane was in the air. He needed to get back to Norman and to Sally. He realized that as far as their struggling relationship was concerned, the ball was now in his court. He needed to reassure her, to let her know he understood why she had returned home from Kansas City, that he understood her children were her first responsibility, and he did understand that on an intellectual level. But on an emotional level, he didn't really *feel* that way, not after spending three nights by himself in a Kansas City hotel thinking about what was to have been.

He had not remembered about the program on stepparenting until he was already in South Dakota. Remembering provided the impetus for his immediate return to Oklahoma. Stepparenting was exactly the subject he should be trying to learn more about, he told himself as he poked around the rubble of the South Dakota tornado and checked on the collapsed tornado shelters, which he discovered had been shoddily built by a disreputable dealer who had since "disappeared."

Neal tried very hard to be optimistic about the stepparenting lecture. He wanted to believe that somehow, someone or something would be able to quell the apprehensions he felt about the whole subject of stepparenting and ready-made families. He owed it to himself, and to Sally, to see if there was any aspect of the problem he was overlooking. Perhaps Larry Behrman would have some insights that would make him more comfortable with the idea. He wanted that. He wanted to believe it would be safe for him to care for Sally's children.

The lecture and ensuing discussion had been informative and thought-provoking but at the same time

were both encouraging and discouraging. Marriages
with one or both spouses already being the parent of
minor children could and did work, Professor Behrman
pointed out to the group assembled in the large lecture
hall, but the pitfalls in such marriages were many. For
every success story, there seemed also to be one of failure. Statistically, the chances of such marriages being
successful were not as good as second marriages that
did not involve minor children.

Privately, over dinner at the restaurant in the Student Union, the professor, a small bearded man with
animated gestures, had been somewhat more encouraging than during his lecture.

"It depends on the people, Neal, and how badly they
want the marriage to work," Larry reiterated after the
waiter had taken their order. "Younger children are
usually easier on stepparents than preteens and teenagers. How much the natural parent without custody is
still in the picture and his or her attitude are factors.
Whether or not the natural parent with custody is
willing to share parenting responsibilities and whether
or not the new stepparent wants to assume them are
important concerns. If the stepparent falls into the trap
of being a sort of ex-officio member of the team with
no clearly defined parenting role, the marriage is
usually in trouble. Of course, sometimes what both
partners want is an aloof stepparent, with the children
being kept pretty much out of his or her way. I really
don't recommend such an arrangement although I
have seen it work."

"At times, I feel myself wishing she didn't have any
kids, Larry," Neal confessed. "I wish we were both
childless and could start our own family, and she senses
this. I'm afraid it makes her very resentful. I just
wonder if I'm a big-enough person, if I'm unselfish

enough to share her with those two kids. They're probably nice-enough kids, too—at least they seem to be, but they're not mine, and I don't know if I'd ever feel that they were. I had a bad experience once before, marrying a woman with a child, and swore I'd never get involved in anything like that again, but I am involved. Am I ever! The lady in question has not one but two kids, and if I don't commit myself to a relationship with her pretty quickly, I'll lose her. I think she's already seriously considering giving up on me and moving away.''

''How long ago was this 'bad experience' of yours?'' Larry wanted to know. As he spoke, his smallish hands were in constant motion, as though he were conducting his own verbal symphony.

''Back in graduate-school days,'' Neal answered, ''but I remember it like it was yesterday. I didn't think I'd ever get over that divorce—the sense of failure, the loss of the woman I still cared about and the loss of a wonderful little boy I had come to love and think of as my own. The second divorce was a breeze compared to the first. Of course, I realize now my second wife and I never really had all that much going for us. In fact, I think we drifted into marriage because neither one of us expected very much out of the other. She didn't want kids, and at that point in my life childlessness sounded like a safe alternative to the gut-wrenching experience I'd gone through in losing that little boy. I never had the high expectations for my second marriage that I had for the first one. And now I'd like to get married again, but the thought of trying to be a father to those two kids worries me so. But I'll tell you what worries me even more than that.''

''A third divorce?'' Larry guessed with a shrug of his

narrow shoulders under his somewhat threadbare brown suit coat.

"Well, that's frightening, all right," Neal admitted. "What woman would want to risk getting involved with a three-time loser? And I don't want to spend the rest of my life alone. But what scares me most of all is that if I do marry the woman in question and it doesn't work out, if I can't be the man that she and her daughters need, she'll end up hating me. I couldn't stand that. I really couldn't."

"It sounds like you're pretty sure of your feelings for this woman, but what about your feelings for the children—other than wishing she didn't have any? I gather you really don't know her children very well," the professor commented.

"No. I don't," Neal said. "Quite frankly, I've pretty much avoided them. I would have felt dishonest pretending I wanted to get to know her family when all along I was wishing she didn't have kids. Oh, the little girls themselves are wonderful—one seems fragile and shy, and the other plump and outgoing. It would be a joy to have two daughters like them. But could I ever feel like their father? Would I ever be able to feel that I was a permanent part of their family? It seemed to me I had to solve the question of whether or not I was willing to try a ready-made family again before I entered into a friendship with those little girls."

"But wait a minute," Larry said, holding his right hand up in a gesture of protest. "We're not talking about children in general. We're talking about two specific youngsters. It seems to me how you get along with those two particular children is certainly a big part of your dilemma. Maybe you'll like them; maybe you won't. Shouldn't you find that out before you decide if you will or won't share their mother with them? Don't you think you ought to give them a chance? You might be surprised. After all, your 'bad experience' was a long time ago, and you're a different person now."

Neal listened intently, uncertain if he accepted everything Larry was saying. Somehow it still seemed wrong to him to "court" Sally's daughters until he was sure he would be able to open his heart to them.

"Such a frown," Larry said, laughing. "I can tell I've burdened you with enough food for thought to last for days. What say we change the topic of conversation to football?"

After they had thoroughly explored over prime ribs the strengths and weaknesses of the two leading contenders for the quarterback position on next fall's Sooner squad and discussed over lemon meringue pie the upcoming Big Eight Conference race, the two men walked across the moonlit campus to Larry's office to pick up a couple of books the human-relations professor wanted Neal to read.

The books were now in front of Neal. *Stepchildren: A Realistic Look at the Ready-Made Family* and *Stepparenting—No Easy Answers* rested on Neal's desk atop a stack of facsimile maps, satellite photographs and uncompleted reports. With a sigh, he opened the second book, propped his feet on his desk and started to read.

Concentration was hard, however, and Neal's gaze kept straying to the clock on the wall, then to the view of the parking lot from his second-floor window. He couldn't understand why Sally and Jerry hadn't returned.

He strolled down the hall to check the radio log in the now-deserted communications center. He saw that the van had been in radio contact with the lab at 9:57 P.M., at which time they had signed off for the night.

Earlier in the evening, at 7:54, they had spotted a twister in the clouds two miles southwest of the community of Binger. Of course, by that hour it would have been too dark to get any photographs. Most of the illumination would have been from lightning, but their notes and instrument measurements would be important.

But that report had been made two hours ago. The drive from Binger didn't take much longer than an hour.

Go home, Neal told himself. He was being a jealous old fool. Sally wasn't committed to him. What she did or did not do with Jerry was none of his business. He wondered how much she had been seeing him. She said Jerry liked her children. Neal could almost see the four of them on little picnics, on Jerry's boat at Lake Thunderbird, taking that trip to the zoo Neal had avoided.

But what if they had car trouble? What if they had been forced to stay over someplace? What if Sally unwillingly found herself in a compromising position with meteorology's most carefree bachelor?

As the minutes dragged by, Neal thought of going out to look for them. He thought of calling the highway patrol. He thought of trying for the dozenth time in the past hour to call them on the van's radio, but obviously their unit was turned off—or they were not in the van. He tried not to think where they might be at this moment.

At 12:45, the van finally pulled into the parking lot. Neal leaned against the window frame and let relief wash over him like a gush of soothing warm water. They were back. Sally was all right. He hastened down the stairs and pushed open the door into the crisp, rain-washed night. He could hear the sound of laughter from the parking lot. The van was parked by a streetlight, and they were unloading equipment from the back of the van.

"Hi, Neal," Sally called when she spotted him crossing the drive.

"Hey, Dad, you didn't need to wait up," Jerry joked.

"When it got so late, I was concerned that you might have had mechanical trouble," Neal said as he approached the parked vehicle.

"No, the old van ran smooth as a top," Jerry said. "We just decided to treat ourselves to a steak dinner after we'd radioed in our last report."

"I see," Neal said, hoping his voice did not sound as piqued as he felt. "Well, how'd it go?"

"Oh, incredible! Just incredible," Sally said, coming over to meet him and throw her arms exuberantly around his neck. Neal returned her embrace, momentarily drawing her wonderful womanly body next to him, his hands on her slim waist. *Ah, the sweetness of her,* he thought. Did she have any idea how her closeness affected him. He momentarily put his cheek against her head and drank in the aroma of her damp hair. Sally's damp hair—someone should bottle the fragrance.

"I'm wet and weary," Sally continued, "and we got rained on, hailed on, stuck in the mud—but oh, such a storm—such a big, magnificent storm. We even spotted a funnel aloft! On my first chase! Isn't that lucky?"

Neal was only incidentally aware of Jerry singing, "How're you gonna keep her down on the farm after she's seen Paris?" And then switching to a paraphrased version of the familiar song: "How're you gonna keep her down in the lab after she's seen a twister?" Neal was much more concerned with the delightful shock of Sally's spontaneous embrace. For an instant he could feel her warm breath on his throat before she stiffened and started to pull away. He moved his hands to her back, clinging to her a few seconds longer, not willing to give her up. He wished Jerry weren't singing his silly song. He wished Jerry were a million miles away. Alone—that's what he wanted to be with Sally.

Pulling away from his embrace and slipping her arm through his, Sally walked the last few steps to the van with him.

"Oh, Neal, I wish you had been with us," she said, the tone of her voice aptly indicating the enthusiasm she felt. "I've been a meteorologist all these years, and tonight I think I just discovered weather, real weather, for the first time. Jerry tells me storm chasers are a breed apart, that you're either one or you're not."

"And the lady is definitely one," Jerry interrupted, racing over to Sally's side and putting his arm around her shoulders like a proud papa—or was it more like a "special" friend?

Sally tilted her face upward to receive a congratulatory kiss from her fellow storm chaser. Neal found himself wondering why Jerry couldn't have been struck by lightning or have run off with the waitress who served them their steak dinner. He wanted to push the man aside and say, "Hey, that's my woman you're fondling." But Sally wasn't his, not yet at least.

Jerry relinquished his hold on Sally and returned to his unloading chores. As he pulled an equipment box out of the van, he explained, "Some of this stuff got wet. Thought I'd get things out and dry them off before I head on home."

"I'll get the parkas and spread them out to dry," Sally said, reaching inside the van.

"I'll do that in the morning," Neal said, putting a halting hand on her arm. The feel of the skin on her bare arm was overwhelming. His fingers sent a dizzying array of sensations to his brain and throughout his body.

Sally paused, then looked at him over her shoulder, her eyes reflecting the street lamp, her look showing she was aware of it, too; she felt the electricity that passed through his fingers where they touched her skin. Her lips parted. "Oh, Neal," she said softly, her voice full of longing.

"Better get your purse from the front, Sally," Jerry called out to her. "I'm going to lock her up for the night."

Casting Neal a soulful look, Sally went around to the front of the van, reached in for her purse, then called out a rather subdued good night to the two men.

"See you tomorrow," Jerry said as he picked up the wooden chest and started for the lab building.

"I'll give you a full report tomorrow, Neal," Sally said as she reached in her purse for her keys. "Jerry says I can do the reporting honors for this trip."

"I'll look forward to it," Neal said formally, all the while thinking he'd rather have her body than her report. Oh, how he wanted her. "I also want to talk to you about this transfer nonsense," he went on, telling himself to keep talking. She wouldn't leave as long as he was talking. Besides, he needed to nip this transfer business in the bud. "You can't mean it, Sally. You have the intellectual curiosity of a scientific researcher. That's become quite apparent in the months you've been working here, and you must continue your graduate work. It would be a damned waste if you didn't, and O.U. has one of the best meteorology programs in the world. You belong here. You can't deny that, especially after today. I recognized that gleam in your eyes, that excitement in your voice when you talked about what happened out there in the storm. You're a born storm chaser."

"It was an incredible experience, Neal," she said, her chin high as she looked directly into his eyes. "I can't deny that. But if there's one thing I've learned in my almost thirty years, it's that you don't always get what you want."

Neal realized she was speaking of more than career goals with her last statement. She was implying you didn't always get the friendship and the love you want, either. How brave she was, Neal thought. Her life certainly had not been easy. She'd had more than her share of tough luck, yet she had managed despite all the disappointments and heartbreaks to make a life for herself and her daughters. And instead of giving her the admiration she deserved for what she had accomplished, he had allowed the family she had fought so hard to preserve to become a wedge between them.

He watched as she unlocked her car and slipped inside. He wanted to stop her. He wanted to talk this transfer business out of her head. He wanted her to stay with him or go someplace with him—anything except leave him, but it was the middle of the night. He realized she needed to get home. She was wet and surely exhausted. If only Jerry weren't there, Neal could have kissed her. Maybe he should anyway.

Neal started toward her car. "I'll buy you a cup of coffee before you drive home," he announced.

"I don't think there's anything open at this hour," she said through the open door. "Thanks, anyway. See you tomorrow. Okay?"

He put his hand on the door to prevent her from closing it. "We still have to have that long talk we didn't have in Kansas City," he said firmly.

Her eyes were the deepest emerald in the semidarkness. Her damp hair clinging against her head gave her a childlike look—like a little girl who had just run through the lawn sprinkler. And there was a vulnerable, childlike quality to the line of her cheek, but her mouth was a woman's mouth, full and expressive. The first time he ever saw that mouth on his television screen, he wondered what it would be like to kiss it, to kiss the beautiful woman to whom it belonged. And now he knew. The experience had been beyond his finest fantasies. She was everything and more. She was a passionate woman who held back nothing of herself. When she kissed him with those soft full lips, it was with such completeness and such promise. With Sally, there were no games, no teasing, no coyness—just honesty and passion, such passion.

"I wondered if we still had anything to discuss," she said, grasping the top of the steering wheel and staring off into the night. "I wondered if you'd ever want to talk to me again after I came home from Kansas City."

She leaned her head against the back of the seat, her shoulders slumping wearily. "Oh, Neal, I'm so sorry the way the trip turned out. You know I wanted to be with you, but I can't promise you something like that won't happen again, not with two children to raise. In fact, you can count on *something* happening a great deal of the time—from spilt milk to interrupted lovemaking. And sometimes my children take so much out of me, I have nothing left to give. But they are *mine*. They are a part of me, and I love them."

Her tears glistened on her sweetly curving cheek. He touched them softly. "I know, pretty lady, I know. Listen, you take the morning off tomorrow. The whole day if you like. You've earned it."

But Neal hoped she wouldn't take him up on the offer. He didn't want her to stay away tomorrow. He didn't want to go the whole day without seeing her. If only he could ask her to come home with him, but that wouldn't be fair of him. He could see the exhaustion settling into her face and body. He knew she would probably say yes if he asked her, but he feared it would be because she felt she had something to make up to him after Kansas City.

And she did look almost grateful when he leaned in the open car door to softly kiss her wondrous lips. Then he drew back and closed the door, allowing her to leave.

SALLY HAD CONSIDERED Neal's offer of the day off when the alarm went off at six o'clock. It was almost two-thirty in the morning when she finally had been able to lower her head to the pillow. She could fetch the girls at her mother's, where they had spent the night, get them off to day school and come back to bed. The plan sounded very inviting.

But then she thought of the annual report that was due in one month. She was anxious to start work organizing the data she and Jerry had collected on their storm chase. Most of all, however, she needed to go to work because that was where Neal was. She touched her lips where his gentle kiss had rested just hours before. Yes, if she didn't even lay eyes on him all day long, she wanted to be in the same building with him. But she would manage to lay eyes on him. She would be in the same room with him, talk to him, watch his eyes and lips and hands, and she was the lady seriously thinking about transferring to another state, she thought hopelessly. How would she be able to bear leaving him? Could she possibly banish herself to a world where the sights and sounds and feel of Neal did not exist?

Neal brought up the subject of a possible transfer before Sally had a chance to approach him. She had put her purse away and started to straighten her desk when he came into her office with two Styrofoam cups filled with steaming coffee. He was the first boss she'd ever had, Sally thought, who brought her coffee.

"Complete your six-month probationary period," he insisted without preliminaries. "It's not fair to the lab or to yourself if you don't stay at least that long. Give the job a fair shot. Give *us* a fair shot to convince you this is where you belong."

"I don't know, Neal," Sally said wearily. "I really don't know. It's too hard on both of us to try and work together when our personal lives are such a disaster. The job—well, especially now that I know I'll get to storm chase—it's everything I want, but I can't keep on with this constant emotional upheaval. I think my mother may be moving to Dallas, and I'm considering moving there also. She's been such a help to me with my children. Maybe I'm too much of a coward to go it alone, but whatever—it does seem like maybe that would be the best thing for my girls and for me."

But as she spoke, she wanted him to reassure her, to offer some plan, some hope that they could make a life together. She didn't want to move to Dallas or anyplace else, but she knew she had to arrive at some decision about Neal. She had to decide if she would continue to see him but forget about marriage—or give up.

Neal was sitting on the window ledge, his long legs stretched out in front of him, his torso silhouetted by sky of the clearest blue punctuated by brilliantly white cumulus clouds. She wasn't the only one who was tired that day, Sally realized. The dark eyes that regarded her so intently betrayed his weariness. He looked as though he had lost weight. Apparently he wasn't cooking Italian for anyone these days.

The memory of the Italian meal he had prepared for

her came flooding back. It had been the most romantic, the most special night she had ever spent with a man. She had fallen in love, not the idealized love of youth that had come and gone in her life several times but the mature love of a woman who had known heartbreak, who had known loneliness, who had tired of meaningless relationships. It was the love of a woman who'd had enough years and enough wisdom to appreciate the sensitivity of the beautiful man in front of her.

Neal was handsome, but not extraordinarily so. He was not socially prominent or wealthy. At one time, she might have thought those things important, but now she realized she respected intelligence and commitment to a career far more than she did riches, social prominence and dazzling good looks. Michael had been a dazzler. She knew now to look at a man's soul.

No one had ever affected her like Neal Parker, and no one had ever loved her so completely. The image of herself she saw reflected in his eyes was a woman she liked. His love uplifted her. When she was with him, she was smarter, more perceptive, more alive. She even felt prettier when his eyes were gazing at her.

He was a man worthy of loving, a man she admired and responded to more than to any other man she had ever met. She understood, however, that the sensitivity in him she so admired, along with his honesty and deep-seated sense of responsibility, was in a way part of what was keeping them separated. He had never tried to mislead her about his apprehension over her children. He worried about doing the wrong thing not just for his sake but because of what it might do to her and those children. He forced himself to consider what might happen in their lives if they blindly rushed into marriage without giving full consideration to the problems that confronted them. She supposed she should be grateful to him, but she was not. Instead, she felt a mother's distress over the seeming rejection of her children by the man she loved.

Could she honestly say, however, if she were childless and he were the one with two small children that she wouldn't be having profound reservations about a long-term commitment to him? Phil had urged her to be sympathetic to Neal's dilemma. He had asked, if she were the one facing the prospect of suddenly assuming a parenting role for two youngsters, wouldn't she, too, be wary?

Sally supposed the answer would have to be yes. She would be wary and probably frightened to death, but she would give it a try. She at least would give herself a chance to care for them. Neal wouldn't even try. They were at an impasse. What else could she do but give up and try to reorganize her life and dreams? And to do that, she would have to put Neal out of her life, something she could never do as long as she worked for him.

"You don't have to make any sort of decision now," Neal was telling her. "If transferring is what you ultimately decide is best, I will arrange it, but fulfill your six months' probationary period first. You owe me and the lab that much, Sally. I'd be hard put to replace you right now in the middle of the annual report, and we've got a visit from the top brass coming up in two months. Our funding for the next two years depends on the outcome of that visit."

Sally took a sip of the hot coffee, relishing its aroma and fresh taste. What Neal said was true. It would be a bad time for her to be leaving the lab. It would be very difficult for anyone to step in and take over the completion of the annual report, and she had assumed a lot of the responsibility for getting materials organized in preparation for the visit by the national administrators of N.O.A.A. She felt proud Neal recognized that if she did leave, her presence would definitely be missed at the lab. And oh, how she would miss the lab! But there were other meteorological jobs to be found. It was Neal who was irreplaceable in her life. He was the first thing she thought of every morning and the last thing at night. Her heart seemed to pound out his name with each beat. He had become part of her.

Chapter Eleven

In spite of her lack of sleep the night before, Sally, with the help of much coffee, made it through the day without great difficulty. However, she definitely was looking forward to a quiet evening with her children and going to bed early.

But that evening when Sally pulled into her mother's driveway to pick up the girls, Vicky and Amy were sitting on the front porch waiting for her. They came bounding acrss the yard as soon as they spotted her car.

"Grandma's boyfriend is here," they both burst out at once as she opened the car door.

"He brought us bracelets," Vicky said excitedly. Both girls extended small wrists to show gold bracelets with their names spelled out in tiny ceramic beads.

"And he brought Grandma flowers and candy," Amy said, the chocolate smeared across her round chin indicating she had sampled the candy.

"And he brought her a bracelet, too," Vicky added solemnly. "Hers doesn't spell her name, but it's real pretty. I didn't know grandmothers could have boyfriends, but Mr. Casey says that's what he is—her boyfriend."

"Well, give me a welcome-home hug and let's go find the lovebirds."

Casey Tinsley was a robust, handsome man with a full head of white hair and a pair of the bluest eyes Sally had ever seen, and he did indeed seem to be her mother's "boyfriend." As she watched the man with her mother, Sally realized he adored Margie, and Margie fairly glowed under his attention. There had been times lately when Sally was concerned with her mother's health, when Margie seemed unusually tired or when she closed her eyes and put her hand to her temple as though momentarily dizzy. But the woman bustling around the kitchen tonight looked as if she had just taken some sort of magic elixir.

Casey and Margie were collaborating on a meal. After the beaming Margie had introduced Sally to "her old friend Casey Tinsley," Sally offered to help with dinner. Obviously a big meal was in the making, and the table in the dining room was set for five. She and the girls were apparently staying for dinner. But her offer to help was not accepted. She was escorted to a kitchen chair and handed a cup of coffee. Sally realized the meal was *their* production, and quite an involved one at that. There was much tasting of sauces and adding of spices.

Sally quickly realized, however, that there was much more going on in this kitchen than two people who loved good food sharing a gourmet experience. A courtship was definitely in progress. By comparing their recipes and preferences, they were discovering common likes and dislikes. Casey raved about Margie's hollandaise. She couldn't sing enough praise of his salad dressing. They were inventing a new way to prepare zucchini. And they were finding out how nice it was being together in the same room, how exciting it was to "accidentally" brush against each other, how delightful it was to share a favorite activity. Sally felt somewhat like a voyeur as she watched the two bustle about. Neither one seemed to have any idea how much they were revealing by their gestures, the way they looked at each other, their obvious pleasure at being together. They would not have been able to conceal their happiness if they wanted to.

But for the gray hair, middle-aged faces and two young children occasionally racing through the room calling Margie Grandma, Sally felt she could have been watching two teenagers on a first date. Many—but not all—of the reservations she felt about having a man enter her mother's life wilted under the sheer onslaught of their shared joy. She wondered if she would ever be completely accepting, however, if her mother chose to remarry. Would the memory of her father always intrude?

After dinner, Casey invited Sally for a walk and firmly but gently turned aside Amy and Vicky's request to accompany them. "No, little ladies," he told them. "I want to spend some time just with your mother. But I'll tell you what, if you'll color me a picture while we're gone, I'll tell you a story about Goldilocks and the three pigs."

When with a peal of giggles, both girls informed him the story was "Goldilocks and the Three Bears," Casey asked, "How do you know Goldilocks didn't meet the three pigs on another walk in the woods?"

After a whispered conference, the girls seemed to decide such a story was worth the bribe and went to get crayons from the drawer in their grandmother's desk. Sally and Casey left Margie to finish up in the kitchen and headed down the front walk.

The remnants of a pink-and-orange sunset still glowed in the western sky and bathed the rising moon in a glorious shade of orange. A tiny breeze stirred the leaves and softly teased Sally's hair. It was a night fit for lovers, she decided, the kind of night she would like to have spent walking with Neal. That was one of the many things she and Neal had not done together, walking in the moonlight. She painfully wondered if they ever would.

"It was on a night just like this that I first asked your mother to marry me," Casey said with a sigh. "We were in the sixth grade, on a hayride. It was my first date. She even let me kiss her on the cheek."

"The *first* time you asked her? Does that mean you asked her to marry you more than once?" Sally wanted to know.

"Probably about thirty or forty times. We sort of went together off and on during our junior-high years—and went steady in high school for one glorious year. But she fell in love with your father and broke my heart. I recovered only when my darling Betty came along. Betty and I had a wonderful life together, and your parents did, too. Your father was a fine man, Sally."

"Did you know him well?" Sally asked.

"Oh, yes. We lost track of each other over the years, but at one time I considered him my best friend. After all, I was the receiver who caught his pass that won the state championship for old Springfield High."

Sally stopped and pointed an accusing finger at Casey. "The Tin Man!" she exclaimed. "You're the Tin Man, aren't you?"

Casey stopped in the middle of the sidewalk and made a formal bow. "Casey Tinsley, alias the Tin Man, at your service."

"My goodness," Sally said, "I heard about that pass for years. 'Ham Bones to the Tin Man.' According to my father, you leaped ten feet in the air to catch an impossibly overthrown pass, eluded a score of would-be tacklers, made a flying dive over a wall of defenders, and scored a touchdown right at the gun.''

"Well, the story got pumped up a little in the telling," Casey said with a delighted laugh. "But it was a pretty good catch."

They fell into step again, heading for a pool of light from a street lamp at the corner. "My father thought you were pretty special," Sally continued. "You were in the army together for a while, weren't you?"

Casey nodded. "Then we lost track of each other. Last time I saw him was the day we mustered out, but I thought of him often over the years. I tried to call his mother once to find out where he was living, but she had apparently passed away by then."

"He used to think of you," Sally said. "I remember him telling the story of that pass and your other football escapades; then he would always finish by saying, 'I wonder whatever happened to the old Tin Man.'''

"I thought of your mother, too, over the years," Casey said. "She always occupied a very special place in my heart. I guess one's first love always does. And when I saw her again at that reunion, something happened inside of me. Instead of feeling like an old man looking back, I felt like a new man looking forward. It was as if we had never been apart. We are so comfortable together, so right with each other. We had a wonderful weekend, and since then, something that had been missing in my life for a long time has returned, and that something is anticipation. I feel that I have a future. I call her every night on the phone, but I want more than phone calls. I want your mother in my life, Sally. And I realize you probably can't quite welcome me with open arms because of your memory of your father, but believe me, I don't expect to take his place. Nothing can alter the part of Margie's life she spent with your dad. It's time, however, she began a new phase.''

"I know that," Sally said softly, reaching out to pull a twig from an overhanging tree. "I won't stand in her way.''

"She worries about you and those little girls," Casey continued. "She doesn't think she should move to Dallas just now and leave you without someone to help with Vicky and Amy. But she tells me you're thinking about moving to Dallas. Any prospect of that happening sometime soon?''

"Possibly. But is there any reason to hurry? Shouldn't you and Mother take some time to get reacquainted?''

"We will," Casey assured her. "I plan to court her right proper. But if she'll have me, I'm not interested in taking too long about making things legal. I'm tired of being lonely, and when you get to be the age of Margie and me, you realize time is pretty damned precious. One never knows just how much of it there's going to be.''

"Why is it I feel like a parent being asked for my child's hand in marriage?" Sally asked as they rounded the street lamp and started back up the street.

"Because your mother needs your blessing," Casey said. "You and her granddaughters are the three most precious people in the world to her, and she would never do anything to damage the relationship she has with any of you. I know she thinks about how much you depend on her to help with the girls. She has been like a second parent to them, and I'm sure she worries about how you would get along on your own.''

"It'd be very difficult," Sally admitted, "but I would never stand in the way of her making a new life for herself. I'll let you know that Casey. I want to be matron of honor at your wedding if you do get married.

And who knows, maybe the girls and I will move to Dallas. From what I've seen so far, looks to me like you'd be a pretty good granddaddy.''

"It would be an honor to serve as stepgrandfather to the grandchildren of Ernie Hampton," Casey said with a touching sincerity that brought tears to Sally's eyes.

They climbed the front steps, but before they entered the house, Sally put her arms around Casey's neck and pressed her cheek against his. "I'm glad you've come along to make my mother happy again," Sally said. "I'll have some bad moments every now and then thinking about my dad and wishing he were still with us, but I'll try not to take them out on you. And now you better go inside and explain what happened when Goldilocks met the three pigs. I think I'll sit out here for a while."

"Don't you want to know what happened?" Casey asked. "Goldilocks got those three little piggies in all sorts of trouble. And when I finish that one, I may have to tell them about the time Little Red Riding Hood climbed up the beanstalk. Or there's the one about Chicken Little and the billy goats gruff. I've been waiting for years for two cute little gals to tell my tall tales to."

"Oh, I'll hear about them later, I'm sure," Sally said laughingly. "I can already tell you're going to be a big hit."

Yes, the girls will adore him, Sally thought as she pushed herself slowly back and forth in the porch swing. It saddened her that it was not her father doing the storytelling, but one could not always write the book. Life had a way of setting its own course. Her father was not there to entertain his grandchildren. Casey was, however, and Sally knew she must accept that.

And Neal was apparently not the man to chase away her loneliness. She'd had to accept that also, and the sooner the better. Not only did she need to get on with her own life, but her indecision could very well prevent her mother from getting on with hers. If Margie wanted to move to Dallas and marry Casey, Sally did not want her to refuse him because she was worried about leaving Sally and her granddaughters.

She and the girls probably also should move to Dallas, Sally decided. Or maybe she should grab the first decent man who came along and try to make some sort of life with him. Jerry had hinted he would be willing to change the ground rules of their friendship from buddy-buddy to romance. Maybe she should think about that. Or Barry from the television station, who had a crush on her and would jump at the chance to make it something more, but as much as she liked him, marrying Barry would be like taking on a third child to raise. There had been other men, however, who would have married her, and there probably would be others in the future.

But what a bad bargain it would be for whatever man she might latch on to. It was a dumb idea, Sally decided. How could she marry someone else when she'd be thinking of Neal whenever she kissed that someone else? Whenever she made love to him?

Marriage for her would have to be all or nothing. She had Michael Storm to thank for that lesson.

THE "WEEKEND MAGAZINE" SEGMENT on which Sally would appear was scheduled to air Sunday night. Jerry announced that everyone from the the tornado project was invited to his house to watch the show and christen his new hot tub. As a result, there was much joking around the lab as to what was the proper state of dress—or undress—for hot tubbing. The receptionist announced she had bought a wonderful new bikini just for the party. And to a general round of groans, Phil indicated he, too, had a sexy new bathing suit he would be wearing.

"After all," he stated proudly, "there's thirty pounds less of me this year than there was last year."

"Yeah," Jerry agreed, "but there's still forty more pounds of you than there were in college."

"I'm working on it," Phil said. "By this time next year, they'll be selling Phil Rankin posters to the women of America."

Sunday afternoon, Sally dug out her old bathing suit and found herself wishing she had gotten more sun on her legs that summer. She had thought she might sunbathe a bit later that day, but knew from the satellite photographs she had seen on Friday afternoon that there would be no sun over Oklahoma today. A monstrous front had already dropped temperatures and brought brisk winds and a cloud cover to the state, with a promise of thunderstorms on Monday. Fortunately, Jerry's hot tub was located inside, in a garden room he had added on to his house last summer, or there would have been no hot tubbing that night.

Instead of a sunbath, Sally took her daughters shopping, then spent the rest of the afternoon helping Vicky with a huge poster she was coloring for her bedroom wall and painting toenails—hers and those on two sets of little-girl feet.

In spite of the fact that Casey was not going back to Dallas until tomorrow morning, Margie insisted Sally bring the girls over for the evening. Apparently the two had promised Vicky and Amy they would all make fudge and Casey would tell a story about the Seven Dwarfs in Never-Never Land.

Sally pulled a loose-fitting caftan over her bathing suit and packed some underwear in a beach bag. After delivering the girls to their grandmother, she was on her way to Jerry's party.

The wind was picking up, and it promised to be a blustery night. And stormy tomorrow. Sally wondered how stormy. If tornadoes threatened, would Neal decide on a chase? This time, she knew he planned to go himself and for her to accompany him. If that happened, she hoped they could go alone. The university's summer semester was no longer in session, and chances were no students would tag along on the next chase if there was one during the month of August.

Jerry handed her a margarita the minute she walked in the door. "My favorite lady's favorite drink," he said with a flourish.

Sally kissed him to an accompaniment of "My turn next" from several of the other men present. Even Neal joined in the chorus. Sally accommodated his request.

"For our esteemed director," she said, then leaned forward, tilted her face upward and planted a pristine kiss on his lips.

In response, Neal grabbed her, causing her to spill her drink on their clothing, and kissed her with melodramatic passion, placing a hand firmly behind her head and one behind her waist, then bending her body backward. Someone rushed forward to take the drink from her extended hand.

Neal's overdramatic gestures were playacting for the benefit of their colleagues, but the kiss was real. With breathtaking intimacy for a public kiss, Neal forced open her lips and plunged his tongue into her mouth. In spite of the watching eyes, Sally had a moment of intense reaction. The soft warm wetness of his tongue, the symbolic entering by a part of his body into hers, the pent-up yearning that came rushing to the surface of her consciousness all served to rob the breath from her lungs and support from her knees.

When at last Neal drew his face back from hers and stared down into her eyes, she whispered an "Oh, my" for his ears only. He seemed to sense her need for support as he helped her regain her footing, and he kept his arm firmly about her waist. Together, they turned to face their audience and offered a simultaneous bow in response to the applause and cheers.

Sally was grateful that the time for the television program had arrived. Attention shifted from her in the flesh to her televised image, and she retrieved her drink and was allowed to sit on a corner of the "conversation pit" that occupied much of the living room in Jerry's professionally decorated, terribly smart house. Her bachelor colleague obviously spent much of his income on his "pad."

The entire group of about twenty, some fresh from the hot tub and wrapped in towels, gathered in the room, drinks in hand, to watch the show. Sally's attention, however, kept stealing to Neal. He was intently watching the program, whose entire content that week was devoted to severe-weather phenomena. How handsome he was in profile, she thought, with his well-shaped head, fully cut dark hair, strong jaw and high forehead. And he had a good nose, not overly large but a masculine nose, perfect for a man of his proportions.

But the most striking thing, she decided, about Neal's face was his intense dark eyes rimmed by thick dark lashes. And at that moment, just as though he sensed her scrutiny, Neal turned and regarded her with those dark eyes. The look that passed between them was totally revealing and made even more intimate by its privacy in a crowded room. With his gaze he said with such force that he wanted her. His message was so powerful that it triggered a chain of involuntary responses in her body. If she had been naked and alone with him this minute, he would have found her open and moist and ready to receive him.

She wished that was how things were, that they were alone and naked and about to make love. *Ah, Sally, what a romantic you are,* she told herself. *You are about to be featured on network television for probably the only time in your life, and all you can think about is making love to a man.*

But then Neal wasn't just *a* man—he was *the* man she adored and loved and with whom she wanted to spend the rest of her life.

With concerted effort, however, she forced herself to concentrate on the television broadcast occupying the vast expanse of Jerry's big-screen television. A segment on hurricanes was just finishing, and the host promised tornadoes would be next. Everyone rushed around during the ensuing commercial, refilling drink glasses and grabbing handfuls of peanuts.

"Okay, everyone, time's up," Jerry shouted as the show returned to the screen. "And now, heeeere's Sally!"

The room grew silent as the segment began with a stock film of past tornadoes, most of it from the National Tornado Project files. Then came a panoramic shot of the view from atop Mount Scott with Sally's voice giving statistics on why the Sooner state had the dubious honor of having more tornadoes than any other region in the world.

The photography was breathtaking. Sally could well understand why the director had been so excited by the simultaneous sunshine and clouds. The bank of clouds was stunningly spectacular against the vivid, blue Oklahoma sky, and the sparkling clear air revealed a breathtakingly beautiful view from atop Mount Scott. The Wichita Mountains rose quite abruptly out of the short-grass prairie land of western Oklahoma, and consequently the view from atop Oklahoma's highest mountain—even though it was small by other state's standards—seemed endless. The roads, tilled fields and small communities were laid out in front like a beautifully detailed relief map. The horizon, as the camera revealed, was visible in three hundred and sixty degrees from the mountaintop.

And there she was, Sally realized as the camera came in for a tight shot of her and the reporter. With her short hair billowing about her face, her jacket collar occasionally blowing up against her cheek, Sally was explaining about winds gone amok in the form of fearsome tornadoes that sometimes plagued this land.

As the segment ended and the nationally known television journalist returned to the screen, Sally was once again reminded that this was network television, which went out all over the country. She was quite used to appearing on television, but her weather programs had always been regional telecasts and never gone coast to coast. She thought about what the show's director had said—that long-lost cousins and old sweethearts contacted people after a network appearance. She didn't have any long-lost cousins, but old sweethearts? With a shiver, she thought of Michael, the sweetheart she had married. For the first time in years, she wondered where Michael was. Had he seen this telecast tonight? For some inexplicable reason, the possibility that he might have been watching distressed her.

Everyone in the room had nothing but praise for Sally's smooth performance. She found the kind words all rather embarrassing, realizing that she had benefited greatly from the skill of a talented director, competent camera crew and highly professional interviewer. But the compliments were nice, especially the one so plainly written in Neal's eyes as he lifted his glass and toasted her.

"Here's to Sally Hampton," he said proudly, "who represents our project so well and so graces our lives."

"Hear, hear," Jerry said. "Now it's time for her to do the honors and formally christen the new hot tub."

They all followed Jerry to his new garden room, and Sally dribbled a few drops of champagne into the bubbling hot tub.

"I christen thee USS *Cyclone*," she said. "May your timbers never spring a leak, and your passengers all have clear sailing."

"Now you have to get in, Sally," Phil urged, "or it won't be official."

Self-consciously, Sally divested herself of her caftan and tested the water with her toe. But the appreciative whistles from the male guests caused her to step down quickly into the tub and immerse herself in the swirling, steaming water. Phil and his wife, Edna, followed her, as did one of the secretaries and her date. As Sally sat on the bench that lined the circular tub, someone with a flair for the romantic dimmed the lights and soon a seductive Neil Diamond song wafted from the stereo speakers.

Sally welcomed the near-darkness. It offered privacy and isolated her from her fellow tubmates, allowing her to relax and completely enjoy the hot swirling water. She leaned her head against the back of the tub and closed her eyes. Almost at once, she could feel the circulating hot waters begin to massage her body and soothe her. She heard Phil's wife comment from the opposite side of the tub that she had never been in one of these things before but was beginning to understand what the attraction was. *My sentiments exactly,* Sally thought, but she was too relaxed to express them aloud.

Then she heard laughter from the living room. Someone had decided to challenge Jerry to arm wrestling. Her tubmates decided to investigate, but Sally was too relaxed to bother.

But she was alone for only a moment. With her eyes still closed, Sally was aware of someone lowering himself or herself into the tub, but she did not open her eyes to discover who was now sitting beside her. Even with her eyes closed, she knew it was Neal's hand that came to rest on her shoulder. How remarkable, she thought, that she could recognize his touch. Was there some special chemical reaction that occurred when his skin touched hers? Were there special receptors in her flesh that responded in such a wonderfully tantalizing way only to the touch of Neal Parker?

She didn't move or open her eyes but allowed the rest of the world to recede while she focused all her attention on the hand that rested on her shoulder. When it slid down her submerged arm, a soft moan escaped from her lips. And her hand rose as though on the currents formed by the water forcing its way from the jets in the sides of the tub. The currents took her hand to Neal's leg. Her fingertips investigated the musculature and hair of his firm thigh. She thought of the way her body had felt after Neal's public kiss. Conflicting emotions stirred inside her. She knew she should be putting the physical part of their relationship on hold until they were able once and for all to define just what that relationship was to be, but the immediacy of his physical presence overwhelmed her. Her fingers seemed to have a will of their own as they slowly, ever so slowly, trailed their way up his thigh until they touched the edge of his bathing suit. Then with increasing boldness, those fingers crept even farther, to where the cloth was stretched tight over a hardness in the front of the garment.

With eyes still closed, she realized a most smug smile was creeping onto her lips. She couldn't help it. Oh, how she liked to know she had that effect on him! Such wonderful honest proof of his desire for her. She positively gloried in it.

"I see that look on your face," he whispered in her ear. "Pretty proud of yourself, aren't you? Well, my lovely, turnabout is fair play."

And Neal's fingers went from her arm to her thigh. His fingertips began tracing light circles on her flesh, each small circle moving higher and higher on her leg. After what seemed an agonizingly long time, the circles were being made on her stomach under her bathing suit. Then a large hand was cupping itself between her thighs.

Sally's hips rose in the water and pushed against his hand. At last, she opened her eyes. Their gaze locked as Neal tugged aside the elastic on one leg of her suit and slid his probing fingers under the fabric. Her legs floated apart as his fingers entered her. Sally felt the smile disappear from her face. She knew the expression that had replaced it matched the naked desire evident on Neal's face.

Looking directly into the depths of his dark eyes, she said softly, "Come home with me tonight. You can help me tuck my daughters in bed; then you can tuck me in bed."

He didn't spoil the mood by insisting she come instead to his childless home. He nodded, his fingers expressing graphically what would happen in Sally's bed with him in it. "It won't cause a problem?" he asked, his voice begging her to say it would not.

Sally shook her head no. "I'll probably shove you out the door before morning so I don't have to explain to them why I have a man in my bed."

Jerry's call to dinner brought a reluctant end to their secret underwater adventures. And a phone call for Neal shortly after everyone had their fill of barbecued ribs and corn on the cob brought an end to the party for Sally.

Neal returned from Jerry's bedroom, where he had taken the call. "It was the radar technician at the severe-storms lab. He's been monitoring the front. It looks like a live one, Sally, and he thinks it's one we might want to chase. Let's go out and have a look."

Sally felt strange going on their nighttime errand dressed in a flowing caftan. But she soon became so absorbed in monitoring the approaching storm via the wonders of Doppler radar that she forgot the inappropriateness of her attire.

She called home to tell her mother to go ahead and put the girls to bed. "And I might go on another chase, Mother, in which case I'll be gone all night. If you get a phone call in the middle of the night, don't panic. It will just be me telling you I'm not going to pick up the girls in the morning. Can you take care of them for me?"

Margie assured Sally there would be no problem, that she would run over to Sally's house now and get some clothing for the girls just in case.

At two-thirty Neal decided to chase. "If we leave now, we can get to the Panhandle by daylight. Then we can follow the storm as it heads down. We'll probably spend most of the day out there," he warned Sally.

Sally was glad Jerry had cautioned her to keep a change of suitable clothing stored at the lab in case she had to take off on a chase without returning home. She changed into her jeans and pullover top and exchanged her sandals for lop-topped boots. She grabbed a light-weight jacket and raced out of the deserted building to where Neal waited in the van.

Before she buckled her seat belt, she reached across and hugged him. "If given the choice between an adventure with you or bedding with you this night, I would have chosen bedding. But I want you to know I'd rather be off on an adventure with you than with anyone else in the world."

Chapter Twelve

"We may really be in for a bad one," Neal announced as they drove down Robinson Street heading for the interstate. "The heavy action is moving over southern Colorado. It looks like one of the largest systems to go through here this year. I called Jerry and Phil and told them, hangover or not, they were to come take the truck out with the robot. We'll have a better chance of spotting any funnels that may occur if we cover two sectors."

Neal suggested Sally crawl in the back and try to sleep for an hour or so. "Then you can relieve me at the wheel, and I'll try to get some shut-eye. We're in for a long day, and I'd hate for us to face it with no rest at all."

Sally stretched out on a foam-rubber pad in the back of the instrument-laden van and pulled a musty smelling blanket over her legs, but she could not force herself to sleep. She found herself reliving the intimacy she had shared with Neal at the party. Just thinking about it brought such remarkable responses to her body that sleep was not even a remote prospect, especially not with the man himself sitting a few feet away from where she was lying.

And how thrilling it was at long last to be storm chasing with Neal. She had longed for this day, and it meant more to her than just going on an adventure with him. For her, being included on this chase symolized his professional acceptance of her as a research meteorologist. No, she was too keyed up even to relax, much less sleep.

After what seemed like an appropriately long period of time, she crawled back into the passenger seat in the front of the vehicle and suggested a coffee stop. But more than coffee, she wanted to sit by him, to talk to him, to savor the pleasure of his company.

"We'll have breakfast in Weatherford in about thirty minutes," Neal told her.

Sally checked the gray sky overhead and surveyed the horizon. There was nothing terribly threatening looking so far, but she could tell the wind was starting to pick up. Turning her attention from sky watching, she allowed herself a pleasurable scrutiny of Neal.

It was such a treat for her to be able without interruption to watch him: his strong tan hands gripping the steering wheel, the flexing of muscles under his knit shirt as he maneuvered the vehicle, the well-developed musculature of his thighs revealed by smoothly fitting Levi's. Sally had always read about men mentally undressing the women they watched and supposed it was an exclusively male pastime. But she found herself mentally undressing the man beside her, imagining him naked and in bed with her—or naked and in back of the van with her. She imagined the look of him, the hard strong maleness of him, and longed to feel his muscles embracing her, wrapping themselves around her. The strength of him tantalized her, and the thought of that strength directed toward making love to her warmed her flesh and heightened her pulse.

It was close to eight o'clock when Neal pulled into a

café on the outskirts of the small town. He pulled a thermos from under the seat to have filled for future coffee breaks. "And we'd better grab a few candy bars and a couple of sandwiches. It's a long way between cafés out where we're heading—and a long way between ladies' rooms," he added, "so be sure to take advantage of the stop. Chasing tornadoes doesn't allow for some of the refinements of modern living you've grown accustomed to."

"Look, Neal, it may not be as easy for females to go behind bushes as it is for men, but I can manage. Let's not pull out the old no ladies'-rooms-out-there bit as a reason why women should stay home and make cookies while the guys go out and have all the fun."

"Well, it's even a long way between bushes out where we're heading," he said as they started across the café parking lot. His tone was good-natured, but Sally could tell that he was genuinely concerned about her comfort and wanted to spare her embarrassment.

"In that case, I'll just have to go behind the van," Sally said by way of reassurance as she put her arm around his waist. "For the rest of the trip, I'm just one of the boys."

At this Neal threw back his head and laughed. "I'd be really worried about myself if the day ever came when I could think of *you* as 'one of the boys.'" And his hand slid provocatively down over her bottom as though to emphasize his appreciation of her feminine attributes.

Sally could tell Neal was anxious to be on the way, and she did not linger over her eggs and toast. After her prescribed trip to the rest room, they were on the road once again. For this leg of the trip, Sally drove and Neal crawled into the makeshift bed in the back of the van.

At noon, Neal once again took over driving duties.

Sally poured them both some coffee from the thermos and handed Neal one of the candy bars.

"Not the most nutritious snack in the world," Sally said as she bit into a Hershey bar, "but it sure tastes good."

"We'll get something a little more substantial at Shattuck," Neal said. "We'll need to stop there anyway for gas and to call in for the latest report on this front. And we need to be deciding whether to head for the Texas or the Oklahoma Panhandle."

"Can't we just radio the lab and ask for a status report?" Sally asked.

"We're out of range," Neal explained. "We'll call in every so often from now on to figure out our route. We'll follow the front south as long as it shows promise."

Sally bit on her candy bar and sipped her coffee, enjoying the mingling of two of her favorite flavors. Although her lack of sleep was beginning to tell on her, she was thoroughly enjoying herself. Ever since she had started working with the tornado project, she'd dreamed of doing this with Neal—just the two of them storm chasing across the prairie. Her sense of adventure was aroused. She was pursuing an exciting new facet of the profession she loved with the man she loved. No matter what happened between the two of them in the future, she would have the memory of this exciting day with him.

She wanted to tell him how she felt—that the day was special unto itself regardless of what came after it—but she was afraid her words would not aptly express her feelings. Instead, she leaned over and touched his arm. He lifted a hand from the steering wheel and covered hers. No words were spoken, but Sally could sense the feelings that passed between them. *How precious such a small gesture can be,* she thought.

Neal made his call from a Texaco station in Shattuck. They were to head toward Borger, Texas. While they waited for their hamburgers at a drive-in, Neal told her what to expect of the Texas Panhandle.

"It's said when God made the world, he made the Texas Panhandle last, but by then, he had run out of everything. He didn't have a thing left: no trees, no flowers, no bushes, no mountains, no hills, no rivers, no lakes, nothing. So he just made some folks who liked it that way and put them out there to live."

"I take it the Texas Panhandle is not one of your favorite geographical regions," Sally said with a smile.

"Oh, quite the contrary. I love it. They have great weather out there, surpassed only by the weather in the Oklahoma Panhandle. Only trouble is, there aren't very many roads to chase around on in the Texas Panhandle. There are precious few ranches and even fewer towns—not much to connect together with roads—and I'm against off-the-road driving on storm chases even in a four-wheel-drive vehicle. It's too easy to get stuck or break an axle, and I want to stay mobile when a tornado might be in the vicinity."

Announcing that he wanted to be in Borger by three and would eat his hamburger on the road, Neal started down the highway as soon as the carhop brought their lunch.

As they drove, Sally began to see what Neal meant about the Texas Panhandle. The land was austere, with only small, scraggly mesquite trees punctuating the emptiness, but the sky was full of stormy weather. It was midday but already as dark as evening. The wind was buffeting the van about, causing Neal to keep a tight grip on the steering wheel. And the sound of the wind rushing past their vehicle lent a melancholy feeling to their journey and served to emphasize the quiet that now prevailed inside the van. It was a heavy quiet. Sally sensed the time at last had come for them to have the talk Neal had promised, the talk they never had in Kansas City. There was no reason to put it off—except fear. What if it was the end for her and Neal? Could she bear it? Not knowing was better than that.

She stole a look at Neal, but he was already glancing her way. "I guess you know I'm in love with you," he said. "It's not the first time I've been in love, but it's the deepest love I've ever felt for anyone, and it scares me. I guess I know if I lose you, I've really lost something special."

Sally said nothing, realizing nothing was expected of her. This was Neal's speech. She stared down at her clutched hands. *He's trying to tell me gently that it will never work,* she thought frantically. *Oh, no, please don't let it be that.*

"I told you about Barbara and that marriage," Neal went on, "but I never got around to explaining about my first marriage. I've been married twice already, Sally."

She sensed him turning to look at her to check her reaction to his announcement, but she continued to stare at her hands.

"I was married the first time when I was in graduate school. My wife had a little boy from a previous marriage. His name was Danny."

Danny. Phil had mentioned someone named Danny. Now she knew who he was. Something in the way Neal said the child's name told Sally a great deal. Neal had loved Danny. With a sinking heart, she knew what was coming.

"I thought Danny was the brightest, cutest, neatest

little kid that had ever been born. I wished I had been his biological father, but I wasn't. I was damned glad to be his stepfather, however, and be a part of his life. He was eighteen months old when I married his mother. He was four when she left me. I miss him still.

"The irony of it was," Neal continued, "that the presence of that child in our marriage seemed to be what ruined it. His mother and I were constantly at odds over his upbringing. She didn't believe in kids eating candy and chewing gum, and I was always giving him treats. She believed in a fixed bedtime, and I was always wanting him to stay up and play—especially on the nights I got home late. But on the other hand, I thought she was too lenient about some things: his behavior in public places or not making him put his toys away. As he got older, Danny discovered he could play one of us against the other. When I'd discipline him, he'd go running to his mother, and of course, she would always prevail. After all, she was the boy's mother, and I was just the guy she had married. At those times, I realized he was her child, not mine, and I sure didn't like the big bad stepfather role. It seemed like every fight Sue and I ever had was over that little boy. And there was the irritant of her constant contact with the boy's 'real' father over visitation rights and reporting to him every time Danny got the sniffles. And I'm embarrassed to admit there were problems when she put the boy first and me second. I guess I wasn't big enough to handle that. I kept finding myself being jealous of a little boy!''

As Sally listened, she lost heart. No wonder Neal was reluctant to become involved with her children. She wanted to cry out to him that it wouldn't be that way if he were Vicky's and Amy's stepfather, but could she promise that? More than ever before, she was aware of the difficulties Neal might face if he did marry her. There would be some bad times ahead for them. There would be disagreements over child rearing. There would be a tremendous adjustment for them all. Neal would have to learn to live in a child-oriented household, and she and her daughters would have to get used to a family situation with two parents rather than one.

Sally believed they could make it. She believed the good times would far outweigh the bad, but that was just a feeling on her part. She had no proof. All one had to go on in a situation like this was faith in a shared future, and Neal did not seem to have that faith.

Neal loved her. She was certain of that. And she loved him, so much it overwhelmed her, but Sally understood that love did not solve every problem that stood in the way of a man and a woman making their life together.

"I made up my mind," Neal continued, "that if I ever tried parenting again, it was going to be with my own children or not at all. And after being married twice, I have this feeling that the third time had better take, or I will spend the rest of my life alone. Sally, you can't believe the time I've spent agonizing over this."

Would it make a difference to him if she assured him they could have a child together, Sally wondered as she listened to him. She realized she would like that very much, to have a child with Neal. She had not really thought much about having other children, but then, given the circumstances of her life for the past five years, two children had been as many as she could manage. Somehow, however, it didn't seem right to bribe him with a promise that she would bear a child for him. It was like saying "You put up with my children and I'll give you one of your own." The decision about

future children should be made only after the four of
them were a working family.

But the conversation was over for now anyway. She
sensed he had more to say, that the story of Danny was
just a preliminary to something else. As much as she
wanted to believe he was going to tell her he was willing
to join her little family, she feared he would have finished by explaining he couldn't handle being a stepfather again. However, the noise from the wind was
making normal conversation difficult, and driving conditions were becoming increasingly troublesome. Theirs
was practically the only vehicle on the road. The wind's
pull on the van had grown more intense, causing Neal to
grasp the wheel even tighter.

Neal swung into an isolated service station whose
sign promised the last gas for twenty miles. "I think it's
time we call in again and get a fix on this thing," Neal
said, "and we should photograph those cloud formations."

The phone call caused them to alter their course.
Neal learned the lab's radar showed several hook
echoes that could mean tornadoes in the southern part
of Ochiltree County and up into the Oklahoma Panhandle. Neal turned north on State Highway 70 across
Roberts County. Sally checked the road map and could
see that Ochiltree County lay immediately north of
Roberts and just south of the Oklahoma Panhandle's
Beaver County. Sally wondered why anyone had bothered to build a road out there. The map did not show a
single town on the fifty-two-mile stretch between
Pampa and Perryton. In fact, there seemed to be only
one town—Miami—in all of Roberts County that was
large enough to appear on the road map she was using.

"At least a tornado out here wouldn't do much damage," she called to Neal over the wind noise.

"Let's photograph from that rise up there and get some instrument readings."

Although they could see two rain shafts, one to the north and another to the northwest, the highway was still rain-free. They were able to make fairly good time, stopping periodically for photographs and instrument reading. Neal stopped once at a ranch house and another time at a country store to call in for a radar report. In southern Ochiltree County, he adjusted their route westward, first taking State Highway 281, then heading away from a southward-moving precipitation shaft and taking a southwestern route on a county road that closely paralleled the ferociously dark squall line.

Neal was "flying by the seat of his pants" now, using his eyes to guide the path, since there was no place to phone in for additional radar reports. They were isolated and alone in a world dominated by a raging sky.

The winds were treacherously gusty and seemed intent on attacking the lone vehicle traveling on the narrow gravel road.

Sally watched intently as the nature of the clouds began to change. The shelf cloud marking the front edge of the squall line began to dissipate, being replaced by wall clouds formed by a lowering of the rain-free cumulonimbus base.

From Sally's perspective, the slow rotation of the wall clouds was evident. If a tornado developed, she realized it would form from those clouds.

Twice they stopped the van on the county road to photograph the cloud formations and take more instrument readings, but the wedge of distance between the road and the suspicious line of clouds began to increase as they continued along their southwesterly route. Sally knew Neal was searching for a bisecting road to turn onto. She couldn't believe how far apart roads were.

She was used to Oklahoma's section-line roads occurring regularly at one-mile intervals, but this was the Texas Panhandle, she reminded herself, where it took many acres of land to support just one cow. Ranches were necessarily vast, and roads were not automatically built at regular intervals.

At last, however, an unmarked road with an oiled surface did offer an exit from the gravel road they were following. Neal turned onto it, and now, instead of paralleling the squall line, the van was heading directly toward it.

Neal followed this road for about a mile before stopping once again for pictures. Sally operated a sixteen-millimeter motion-picture camera, and Neal took stills.

She saw it first through the lens of her camera, about two miles away, a thin needle of pale clouds dropping down from the darker clouds above. She kept the camera running but sidestepped close enough to Neal for him to hear her above the noise of the wind.

"Neal, to the right at two o'clock," she yelled, using the imagery of the clock face to direct his gaze toward the snakelike vertical formation.

He responded by directing his camera with its powerful zoom lens where Sally had indicated. But not for long. The twister was growing before their eyes and growing darker as it sucked debris into its vortex.

The funnel cloud seemed to be taking a route that would miss them by at least a mile, perhaps two, but Neal was not taking any chances.

"Let's get back to the county road," he yelled. "We can take more pictures there."

Sally understood that Neal wanted to be in a position where they could drive away from the path of the storm at right angles rather than be put in the more dangerous position of outrunning it.

Neal executed a tight U-turn, and very quickly they were back on the county road. Once again, they exited from the vehicle and got their cameras into action. Sally realized the film they were taking would be some of the most valuable that had been acquired this year, perhaps for several years. She was thrilled, awed and a little frightened, even though the storm was at least a mile and a half from where they stood.

Still the funnel grew and blackened as it sucked more dirt and debris into its mouth. And it had definitely changed its direction. Sally was certain that if they were not directly in its present path, they were too close for comfort.

She was relieved when Neal tugged on her arm and indicated it was time for them to depart.

She climbed into the van, stored away the cameras and fastened her seat belt.

As Neal turned the key in the ignition, Sally watched the funnel continue to grow and move even closer to their present position. She realized that little more than a mile now separated them from the death-dealing force concentrated in that fearsome rotating cloud. The engine turned over, but the rear tires spun in the soft dirt of the shoulder. The van lurched forward as the tires spun free, and the engine coughed and tried to die.

Quickly, Neal pumped the accelerator, giving the engine more gas. The engine seemed to recover, and to Sally's intense relief, the van moved forward. But they had gone only a few feet when the engine sputtered.

The noise from the wind had so heightened that Sally could hardly hear the expletive that erupted from Neal's lips as he reached for the ignition and attempted to restart the engine.

It turned over. Once. Twice. A third time. Then sputtered again and died.

Neal tried again. Each time he attempted to restart the engine, it became less responsive. The twisting, spinning cloud was coming ever closer. It had changed course. Sally was certain it had. The funnel itself might still miss them, but what about the debris? Sally knew how much danger there was from the lethal flying debris that accompanied tornadoes. She'd read of pieces of straw being driven through telephone poles, of pebbles becoming hurtling bullets, of boards being driven through concrete walls.

A fourth time Neal tried to start the engine. And a fifth.

Then he quit trying.

"Out!" he yelled. "Leave everything. There's a culvert about fifty feet back up the road. We've got to run for it."

Sally had never run track faster than she ran down that dirt road, even though her every instinct told her to run in the opposite direction—not toward but away from the horrible monster that could eat her body in an instant.

She leaped down in the culvert and, following Neal's lead, took refuge in the huge pipe that ran under the road and connected the two sides of the culvert.

They crouched side by side in the corrugated metal pipe. Neal's arms were around her. They seemed to be safe—but the roar, the deafening roar was so close now. It did sound like a freight train just as she had always heard. It sounded like a dozen freight trains getting closer and closer! The ground shook all around them. The violence of the storm flowed through her body from the very earth around them.

She felt the hair on her arms rise and her flesh crawl in response to the electrical field created by the rotation of the tornadic winds.

And darkness engulfed them as both ends of the metal pipe were obliterated by the rising dirt being sucked into the mouth of the awesome force passing over their heads.

She buried her face against Neal's chest. Death was passing overhead. Fear engulfed her like a suffocating blanket. Her only comfort was from the closeness of this man.

Fear began to erode the confidence she had in their makeshift tornado shelter. What was to prevent the winds from sucking them from their hiding place? From ripping up the roadbed and taking them, pipe and all?

Such force! It pushed in on her. The pressure pushed against her lungs and robbed her of air. She was paralyzed with the pressure, and the incessant roar made her eardrums feel as though they were breaking. There was no other sound in the world but that horrible roar.

Was she going to die? Was this the end of her life?

With a crushing ferociousness, Neal pressed her against his body as if to ward off the demon that surrounded them. If death came, they would meet it together.

Sally closed her eyes. There was no light to shut out, but by doing so, she tried to draw herself more fully into Neal's circling arms, to shut out the noise and the fear. Then she realized there was another sensation for her in all this terror. She could feel Neal's heartbeat. She concentrated on it instead of the roar.

AND THEN IT PASSED. Sally wondered if they had been inside their corrugated shelter a minute or an hour. They stayed on for a time until the roar was completely gone and peace descended upon the land.

Sally followed Neal from the pipe. Rain was starting to fall, quickly settling the dust around them.

Elsewhere, Sally realized, she would have emerged to an altered and devastated world, but the barren landscape of this particular corner of the globe offered up little for destruction. A few mesquite trees to uproot — that was all.

Or at least Sally thought it was all until she looked around to see what damage the van had sustained.

There was no van!

Sally was thunderstruck. She made a complete turn. It had to be around here somewhere. It had to be!

But it wasn't. The van was literally gone with the wind.

Suddenly the full knowledge of how close they had come to death's door hit Sally so powerfully her knees buckled and she found it difficult to breathe. Neal grabbed her and lowered her gently to the ground. He hovered over her, cradling her in his strong arms, rocking her back and forth, murmuring comforting words to her.

There in the rain, beside a remote country road in the middle of the emptiness that was the Texas Panhandle, they clung to each other. They seemed to be the only people in the world. The rain was pelting them, drenching them, but they did not move.

Sally was cold and wet, but the very fact she could feel cold and wet meant she was still alive. She rejoiced in it.

IT SEEMED AS IF THEY HAD WALKED FOREVER before twin beams of light announced an approaching vehicle.

Please let them stop, Sally thought fervently as Neal stepped out onto the road and waved.

It was a pickup truck — a very old pickup truck.

Sally walked over to the vehicle when it stopped and leaned against its side while Neal talked to the driver through his open window. She was vaguely aware of his explanation about the tornado, about needing to get to a town and the lady being about to drop.

I am, Sally thought. *If this man doesn't let us in that truck, I will drop right here on the road. I don't think I can walk another step.* Her feet inside her drenched boots felt as though they were made of cold, hard lead. No muscle in her body was free from aching weariness. And she was so cold, so wet and cold.

Apparently the truck driver was willing to give them a ride. Neal took her arm and helped her inside. Soon she was wedged between Neal and the driver in the small elderly truck, and a blanket that smelled as though it had previously covered a horse was wrapped around her shoulders. Its warmth was most welcome.

The ride was jostling. Sally would wake from time to time and take a look at the unchanging landscape revealed by the narrow wedge of illumination from the truck headlights.

She had no sense of how much time had passed when the truck finally reached a dark little town that occupied two blocks on either side of a wide street. There was an ancient tourist court at the end of the two-block-long town. Lone Star Courts. Sally couldn't have been more relieved if the sign announced they had arrived at the Waldorf-Astoria. She knew warmth and dryness and a bed awaited her. That was all she asked.

Neal was incredibly wonderful. He peeled the wet clothes from their chilled bodies and hung them over the chairs to dry. He started the shower and helped her inside the stall.

"Do you need help in there?" he asked.

Sally nodded yes, and Neal stepped in with her. They stood for a long time clinging to each other under the spray of marvelous warm water. Slowly the warmth from the man and the water seeped into her chilled body.

With great ceremony, Neal soaped her body and rubbed it with a frayed washcloth. As they bathed, he talked to her of love and caring. He spoke of the fear he had felt for them both as the tornado passed over their heads.

"I kept thinking about those two little girls," he admitted. "What if I didn't get you home to them? That scared me more than anything else."

Sally was touched by his words to the point of pain. Tears mingled with the water cascading down her face. Sally was too exhausted even to talk, but she took such extreme joy in his words, in the sound of his voice. There was no other man like this man, not in the entire world. She loved him so much she thought she would burst with it.

He dried their bodies with threadbare towels and then half carried her to the waiting bed. After tucking the covers around her, he brought her the Coke and candy bar he had gotten from the vending machines in the motel office when he had checked in.

"I wish I could get you a real meal," Neal said. "According to that grumpy old guy who rented us the room, there's nothing open at this hour."

"I'm not really hungry," Sally said.

"No excuses," Neal said firmly. "It will give you a little blood sugar and make you feel better. Really it will."

Sally obediently nibbled on the candy bar and took a few sips of the soft drink, and after a few minutes, she did start to feel better. She realized how totally drained of energy she had been.

"Are you feeling any warmer?" Neal asked.

"I'd feel warmer if you were in here with me," Sally said softly.

It was with such tenderness that Neal made love to her. He treated her as though she were the most fragile creature on the face of the earth. Sally had never known such love.

Afterward, with her back to the sleeping Neal, she wept. She had braved the greatest of storms with this man, but there seemed to be no end to the storm that raged within her. She wanted to be with him always, but he had to want a life with her *and* her daughters. She loved him so desperately, but soon their night together would end, and they would part.

Could she continue to be with him like this—to have an affair with him, to live only for the present? In her heart, Sally sadly acknowledged that she could not do that. She could not stand the pain of having only part of him and always be leaving him, always be saying goodbye.

She was part of a family, and Neal wanted only her. It was not meant to be. But tonight, she was weak. She turned to him and touched his face. Tonight she wanted him to love her again and again.

SALLY AWOKE to the pattern of sunlight stripes streaming between venetian blinds. Instead of Neal, her carefully folded clothes occupied the opposite side of the bed. They had been laundered and smelled of fabric softener.

And awaiting her in the bathroom was a new toothbrush, a comb and a tube of lipstick. Sally was grateful for Neal's thoughtfulness. He had obviously been up and about early this morning. Or maybe it was just that she slept so late, Sally thought, wondering what time it was. Her rain-soaked watch had quit working, and she had no idea if it was early morning or nearly noon.

Dressed in clean but wrinkled clothes and grateful for the touch of color that the tube of lipstick provided her clean but unmade-up face, Sally left the cottage in search of Neal.

A familiar pickup truck bearing the logo of the National Tornado Project was parked in front to the adjacent diner. Neal had apparently been able to contact Jerry and Phil. Sally was relieved to know they would have a way back to Norman.

Sally joined the three men inside. They had just finished their breakfast but lingered over coffee while she downed a hearty meal of pancakes and bacon. The four of them compared notes on their previous night's experiences. Although they had been chasing in the same county, Phil and Jerry had not sighted any funnel clouds but had gotten blown around quite a bit.

They all mourned the loss of the photographs and motion picture film that were in the van. "The thing formed right in front of the cameras," Sally said, "and we had documented the whole thing, a whole series of photographs and readings of the storm that spawned the tornado. It makes me sick to have lost it. I wonder if the van will ever be found or if its pieces are scattered all over Roberts County."

"But at least you two are okay," Phil said, his round face full of concern for the close call his friends had experienced.

"Neal's quick thinking kept us out of trouble," Sally said with a smile in his direction.

"Yeah, but Neal's jackrabbit driving habits got us into trouble in the first place," Neal commented ruefully. "I just plain flooded the van's engine. I think we are going to have to reformulate our chase safety rules—no turning off motors during severe weather. Leave the motors running just in case a quick exit is called for."

After a little more shoptalk, the four of them began a long, cramped ride home in the cab of the pickup truck that took the rest of the day. At least it was a one-ton vehicle with a much larger cab than the truck she had ridden in last night, Sally thought, but it was not designed for four, especially when one passenger was the size of Phil. The men started taking turns riding in the back. That helped, but the ride seemed endless.

It was shortly before five o'clock when the truck pulled in the laboratory parking lot and pulled in beside a long, black Lincoln Continental.

The four weary meteorologists speculated about whom the expensive car might belong to as they made their way into the building and automatically stopped at the receptionist's desk to pick up their messages.

The receptionist, a small Oriental woman, greeted them with wide eyes. She nervously handed them the slips of paper with their calls on them. She cleared her throat and said, "Ah, Sally, there's someone here waiting to see you. He's been waiting all afternoon."

"Oh? Who is it?" Sally queried.

Avoiding Sally's gaze, the flustered woman gestured toward the small lounge area across the hall, indicating where Sally would find her visitor. In a puzzled voice, she answered Sally's question.

"He says he's your husband."

Chapter Thirteen

Sally froze. Even her breathing stopped momentarily. Michael? Here? He was the last person in the world she wanted to see. She felt the gaze of the others upon her as they waited for her reaction.

She wouldn't see him. She would have someone tell him to go away. After five years he couldn't come waltzing in here and announce that he was her husband and expect to see her. What could he want?

Damn him!

Neal was touching her arm. "Do you want to see him? Would you rather I tell him to leave?"

Sally squared her shoulders. "No. He'd probably just come back again. I'll take care of it."

Michael was standing when she entered the small lounge. He must have heard them come in.

"Hi, Sal," he said casually, as though they had parted only yesterday. "You been sick? You look awful."

"Charming as ever, I see," Sally said sarcastically. "What do you want?"

"What? No word of greeting for your long-lost husband?" Michael opened his arms as though he expected Sally to fly into them.

"What do you want, Michael?" she repeated.

He was still very handsome, Sally realized, perhaps

even more so. No longer boyishly slender, he now possessed a filled-out man's body. But there was something else about him that had changed—his demeanor. There was a new cockiness she had not seen before. Of course, he had always been brash—and irresponsible. For a long time, she had put up with him in spite of his faults, deciding their marriage was a trade-off of sorts: she put up with his faults; he put up with hers. However, their life together had not been all bad. She had loved him once. But the Michael that stood expectantly before her somehow made her flesh crawl. He looked so uncaring, even sinister. She knew before he said another word, he was up to no good.

His hair was cut fuller—with sideburns. His clothes were flashy: a white sport coat and necktie with a black shirt, black slacks. And he had several large showy rings on his fingers. Sally decided he looked like a gambler. She wondered what he could possibly want with her—but she was almost afraid to find out.

"What do I want? Why, I want to see you, of course," he said. "Can't a guy stop in to see his wife if he wants to?"

"Ex-wife," Sally said flatly.

"Yeah, I noticed the Sally *Hampton* bit on that television program, but I never signed any papers. I thought maybe we were still married."

Sally could not believe what she was hearing—that he thought he might still be married to her yet had made no effort to contact her in all this time. That their marriage had meant so little to him! That he could be so irresponsible he didn't even bother to find out if he was still married or not!

"When the charge is abandonment, the signing of papers by the errant spouse is not required," Sally said curtly.

"Well, I'll always think of you as my little old wife," Michael said, attempting to take Sally in his arms.

Sally pushed him away, amazed at how much strength her weary body was able to muster. "What do you want, Michael?" she said vehemently.

"To offer you a job, honey," he said with a broad snake-oil-salesman smile, choosing to ignore her rebuff. "Right up your alley, too. Meteorology. My business associates saw you on television and about wet their pants when I told them you were my wife. We've gotten together a scheme to sell tornado-warning devices to homeowners. Sounds an alarm when a tornado is near and ought to go over really big in this part of the country. And with you being a local celebrity and tornado expert, you'd be a natural to do some television spots advertising our little machines. You really looked great on the tube, Sally baby—although I can't say much about the way you look right now. You really should iron your shirt at least."

Sally wanted to hit him—or throw something at him. He always had been so critical of her. Always. She hated the way he made her feel.

"Are you speaking of the shortwave devices tuned in to a central forecasting system?" Sally asked. *Keep it impersonal,* she told herself. *Tell him no and get him out of here.*

"No, ma'am. These amazing little machines with their newly developed laser sensors are so attuned to the environment that they are able to warn homeowners if there is a tornado or the threat of a tornado within a ten-mile radius."

"There is no such device," Sally announced flatly. "I wouldn't touch a con game like that with a ten-foot pole. Now get out."

"I wish you'd reconsider," Michael said smoothly as

he perched himself on the arm of a chair, obviously with no intention of leaving. "It might be to your advantage."

"You couldn't pay me enough to be involved in such an undertaking," Sally said, trying to keep her anger in check.

"Now, I wouldn't feel right about this unless you took some time to think about it," Michael said glibly. "I'll just wait around here for a few days while you make up your mind. It'll give me a chance to see my babies. I'll bet they've really grown. They'll be real surprised to see their old dad."

See his *babies*? Did he really say that? Sally felt as though her blood had turned to ice water. She wanted to scream at him and tell him that if she had anything to say about it, he would never see those girls again in his entire lifetime.

"And if I go along with your scheme...?" she questioned.

"Ah, you always were a smart little lady," Michael said with a falsely hearty laugh. "Well, if you agree to come to Houston for a week and do some television work for us, I think I can forget about seeing my children this trip. Otherwise, I might demand my visitation rights—you know, take them on trips and all that sort of thing."

"That's blackmail," Sally said between clenched teeth.

"Call it what you want, Sal. That's my proposition. With you as part of the package, my associates will agree to overlook a small problem of missing funds. So I don't intend to take no for an answer."

Sally felt as though she were deflating—like a balloon that someone had poked with a pin. The taste of bile rose in her mouth, and she took a step backward to put more distance between herself and the corrupt creature standing there smiling at her. It was as if an alien being had taken over the body of Michael Storm. She fervently wished she had never had to see this Michael, for in spite of the fact that he had walked out on her and their daughters, Sally still had managed up to now to maintain a degree of affection for the Michael she had once loved. She remembered fondly the youthful time they had shared before they were married, but this corrupt man standing in front of her was robbing her of even that.

Could he do that—demand to see the girls, spend time with them, take them on trips? The thought of her daughters with this man sickened her. Surely he had no legal right to visitation, not if he had never paid any child support and never attempted to see or contact his children in five years. But he was their father, and maybe he could pay child support now. Maybe he was rich enough to pay up all that back child support and demand his rights. That expensive car out there must belong to him, and those rings on his hands looked real enough.

Surely no court in the land would grant him visitation rights. Of course it wouldn't. But what if she was wrong?

Frantically, she searched her mind for something to say to him, something that would make him go away. She opened her mouth to speak, but nothing came out.

It was Neal who spoke instead—from behind her. Sally spun around to see him standing there, drawn up to his full height, his face full of rage. But his voice was calm.

"Mr. Storm, I would tell you most graphically what you can do with your proposition, but I don't talk like that in front of Miss Hampton. I do have something to say to you, however. Now, listen, and listen well. I plan to call a judge who is a very good friend of mine. A judge can issue a restraining order forbidding you from seeing Sally's daughters, and if you choose to ignore that order, a police officer will come and put you in jail. Now, I could be wrong, but you don't look to me like someone who would like to meet a policeman right now. They tend to be nosy, you know, and run checks on suspicious characters who drive big black Lincoln Continentals—that is your car out there, isn't it?—and have questionable means of support.''

Sally wanted to cheer or cry or kiss Neal—or all three. After all these years of fighting her own battles, how marvelous it was to have help for this one.

Michael blanched somewhat under Neal's onslaught but did not retreat. "Hey, buddy," he said with great bravado, "those kids aren't just Sally's, you know. They're my kids, too.''

"No, they're not," Neal said. "You forfeited any right to those children when you left them. You wouldn't even know those two girls if you saw them on the street, and they certainly wouldn't know you. Being a father has a whole lot more to it than a biological act. That's probably the least important ingredient of fathering. Only a man willing to be there day in and day out through sickness and bad times and to be a part of their lives no matter what deserves the father label.''

"Oh, and I suppose you're some kind of grand champion specimen of fatherhood," Michael challenged.

"No, I'm not. I don't deserve the label, either—at least not yet. But I feel sorry for someone like you who had a chance at it and threw it away. I hope I'm wiser than that. Now, if you'll excuse Sally and me, we'll go call that judge.''

Michael stood staring at them, hate distorting his face. Then his twisted mouth let forth with a violent stream of obscenities. Only Sally's restraining arm kept Neal from hitting him.

She looked at Neal, her eyes beseeching. "Let him rage," she said as she pulled him toward the stairway. "You've won. He'll leave."

Sally was right. Very shortly, the roar of a high-powered engine could be heard from the parking lot. Then the sound of screeching tires pierced the air.

Michael was gone.

Sally felt profound relief—and such sadness. Michael, her beautiful Michael, he could have been a different man.

SALLY WANTED TO RETURN to the sanctuary of her own home after the traumas of the past two days—after learning why Neal wasn't interested in becoming a father to her children, making love to him for what was probably the last time, and confronting her former husband. She needed to go home and regain her equilibrium. She needed to touch her children.

Sally's car was still at Jerry's house, but Neal insisted he drive her home rather than run her by Jerry's. "I'll take you home. You can pick up your car tomorrow," he told her. "Right now, I just want to get you straight home. You need a bath, a brandy and bed—in that order."

"I won't argue with that," Sally said wearily. "What an unbelievable two days this has been! I feel numb."

Sally leaned against Neal in the privacy of his office. "Thanks, Neal, for stepping in downstairs. I can't tell you how grateful I am. You really came up with the right threat. It's a good thing you know a judge."

"Judge? Ah, yes, my good friend Phil Rankin. Judges dog shows on weekends," Neal said casually.

"But I thought you meant . . . but downstairs you told Michael . . . . You mean you were bluffing?"

Neal shrugged his shoulders. "Well, not exactly. I would have gotten hold of a judge if he had caused further trouble, but it just wouldn't have been a judge I happen to know."

Sally hugged his neck. "You never cease to amaze me, Dr. Parker. Now, if you don't mind, I'd like you to take me home. I've really had it."

Very quickly, they were heading up Interstate 35 toward Oklahoma City. Neal was also taking Phil by his house, and the plump man was already snoring in the backseat. Sally's body was stiff and aching after the crowded drive across Oklahoma in the cab of a pickup truck with three other people. And her emotions were in complete turmoil.

Michael. She still couldn't believe it. All he had left was his looks. Anything laudable about her former husband had vanished. She would probably never see him again. Surely now, Michael was truly gone from her life, thanks to Neal. Sally was so grateful for his help. She didn't want her daughters ever to meet their biological father. Ever. She wanted to spare them that.

She tried to tell Neal how she felt, but he wouldn't have it. "Listen, Sally, you don't owe me any thanks. I'm sorry the guy came and upset you so, but I can't tell you what pleasure it gave me to help you out of that mess. Now, you've had enough to worry about without trying to make pretty speeches to me."

He turned on the radio to spare her further conversation. Sally was grateful. She was too tired to talk, too tired even to think and too tired to deal with what lay ahead for her and Neal.

They did not speak again during the twenty-minute ride, but Neal reached over and pulled her to him. She spent the rest of the ride with her head against his shoulder. How natural it felt, so safe and warm. If only she could spend the rest of her life at this man's side.

They dropped Phil off in south Oklahoma City, and it was after six when Neal pulled in her mother's driveway. She was surprised to find that in spite of her weariness, she did not want him to leave. But as she extended a somewhat awkward invitation for him to wait while she got her children, then come to her house and have something to eat, she was interrupted by two young voices calling to her.

Vicky and Amy were racing out the front door and came rushing down the front steps. Something in their voices filled her with alarm. She jumped out of the car.

"Grandma's sick," a frightened Vicky told her mother.

NEAL STAYED WITH THE GIRLS while Sally rushed her very ill mother to Baptist Hospital. Margie was weak and her breathing shallow. On the way to the hospital, Sally kept up a continual stream of chatter. "We'll be there soon," she said over and over. "I'll get you taken care of soon. You'll be okay. Just hang in there."

At first Margie responded to Sally's reassuring words, but her voice grew weak. It became increasingly difficult for her to speak and even to move. She slumped over in the seat.

By the time Sally pulled into the emergency-room entrance of the hospital, her mother was paralyzed.

NEAL STOOD in Sally's living room looking down at two solemn-faced little girls. A large solitary tear rolled out of the right eye of the smaller girl and down her pale cheek. *Poor little kids,* Neal thought, *having their grandmother get sick and being stuck with the likes of me.*

"Well, kids," Neal grimly told the two wary children, "Looks like it's time for you and me to become friends. Which one of you is Amy and which is Vicky? I guess I didn't pay too much attention when we met before."

SALLY WATCHED in numb horror as the emergency-room crew worked over her mother: hooking her up to a heart monitor, starting intravenous fluids, giving injections.

She looks so bad, Sally thought. *Is she dead already? But she can't be, she just can't be. My* mother. *I love her so much. Casey loves her. We all need her so. Oh, please, don't let her die.*

LATER, SALLY LISTENED carefully, trying to comprehend what the surgeon was telling her. Her mother had an obstruction in her carotid artery and needed immediate surgery, the kindly woman carefully explained. She would not tell Sally that everything be all right. Sally was so very frightened.

Yet, through her anguish, the mothering part of her was still operational. She was obviously going to be tied up at the hospital indefinitely, and she had to make arrangements for Vicky and Amy. She called the woman who had cared for the girls during her ill-fated trip to Kansas City. The woman's daughter answered the phone. Her mother was on another job.

Sally called Barry. He was not home. She called the television station and learned he was on vacation.

She thought of calling an agency. Or there was her next-door neighbor. Sally had never left the girls with her neighbor before, but perhaps in an emergency, the woman might be willing to help out. Or there was Jerry. The girls always got along well with Jerry.

Sally called home to let Neal know she would have a relief person there as soon as she could.

"That's not necessary," Neal said. "I can manage."

"But Neal, I'll probably be here for days."

"I said I can manage," Neal said, not concealing the irritation in his voice. "Now quit worrying about Vicky and Amy and tell me about your mother."

"Oh, Neal, she may die."

The fear and exhaustion got the best of her. Sally sat there weeping in the phone booth in the hospital lobby. Upstairs, they were preparing to operate on her seriously ill mother. Whatever reserve she had left abandoned her.

"Sally, honey, I wish I were there with you," Neal said. "I wish I could hold you and comfort you, but I think what you need most right now is to know your children are taken care of. And you're strong, stronger than you realize. And remember, there are two little gals and one big guy here who love you very much."

Sally called Casey Tinsley in Dallas. She tried to explain calmly what had happened to her mother, but her voice broke. She was fresh out of bravery.

"I can't believe it," Casey said. "She was fine when I left her Sunday afternoon. Look, Sally, I'll be there as soon as I can make it back up the highway, and if she regains consciousness before I get there, will you please tell her I love her?"

Margie made it through the surgery. Casey was there with Sally when the surgeon made her report. She was still guarded, saying ominously, "The next forty-eight hours should tell the story."

At seven-thirty the next morning, Sally met Neal and the girls in the lobby. Neal handed Sally an overnight bag with a change of clothes and some toilet articles. "The girls packed this for you. Seemed like they knew just what you'd be needing."

"Oh, they do," Sally said as she hugged her daughters. "They are the smartest, best girls in the world."

Neal handed Sally a comb and brush. "We did pretty well on the dressing part, but I wasn't very good with hair. Maybe you'd better spruce them up before I take them to day care."

They all sat down in the lobby while Sally braided two blond heads. Then the girls gave Sally a folder of pictures they had colored for their grandmother.

"Neal helped us write words on them," Amy said.

"I'll give them to her when she wakes up," Sally promised.

She sent the girls off to get some gum from a vending machine so she could have a private moment with Neal. Once again, she offered to get someone else to come in and take care of her daughters.

"No need," Neal said curtly.

"Don't you need to get out to the lab?" Sally said. "I know how busy everything is right now with the annual report due and the upcoming V.I.P. visit."

"I'll run down this morning while the girls are in day care. I can bring some stuff home to work on and keep in touch by phone. If worst comes to worst, the girls can go with me if I need to be there in the evenings."

"Oh, Neal, are you sure you want to do this? I could call an agency and get someone."

He reached for her hand, turning it over and gently caressing her palm. "Would you rather have a woman from an agency care for them than me?" he asked.

"No, I really wouldn't. I've never used an agency,

but you've never taken care of little girls before, either. It can't be very nice for you. Are you sure ... ?''

He put a fingertip to her lips, hushing her. "I'm sure. If the girls can put up with me, I can put up with them."

Neal seemed grimly determined to care for her daughters. Sally did not feel right about the arrangement. She knew how Neal felt about her children, and she knew how badly he needed to be at the lab. But she was too worried and weary to argue.

She watched through the glass doors as her two small daughters left the hospital with the very tall man. The three of them stood on the curb waiting for the traffic to clear so they could cross to the parking lot. Sally noticed Neal's startled reaction as Amy automatically slipped her hand into his before they started across the street. After a second, he reached out and took Vicky's hand, too. The three of them, hand in hand, crossed the street and marched between the rows of cars.

It was two days before Sally felt she could leave her mother's bedside for even a short period of time. Margie was still listed in critical condition, but her physician was at last openly optimistic about her recovery. Sally borrowed Casey's car and drove home.

When she opened her front door, the unmistakable aroma of oregano greeted her. The house was curiously quiet. Usually, this time of day, the television would be blaring the late-afternoon children's shows. As she crossed the hallway, she was startled to see a very familiar Oriental rug in front of her fireplace. And two rag dolls were watching a blank television screen from an atrocious bean-bag chair. Sally wondered if Neal was so attached to his rug and chair that he couldn't leave home without them. One would think he had moved in.

Neal and the girls were so engrossed they didn't even notice Sally watching them from the other side of the service opening into the kitchen. The unbelievably cluttered kitchen looked as though a tornado had swept through, but the three apron-clad occupants seemed quite calm. Vicky with flour on her nose and in her hair was standing on a stool kneading bread dough. Amy was intently wielding a carrot peeler at the kitchen sink. And Neal was at the stove tasting a tomato sauce that was the apparent source of the wonderful aroma.

"When you finish peeling the carrots, you need to grate some mozzarella," Neal told Amy.

Amy nodded seriously. "I wish Mommie and Grandma could come home and eat some of that merrynerry."

"Marinara," Neal corrected. "We'll freeze some for them. Don't worry, we'll make a real feast when your mother brings your grandma home from the hospital. We'll decorate the house and serve them a six-course meal. The whole nine yards. Hey, more elbow grease in that kneading, Vicky, and try not to get so much flour on the floor."

"Can we sing some opera for them?" Vicky asked.

"You bet!" Neal said emphatically. "But we'll really have to practise a lot."

With tears streaming down her face, Sally watched the unlikely trio burst into the "Mi chiamano Mimi" aria from *La Boheème*. In Italian! Neal's wavering but robust baritone and the childish voices of her daughters rose and fell, filling the cluttered kitchen with their song.

"Hey, we're getting better." Neal said seriously. And he leaned down, kissing first the back of Amy's neck and then the back of Vicky's.

"Know something, girls? I've discovered one of my favorite things is little-girl necks."

"Won't Mommie be surprised when she finds out we've learned how to cook and sing opera?" Amy asked.

"Oh, yes," Neal said. "I've got all sorts of surprises planned for your mommie."

"I'll sure be glad when she gets home," Vicky said with a sigh.

"Me, too," chimed in Amy.

"Me, too," Neal added with a sigh of his own. "Me, too."

Discover the new and unique

Harlequin
Gothic and Regency
Romance Specials!

Gothic Romance	Regency Romance
DOUBLE MASQUERADE	TO CATCH AN EARL
Dulcie Hollyock	Rosina Pyatt
LEGACY OF RAVEN'S RISE	TRAITOR'S HEIR
Helen B. Hicks	Jasmine Cresswell
THE FOURTH LETTER	MAN ABOUT TOWN
Alison Quinn	Toni Marsh Bruyere

A new and exciting world of romance reading

Harlequin Gothic and Regency Romance Specials!

You're invited to accept 4 books and a surprise gift Free!

Acceptance Card

Mail to: Harlequin Reader Service®

In the U.S.
2504 West Southern Ave.
Tempe, AZ 85282

In Canada
P.O. Box 2800, Postal Station A
5170 Yonge Street
Willowdale, Ontario M2N 6J3

YES! Please send me 4 free Harlequin American Romance® novels and my free surprise gift. Then send me 4 brand new novels as they come off the presses. Bill me at the low price of $2.25 each —an 11% saving off the retail price. There are no shipping, handling or other hidden costs. There is no minimum number of books I must purchase. I can always return a shipment and cancel at any time. Even if I never buy another book from Harlequin, the 4 free novels and the surprise gift are mine to keep forever.

154 BPA-BPGE

Name _____ (PLEASE PRINT)

Address _____ Apt. No. _____

City _____ State/Prov. _____ Zip/Postal Code _____

This offer is limited to one order per household and not valid to present subscribers. Price is subject to change.

ACAR-SUB-1

Readers rave about
Harlequin American Romance!

"...the best series of modern romances
I have read...great, exciting, stupendous,
wonderful."
—S.E.*, Coweta, Oklahoma

"...they are absolutely fantastic...going to be
a smash hit and hard to keep on the
bookshelves."
—P.D., Easton, Pennsylvania

"The American line is great. I've enjoyed
every one I've read so far."
—W.M.K., Lansing, Illinois

"...the best stories I have read in a long
time."
—R.H., Northport, New York

*Names available on request.